BLUE CHIPPER

ALSO BY GEOFFREY NORMAN

Midnight Water

Sweetwater Ranch

BLUE CHIPPER

A Morgan Hunt Novel

Geoffrey Norman

William Morrow and Company, Inc.
New York

It is the policy of William Morrow and Company, Inc., and its imprints and affiliates, recognizing the importance of preserving what has been written, to print the books we publish on acid-free paper, and we exert our best effors to that end.

Library of Congress Cataloging-in-Publication Data

Norman, Geoffrey.
    Blue chipper / Geoffrey Norman.
        p.   cm.
    ISBN 0-688-11654-X
    I. Title.
PS3564.O5645B57   1992
813'.54—dc20
                                                                        92-14284
                                                                        CIP

Printed in the United States of America

First Edition

1 2 3 4 5 6 7 8 9 10

BOOK DESIGN BY LYNN DONOFRIO DESIGNS

For Marsha

BLUE CHIPPER

1

Tom Pine insisted, and since it was Friday night and I had no plans, I gave in, even though I've never been much of a basketball fan. Especially not high-school basketball.

"This kid has it, Morgan. Really has it," Pine said. "They'll be comparing him to Oscar Robertson and Michael Jordan one of these days. And you'll be able to say you saw him when he was just a baby but already had all the moves."

I'd always believed you should witness greatness whenever you get the chance. I'd stayed over in Chicago once to watch Gayle Sayers run with a football and had driven two hundred and fifty miles out of my way to listen to John Coltrane play music. It had cost me a night's sleep but I do not remember how tired I was, only that haunting, melancholy sax.

"All right," I said. "Where should I meet you?"

Pine told me how to find the school. I said I would meet him in the parking lot at 7:30.

"We'll find us something to eat after the game," he said. "Maybe some ribs."

"Sounds good." Tom Pine could clean a rack of ribs without stopping for air. I'd seen him do it.

"See you at the game," he said and hung up.

I put away my tools. I'd been cleaning old brick for a hearth that would be the final touch in the room that was technically my study, but which I was calling my drinking room. When I finished, it would have floor-to-ceiling bookcases on one wall. A fireplace on another. A bay window that looked out on the river. Oiled oak floors, a big desk, an armchair for reading, and a small butler's table where I would keep a decanter and a few substantial glasses. On winter nights, I would build a fire in the fireplace, pour whiskey from the decanter into one of the heavy glasses, sit in the armchair with a book on my lap, and experience a kind of peace.

Like a lot of people, I'd spent a lot of time looking for that—a kind of peace. But a lot of my life had gone the other way, into the two black holes of the twentieth century—war and prison. I'd been a soldier, then a convict. Now I was a carpenter, trying to finish this room, and at the rate I was going, it would be next winter before I built my first fire and took my first drink of whiskey in the drinking room. The hearth was coming slowly.

But I was relieved to quit for the day. There was no point in trying to hurry a twenty-room house. I'd bought the place as a long-term project—with money I'd made in prison betting the price of soybeans and feeder cattle—and it was shaping up to be just that.

I showered and changed. It was cool enough in the panhandle of Florida for a wool sweater. I went out on the porch to breathe the evening air and watch the river. Swarms of ricebirds flew low over the marsh, three or four hundred birds to a flock, against a sky that was a deep violet just before going black. A few early stars showed like precise, laser-bored holes in the purple dome.

The river flowed silently and sluggishly past the house, which was on the high bank across from a marsh of needleweed and saw grass as expansive and monotonous as a prairie grain field. The river was named Perdido by the Spanish. The word means "lost" and it was, no doubt, easy enough for the Spaniards to lose the insignificant little stream, one of many on this long and pointless coast. They'd found no gold here. No jewels. No skins. No plunder of any kind.

From the time of the Conquistadors on, nobody has ever prospered by exploiting the panhandle of Florida, unlike the southern part of the state, which has been looted, raped, and poisoned until money is the only thing it has left to offer. Money and drugs. Shop or get high.

There are pockets of the panhandle where the disease has metastasized—where the condominiums soar up out of the sand dunes and the ladies shop in air-conditioned malls and the men dock their boats at lavishly appointed marinas where the restaurants take fish that would have been used for crab bait a few years ago and serve it in blackened butter. But for the most part, the panhandle is still a backwater. Rural, southern, poor, and unsophisticated. A forgotten place of sluggish rivers. Ideal for someone like me.

Lost, my ass, I thought. The river was right where it has always been. You just had to know where to look.

I had no problem picking Tom Pine out of the crowd in the high-school parking lot. There were plenty of other black men around, but none his size. Tom is six four and weighs two hundred and forty pounds—give or take twenty, depending. He'd told me once that he was "born big, almost eleven pounds." He weighed more than two hundred by the time he was in high school.

"Hey, Morgan," he said in a voice that rumbled like a train. "How you holding up?"

"Good, Tom." We shook and I thought, as I always did, that his bones were drawn to different specs. If his skeleton were built out of two-by-fours, then mine was made of screening nailers.

"You remember Phyllis?" Pine said, nodding to the woman who was at his side.

"Absolutely."

Pine's wife is slender and delicate, with an alert, intelligent face that is also pretty, though that is not what you first notice. Her poise and concentration strike you right away, and you sense that she would never lose track of a conversation or forget a name or miss an appointment. She works with kids who have trouble learning. I don't know for sure if she is good at it or not, but she certainly has the temperament.

"Good to see you again," she said and smiled. It was a detached and formal smile. She didn't entirely approve of me or trust me. Tom Pine is a sheriff's lieutenant, and spending an evening with me was a little like bringing work home from the office. But she would never say so.

"Good to see you," I said.

"Let's get on inside and get some close seats," Tom said, and led the way into the small, hot high-school gymnasium.

*   *   *

We sat in the bleachers and watched while the teams went through their warm-ups and the cheerleaders tried to get something going with the crowd. A kid down under one of the baskets pounded out a rhythm on a bass drum and the cheerleaders did a little strut and chanted.

The crowd probably amounted to seven or eight hundred people, not much by the standards of big-time sports, and it was split just about evenly between black and white. Almost all of the players out on the court, wearing their warm-ups and lazily putting up fifteen- and twenty-foot jumpers, were black.

"See the kid at the top of the key," Pine said, "the skinny one, color of coffee with two creams?"

"Hush," Phyllis said and stuck an elbow in Tom's side.

"What should I say?" Tom said, smiling. "You want me to call him a high yellow?"

"*You.*"

I looked at the kid, and while he was just about exactly the color of Tom's description, most people wouldn't quite rate him skinny. If you thought of Tom as a bull, and I did, then it would be consistent to think of this kid as some kind of large, predatory cat, one of those animals that is both fast and strong so that you don't think of them in terms of speed or power but of some combination that does not have a name.

During the warm-ups, the kid took his time and moved with the lazy grace of one of those big cats just after it has come awake from a nap and is stretching and warming up for the hunt.

He picked up a ball and raised it over his head. His feet left the floor and he rose effortlessly. At the top of the leap, he moved his fingers and wrists as though they had been cocked and the ball left them on a soft arc. It traveled twenty feet and touched only string.

"You're gonna see a show," Pine said. "A sure-enough show. The only thing wrong with it is the level of competition. It'll be like a thoroughbred running against a bunch of plow horses. Next year, when he goes off to college, he'll be playing against a little better talent. It'll make him play better. Guarantee it."

"Where's he going?" Phyllis said.

Pine shrugged. "I don't know. I hear he can't make up his mind. But I'll tell you this, he could write his own ticket. The coaches are all around him like dogs sniffing a bitch in heat."

"*Tom.*"

"It's true."

"Be a gentleman. Please."

Pine smiled, touched her arm with a kind of delicacy that looked awkward in a man so large, and said, "I'm sorry. I'll be good."

"All right," Phyllis said, with only a little frost left in her voice.

"Somebody told me that Princeton was over at his house last weekend. Tomorrow it'll be Duke. North Carolina would camp in the yard if he'd let 'em."

"Smart kid, then?" I said.

"Smart enough," Pine said. "Books and libraries don't scare him the way they do some of these kids. He works like he's got plans besides just playing ball. You know what the recruiters and coaches call a kid like him?"

"What's that?"

"A blue chipper. A solid bet. He's the kind of kid who, if you get him, won't steal cars, burn the library down, or flunk out of school. And if you give him four other players who aren't just warm bodies, then he'll win you a championship."

"That good?" I said.

"He's a fine young man," Phyllis said emphatically. "Everyone who knows him is very proud."

"Yessir," Pine said, "he's a real Eagle Scout. And in a minute here, you'll get to see him fly."

The kid, whose name was William Coleman, played basketball like I had never seen it played before. Like Tom Pine said, he needed to move up a class or two in competition because when he was up against other high-school kids, he could have been playing all alone.

On the first play of the game, after the other team got the tip, Coleman went up for a rebound, and while he was still in the air he was looking downcourt for the outlet man. None of his teammates had those kinds of instincts, so there was nobody to pass the ball to. Coleman protected it until he was clear, then began dribbling downcourt so effortlessly that he might not have had the ball. His eyes were on the action under the basket and he was looking for the open man. When he found him, he was so quick with the pass that the man he threw it to was surprised and dropped it. The ball went out of bounds.

Next time down the court, he dribbled and looked for the
open man again. A defender came out to pick him up at the top of
the key and got too close. Coleman gave him a little shoulder one
way and when the other kid took the move, Coleman went around
him like he was nailed to the floor. He went up a foot or two inside
the foul line, rising like he had been launched, raised the ball over
his head, and at the top of his arc brought it down through the rim
like he was driving piles. The rim shook for ten full seconds and
the crowd went wild.

"Oh, son," Tom Pine said, "he's hot. Them other boys are
going to have to use a rope to hold him down."

The other team missed a shot, and once again Coleman
brought the ball downcourt, looking all the time for an open man.
This time, when the defender came out, he gave Coleman a cush-
ion. So when none of his teammates broke clear, Coleman went
up with the ball over his head, cocked his wrists, and put up a
feather-soft jumper that traveled a perfect curve and dropped
cleanly through the net.

Over the bedlam, Pine shouted, "Forget the ropes, them boys
need *chains*."

On the way back downcourt to play some defense, Coleman
looked at the floor, his face completely blank, almost as though he
were embarrassed by his own performance, ashamed of himself for
showing off and reducing the other nine players on the floor to so
much scenery.

"One of the best parts," Pine said, "is that there is no pork in
the kid. I've never seen him hotdog it."

"Isn't he wonderful?" Phyllis said.

"Never seen anyone like him," I said.

The half went quickly, with Coleman scoring most of the
points. He even blocked a couple of shots and stole some passes.
He was everywhere, and the game stopped being any kind of
contest and turned into a one-man performance, a tour de force,
which didn't seem to bother the crowd at all.

In the second half, the other team began to foul him.

"Coach must have got on 'em in the locker room," Pine said,
"told 'em if they couldn't stop him then they had to at least hurt
him."

From what I could tell, Coleman couldn't be rattled. He sank
easily eighty percent from the line and the game ended in a rout.
While cheerleaders and his teammates smiled and hugged and

generally whooped it up, he shook some hands and let the fans pound his back and shoulders without smiling much or saying, it seemed, anything at all. His eyes looked a little out of focus and you could see that some essential part of him was not in that gym at all but off in some other, solitary place.

As soon as he could break away, he trotted off to the showers.

Tom worked his way through milling people toward the door. The crowd seemed to part around him and Phyllis and I followed in the vacuum. The air outside was thirty degrees colder and immeasurably cleaner than the stuff trapped inside the gym.

"Man," Pine said, "feels good to be out of there."

"I wonder why they turn the heat up so high in the first place?" Phyllis said.

"It wasn't the furnace," Pine said. "It was all them bodies."

We walked to their car, and while he unlocked the door Tom said, "Come on and follow us. We'll go get something to eat."

"Thanks, Tom. I'd better pass." I didn't think Phyllis wanted me around when the alternative was having Tom to herself for an evening.

"Come on now. You gotta eat."

I noticed the look of relief that passed over Phyllis's face when I shook my head.

"Yes," she said, smiling politely. "Come on and join us."

"I've got an early morning," I said. "Some other time."

2

I took the highway west away from town and out toward the pulpwood portion of the county, where the subdivisions and trailer parks gave way to patch farms with little clapboard houses and a couple of outbuildings. The lights were on in most of the houses and, invariably, the glow of a television showed through one of the windows. After a few miles, I turned off on a county road that ran south toward the Gulf. The land seemed to sink on either side of the highway until it felt as though I were traveling along a levee that was flanked by cypress and gum swamps broken by the occasional small pond, its smooth black water reflecting the beams of my headlights like startled eyes. In thirty minutes, I reached the driveway to my house.

I parked the truck under the branches of a live oak and stood outside for a few minutes enjoying the air and the smell of the river, which was just tidal enough to give off the specific odor of salt and shell when the water was low. There was no wind and the sky was full of stars. It was the sort of night when you stay outside until you begin to notice the cold, the kind when any house seems lonely, especially one with twenty rooms.

Ordinarily, I would have called Jessie Beaudreaux, who lived up the river a mile or two. We had begun as correspondents when I was still in prison. She had read about my case in the papers and had even done some letter-writing to help with my pardon. After it came through and I got out, Jessie and I became friends. Eventually, we became something more than that, which was easily one of the best things that has ever happened to me.

But Jessie was not home tonight. She was off at a conference in south Florida and would not be getting back for a few more days. I knew the hotel and I thought about calling her there. But I decided against it. I didn't care if she knew that I was thinking about her—even missed her—but I didn't want her to think I was checking up on her this time of night. Since I got out, I have tried hard to learn how to do a few simple things. I try to keep a leash on my temper and I try not to come on too strong. I did not want Jessie to feel like I was crowding her. Not ever.

So when I started to feel the chill enough that I was shivering, I went inside, made something to eat, read for a while, and went to sleep early and alone.

In the morning, I got up and ran three or four miles when it was still early enough to startle the crows off their roosts. They let me know how they felt about that.

As I came back up the drive, trying to sprint like I was going for the tape, I saw another truck parked under the live oak next to mine. There were two dog boxes in the bed of the truck and a man next to it, leaning against the hood. Something in his posture suggested that he had been waiting a while and wouldn't mind waiting a lot longer, that he was a man with a lot of patience.

When he heard me pounding up the drive, he straightened up.

"Go boy, *go*. Dig out. *Move those legs*," Nat Semmes shouted.

When I got to his truck, I stopped running and said, between breaths, "Morning, Nat."

"Come on, come on," he said. "Catch your breath and grab your shotgun. Morning this pretty, we need to go bird-hunting."

"Okay. You want some coffee?"

"Had some. But I'll take a half and drink it while you're in the shower."

"Come on in," I said and led the way.

I poured his coffee, then showered quickly and changed into some Carharts and a canvas shirt, laced my boots, and got my gun out of a closet. When I finished my drinking room, I'd build a proper gun case and then fill it. For now, I had just the one bird gun, a model 21 Winchester. It was a beautiful piece, both quick and sturdy, and probably the finest thing that I owned. It was a gift from Nat Semmes.

He gave me the gun because I wouldn't take his money. It was a situation between us. Not a problem, exactly. Not something we even talked about any longer. More like a conflict we had resolved to work around in intricate, mannered ways, like an old married couple that has learned what ground is dangerous and avoids getting out on it.

Nat Semmes was a lawyer who did his best work on desperate, dead-end cases . . . like mine. If it had not been for the work he had done for me, I might still be behind the wire for killing a man who probably deserved it, even though I hadn't intended to go quite that far. When the case was wrapped up with a governor's pardon, Nat had presented me with a bill that was absurdly low. I tried to pay him more but he would not take the money.

As a condition of my release, Nat had said he would give me some work. There was not much civilian employment for people with my background. Nobody was hiring experts in small arms, tactics, long-range reconnaissance, and the like. But because I'd been pardoned I could qualify for a private investigator's license in the state of Florida, and Nat was good enough to throw some work my way. He said it was a favor to him but I felt like I was the one who should be grateful. Working for Semmes meant action and, in spite of myself and all my resolve, I still had an incurable weakness for action. Working for Semmes meant it would be legal . . . mostly.

The problem came up when he tried to pay me. I told him to take his check and put it somewhere safe. He dug his heels in and so did I. Finally, he said that he would put the money in some kind of escrow account. Then he asked me if I had a will. I said no. I didn't have any heirs.

"Well, that means the government gets it and that is something no patriot can stand for. You are going to have a will. Sit still and think about who you want to get all your worldly goods when you pass from this vale of tears. Try to come up with somebody, or some outfit, that isn't totally worthless."

He drew up a one-page document in all the usual boilerplate, and when it came time to fill in the blanks, I named the Nature Conservancy, Ducks Unlimited, and a little outfit that works with

Vietnam refugees as the heirs to my vast holdings. Now, when I do work for Semmes, the money goes into the escrow account where it builds interest for my estate.

But Nat wasn't entirely satisfied. Probably he thought I had gotten over on him somehow and Nat Semmes does not like to lose. So after we had been bird-hunting a couple of times and he had seen the old pump gun I was using, he decided I needed something better and gave me the Model 21.

"It's a gift, Morgan," he said. "And a gentleman does not turn down a gift."

If I ever stopped being a gentleman in Semmes's eyes, then I would stop being his friend. That was insupportable, so I took the gun. One round to him.

Semmes was waiting for me in my unfinished drinking room. He stood in the middle of the floor surveying things. He was a lean man, with long arms and legs. His thin, angular face seemed blandly curious and detached and you might think there was not much going on behind it until you looked at his eyes. They sat deep in his skull and were almost intimidatingly alert, reminding you, inevitably, of a hawk. Nat Semmes was always thinking and taking things in. The slightly passive expression was a mask that hid an intense, combative personality that showed in perfect, startling relief when he was at work. As much as anyone, I could appreciate what went on behind the tame mask of Semmes's face and what showed in those active eyes.

"I'd say you're really getting it done," he said approvingly. "You must be working night and day."

"Not a lot going on to distract me," I said.

"You complaining?"

"Maybe a little."

We went out to the truck, got in, and drove back down my driveway, crushing oyster shells under the tires, then turned onto the blacktop. Nat immediately floored it and the truck gathered speed.

"So you're getting a little bored, are you?" Nat said.

"Anything gets old after a while," I said. "You know how it is."

He nodded thoughtfully. "Well, I wish I had some work for you, but lately everything has been pretty routine. I'm kind of bored myself."

"I find things to do," I said. "Amazing the number of interesting diversions just lying around out there. Last night I went to a basketball game."

"Oh yeah?"

"Panthers and War Hawks," I said.

"You saw William Coleman, then. Did he score fifty?"

"He could have. How'd you know about him?"

Semmes smiled. "How could anyone living around here *not* know about him? He's the biggest thing to happen in this part of the world for years. The kid is on the front page of the local *Astonisher* more than the president."

"You ever seen him play?"

"Couple of times. I've known him for a while. Know his family. He's a good kid. A *solid* kid. Almost too serious for his own good. Not everyone in the family turned out that well. That's how I know them."

"Uh-oh."

Semmes nodded. "He's got a brother who is on a trajectory that is sure to land him in Raiford. I helped him out of one jam but that was just postponing the inevitable. I did it for his mother, actually."

"His mother?"

"Yes. She's one of her son's victims. Lived a life of work and woe—cleaning up after white folks—so she could do right by her children. William turned out just fine. There was a daughter and she's okay, too. But the other boy is one-hundred-proof trouble. Caused her nothing but pain. She asked me for help and I couldn't turn her down."

I nodded. That sounded like Semmes.

"I bargained the charges down. Got him probation. But the kid is past helping. Doomed, you know."

"Maybe," I said. "But the family won't be poor forever."

Semmes nodded again, downshifted, and turned off the blacktop onto a road that wasn't much more than two well-worn grooves through a five-year-old clear-cut.

"Yes," he said, "I suspect that there are pro teams that would take him right now and pay millions for the privilege. But his mother made him promise her that he'd go to college and finish. And he's the kind of kid who will keep his promise. I'm glad you got to see him, Morgan. He's the sort of kid who gives you hope. Plus he's just a goddamned joy to watch on a basketball court."

"He is that," I said.

"Best I've ever seen," Nat said and stopped the truck at a fence that ran along the perimeter of an overgrown milo field. He killed the engine and said, "Okay. There ought to be a covey or two in here. Let's put the dogs on the ground and take a look."

The dogs were a couple of young pointers, Bonnie and Lou by name. You want to give a bird dog a name that comes out of your mouth easy when you have to yell. These dogs were both liver and white, so lean they seemed like nothing more than bone and hide. They bounded out of the dog boxes and hit the ground running.

There was still some frost on the ground. The air had warmed but it was still not hot. No need for a coat, just the shirt and the vest and the warmth that came with walking at an easy pace behind the dogs as they worked the clear-cut, back and forth, trying to pick up scent and checking over their shoulders now and then to make sure we were keeping up.

They found scent just as I was starting to think the clear-cut was barren and we ought to be across the fence in the milo, where there was a lot more to eat.

"Got a point," Semmes said calmly.

"Okay."

"Easy, Bonnie. Careful, Lou. *Careful.*"

The backing dog wanted to creep in just a little closer but the sound of Nat's voice steadied him and he stiffened.

Nat and I moved in past the dog, which held as though it had been welded to the spot. I could see the rhythmic rise of its chest but no other movement. Then we drew up next to the dog that had made game. It did not move. We took another six or seven steps and the covey came out of the dense brown grass as twenty separate pieces of one sudden explosion that, as always, froze me for one startled second before I began to bring my gun to the shoulder and push the safety off.

I heard Nat shoot while I was still pushing the barrel to catch up with the farthest bird on my edge of the covey. I caught him and tracked him and touched the trigger. The bird dropped conclusively, leaving a small cloud of feathers in the air where he'd been. I heard Nat shoot again as I moved the barrel back and tried to track another bird. By the time I was on, the bird was out of range and I pushed the safety back on and lowered the gun. A few feathers still drifted like pollen where my bird had been.

"Lou, Bonnie," Semmes yelled and blew his whistle. "Come on and hunt dead."

The dogs broke like they'd been let off chains and were out in front of us in an instant, nosing through the grass.

"Well?" Semmes said.

"One. How about you."

"I got lucky."

"Right," I said. Nat had grown up doing this. It was an essential part of him and he did all the essential things very, very well.

After a minute or two, the dogs had found all three birds. Nat tossed mine to me and I caught it. The bird felt light but compact and sturdy in my hand. It was missing some feathers and beaded, here and there, with drops of blood. I admired its rich, subdued colors—several tones of browns that only occur in the woods, along with a soft, creamy shade of white—then dropped it in the pouch of my vest, broke my gun, and reloaded. Nat was kneeling and rubbing the dogs' ears, telling them they'd done well. A kind of lazy calm had returned.

By noon, we had killed six birds and the day had warmed enough that the back of my shirt felt damp and the dogs were losing their concentration and needed a rest.

We walked back to the truck, gave the dogs some water, loaded them in the boxes, and drove back out to the highway to get some lunch.

We ate on the front porch of a general store. Sardines, soda crackers, apples, and canned drinks. The store sagged here and there and was crying for paint where the wood was not covered up with rusting old tin signs for chewing tobacco and soft drinks. There were a few written notices tacked up near the door, most of them political.

"In the old days," Semmes said, "there would have been a couple of Klan posters up there. You don't see those anymore."

"Well, that's progress," I said.

"I suppose," Semmes said and drank from his can of Coca-Cola. "But they've got a man over in Louisiana still selling that old snake oil. He took off his sheets, got a face lift, and learned how to not say *nigger*. But the genes bred true. He damn near got elected governor and before that, he just about made it to the United States Senate."

"That sounds like the right kind of company for him," I said.

Semmes smiled and shook his head slowly. "Can't be cynical about these things, Morgan. Got to have hope. Keep the faith. At least he's out of the sheets and he can't say *nigger* even if that's what he means."

"Progress?" I said.

"You measure it in millimeters, not in miles. William Coleman might play ball next year for some school that wouldn't have let him on the campus a couple of generations ago, unless it was to haul off the garbage."

"Wonder where he will go," I said.

"That's just about the only thing you hear people talking about where I go for lunch. They figure if the U can get him, it'll mean a solid shot at the national championship. They say he's the player they need to turn it all around."

"You think he'll go to the U or one of the other schools around here?"

Nat shrugged. "Would *you*?"

"I'd get the first train out of town, Nat. And I'd take my mother with me."

"Me too," Semmes said and threw his empty Coke can in a trash barrel that was already full to overflowing. "But he may stay around. He told me, when I was out there once, that he can't make up his mind. This is home and he never really wanted to leave, but that he might be able to get a better education if he passed on the U and went somewhere else. Hard for me to believe. The ditches around here are full of snakes like David Duke but William and his mother still think of it as home and don't want to leave. You wonder how we can ever make it right with people like that."

"Get rid of the snakes."

"How?"

"One at a time."

Semmes laughed. "All right. But first, let's see if we can kill us a few more birds."

We hunted the high, sandy ridges for most of the afternoon. It was warm now. The dogs were getting tired and my legs felt heavy. But we found some birds. Enough to keep it interesting.

By the time the rim of the sun was touching the tree line, we had a dozen birds between us.

"We could probably find one more covey," Semmes said, "but I expect I ought to quit. I've got a dinner party tonight."

"Fine with me," I said. "I've had enough." It had been a good day and I didn't feel the need to wring every drop of juice from it. The dogs would have gone right up until dark and beyond, even though they were moving at about half speed and their tails were bloody where they had whipped the briars. They each drank a bowlful of water, and when we loaded them into the boxes they lay down and went immediately to sleep. It felt good to slide into the front seat. We'd probably walked ten miles and I felt a deep but satisfying ache in my legs.

When we pulled up in front of my house, Semmes said, "You might as well keep these birds, Morgan. I've got a freezer full of them."

"Nope."

"You'd be doing me a favor. I don't want to clean them."

"Not going to do it, Nat."

After we'd argued about it a little, I settled for keeping four of the birds.

"You want to come in for a drink?" I asked after we'd divided the bag.

"Nothing I'd like better," he said. "But I'm already running late."

"Okay. Enjoyed the hunt. Thanks for coming by."

Semmes dropped the transmission into reverse, waved, and drove back down the driveway. I went inside and ran a couple of patches down the barrel of my shotgun, wiped the surfaces down with an oily cloth, then put it away. I cleaned the birds in the kitchen, first plucking them as carefully as I could to keep from tearing the skin, then burning off the pinfeathers in the flame of a candle. I snipped the wings and feet with a pair of shears, cut off the heads, then opened each bird at the vent and scooped out the offal with my fingers. It smelled like wet decaying earth with some additional, pungent element. I saved the livers, then rinsed the cavities and dried them with paper towels, placed the little fist-sized carcasses into a covered bowl, and put it into the refrigerator. Nat hangs his birds for three or four days, like the Europeans, before he cleans them, but I have never been able to taste the difference in aged birds and I like to get things done and then forget about them. Having birds around that needed to be cleaned would just nag at me.

I took a long, hot, soapy shower, ate a bowl of chili, and got in bed with a book. Except for an irritating sense of boredom and a slight case of the Saturday night blues—from missing Jessie, I suppose—I felt just fine and I was asleep at an hour when most people were just getting down to the serious business of Saturday night.

3

The phone rang sometime after midnight. My feet were on the floor and I was looking for something to put in my hand before I realized it was the telephone that had shocked me awake.

"Ashamed to call this time of night," Tom Pine said.

"Don't worry about it."

"Wouldn't do it unless it was important."

"What's the problem, Tom?"

"I need you to ride somewhere with me. Can you do that?"

"Sure. I believe I'm free for the next couple of hours."

"I'll be around for you in about three zero," he said, then hung up.

I got into some clothes, put some cold water on my face, and heated up the last of the morning's coffee. It was black as tar and tasted worse than it looked. Coffee without pretense, I thought. But it did what I wanted it to do and I was wide awake by the time Pine's cruiser eased up my drive and stopped under the live oak.

I went out and got in on the passenger side. A shotgun sat on a rack between us. It was flat black, with a hard plastic stock and a short barrel, an entirely different piece from the one I had been using on small birds. This was a weapon with no elegance, only brute function.

When I closed the door, Pine dropped the car into gear and

said, "I appreciate your coming out this time of night. I wouldn't ask if it wasn't important."

"I know."

"This time of night always reminds me of going out on night patrol. Laying an ambush and lying there with the mosquitoes and leeches sucking on you while you wait for something that never comes . . . *almost* never, anyway. It always surprised me when Charlie did come easing down the trail, like ghosts or something."

Pine and I had walked some of the same hills at different times. That was a long time ago and seemed longer, part of a past that neither of us could quite believe had actually happened. This time of the morning, though, it seemed more plausible.

"Just about the time that you and Phyllis and I were watching the basketball game the other night," Pine went on in his deep, grave voice, "there was a killing over in one of the projects. Nothing unusual about that. It's a rare night when we don't have something go down in those places. The action there is more predictable than any night ambush ever was.

"We didn't handle this one, since the project is inside the city limits. It was property of the Pensacola police." Pine said this without any change of expression, but I knew that relations between the sheriff's department and the city police were generally hostile.

"They picked up the killer without much trouble and they're holding him at the city pound until Monday morning, when they'll let him talk to one of the public defenders. Nothing unusual in that. We do the same thing, especially on weekends. A few hours in jail will take some of the piss and vinegar out of these punks, especially if they're high when you pick them up. They go through withdrawal and start thinking that maybe if they're nice to you, you'll be nice to them. By the time they talk to the public defender, they're ready to strike a deal."

Pine accelerated and the cruiser's engine seemed to growl like a big, angry cat. Pine steered effortlessly and the wheel looked small, almost dainty, in his massive hands.

"Turns out that the man they're holding down at the city jail for murder is named Jackson Coleman. He's the older brother of William Coleman, the kid we watched play basketball the other night."

"I've heard about him," I said.

"From Nat Semmes?"

"That's right," I said. "Just this morning, in fact. Nat says he's bad medicine."

"More like poison," Pine said with a note of contempt. "Jackson Coleman is a small-time dealer and hustler who would rather die and rot in the sun than do hard work. His daily goals amount to getting high and stealing enough to afford it. I'd like to put a bounty on him and all the others like him. Bring in an ear and a couple of fingers and you get a brand new fifty-dollar bill to spend. Nobody in the world would miss him, except his mama. She's the one who called me."

"Did he call her from jail?"

Pine did not answer right away and in that silence, there was a world of significance.

"That's why I came looking for you."

I didn't understand that, so I waited for him to go on.

"Jackson the punk hasn't talked to anyone yet, at least not according to the desk sergeant I talked to down at the city police. The sergeant's a friend, and when I asked him about it he said the kid hadn't made any phone calls or talked to anyone yet. I made it sound like we might have something they could use and it was just a courtesy call. He didn't think anything of it. Said good-bye and went back to his coffee."

"Then how did his mother find out?"

"That's the strange part," Pine said. "Everything else is just as normal as sunrise. Jackson finally does what everyone knew he'd get around to doing sooner or later. A two-bit drug deal gets crosswired and he greases some creep who is just like him. Blind man could have seen that coming. Then, because Jackson doesn't have the brains to get out of his own way, he gets picked up before the body is even cold. They warehouse his sorry ass down at the city pound for the weekend and decide not to let him make any calls . . . all strictly routine.

"But earlier tonight, a man comes out to see Jackson's mother at her house. A white man, it so happens."

*   *   *

The white man had reddish sort of hair, Jackson Coleman's mother said. Curly and not too much of it. The skin on his face was roughed up and red, and he was getting heavy in the middle, so his shirt wouldn't stay tucked in neat and flat behind his belt.

Dinah Coleman sat in a very old wing chair while she told me this. The fabric that covered the chair was worn thin as tissue and the wood was bleached out from years of sunlight. It was, no doubt, the most comfortable chair in the house, the one she sat in to rest her legs after a hard day.

The rest of the furniture was mismatched and old. There were school pictures of her children in ceramic frames on the tables. Pictures of William, carefully cut from newspapers and game programs, on the wall. The floors were bare and spotless, the kind of clean that doesn't come with merely pushing a broom or a vacuum over them but from hard scrubbing, done on hands and knees with a coarse brush and strong soap. The entire house had a furious, determined cleanliness about it. And all that hard work had taken its toll on Dinah Coleman.

She was a thin woman. The mothers of men like Jackson and William Coleman are either very fat or very thin. I knew this from seeing them on the weekends when they came to visit their sons in prison. The fat ones had given up on everything but eating, I guessed, and the thin ones had given up on everything but suffering and work. There was nothing to Dinah Coleman but bone and skin and what remained of her vast, hard will. Her face was small and pinched and her hair was a dull, pewter gray.

"Did he tell you his name, Mrs. Coleman?" I asked. She called me Mr. Hunt, because she would never think of calling a white man anything but Mister, and I called her Missus, because I thought she deserved at least that much respect.

"No, sir," she said, shaking her head wearily. "He just said he was a friend of Jackson's and wanted to see could he help him out."

"Did he tell you how he knew that Jackson was in trouble?"

"No, sir," she said. Her hands were folded in her lap, her bent and bony fingers woven together as though she were ready to pray. "He just came in here and said that he had bad news to tell me about Jackson. Said the boy was in jail for a killing but he might be able to help him out. He said that Jackson would likely go to the electric chair without somebody to help him."

"How was he going to help Jackson?"

She thought for a moment and probably would not have answered that question—or any other from me, for that matter—except that Tom Pine, who was waiting outside in the cruiser, had told her she could trust me. Plainly, she still wasn't sure, but finally she answered wearily, "He said he might be able to talk to the prosecutor. Jackson didn't have to be charged for first-degree murder, he said, if the prosecutor had a reason to make it something else. Manslaughter or maybe even self-defense."

"What kind of reason, Mrs. Coleman?"

"He said a lot could depend on where William—that's my youngest—went to school to play basketball."

"I saw William the other night," I said. "He's a great player. Greatest I've ever seen."

"There's a lot of them saying that," she said, with the faintest note of pride. "They've been coming around here a lot, making all kinds of promises. None of them as big as this."

"No," I said.

"This man made it sound like he could do something. Full of confidence, you know. Talked to me like I was dumb and slow, explaining everything twice even though I could see he just hated being in this house and wanted more than anything to get out and be somewhere else."

"Did this man say where William should go to school?" I said.

"He said the prosecutor was a strong university man and he'd be pleased if William played there."

"What did you tell him?"

"I said William hadn't made up his mind yet and he told me to talk to the boy and tell him how important it was for him to go to the university. Then he said he'd talk to me again and he got out of here like the place was on fire."

"What did you do then?"

"I called down to the jail to see if they had Jackson. They wouldn't tell me. Hung up on me. So then I called Deputy Pine. I've been knowing him since he was a little boy."

"Have you talked to anyone else?"

"No, sir. Just you."

I thought for a minute, then said, "Mrs. Coleman, it might be better if you didn't say anything about this to anyone else. Not for a while, anyway."

She looked at me skeptically. She had no reason to think I was on her side, that I wouldn't do my best to cover the tracks of the man who had come into her house offering to trade one of her sons for the other.

"Mrs. Coleman," I said, "I'm not a lawyer, but I work for one. Nat Semmes."

"He's a good one."

"Yes ma'am, he is. And just as soon as I can, in a couple of hours, I'll call him and tell him what you told me. He'll know what to do."

"Mr. Semmes helped Jackson once before. He's a good man, Mr. Semmes is."

"Would you keep this to yourself until I've had a chance to talk to him? One of us will talk to you after that. Later this morning sometime."

"I'll do what you think best, Mr. Hunt," she said firmly, "long as it doesn't hurt my boy. I suspect he'll be safe where he is for a few more hours."

"If the man who was here earlier comes back," I said, "stall him. Tell him William is thinking about it. And don't tell him about me or Tom Pine or Nat Semmes."

She nodded slightly as though she did not have to be told any of that. I got up to leave, wanting to say something that would reassure her and give her some hope. But I'd done just about all that I could do by bringing Nat Semmes's name into the conversation. So I thanked her and said I would be in touch soon.

"I thank you for coming out, Mr. Hunt," she said. "This time of morning and this part of town."

"I'm happy to do it, Mrs. Coleman," I said. "And I hope that things work out."

"I do too. Jackson hasn't had nothing in his life but trouble. My other children had something to prop them up and keep them out of trouble. But not Jackson. He's the one that needed something the most and all he's had is trouble. I pray for that boy. The others will be all right but he needs help—God's help and every other kind."

"I'll do what I can," I said. I couldn't speak for God.

"I appreciate that, Mr. Hunt. Truly."

4

When I came out of the front door, Pine was resting his big head against the back of the cruiser's front seat. His eyes came open instantly and he straightened up and started the engine before I could open the door. He dropped the cruiser into gear and started down the small street of tired frame houses, all of them still dark with one hour to go before dawn on a Sunday morning. A few blocks away, there were places still serving whiskey. Cards and dice games were still being played, some drug deals still going down, and a hooker or two still trying to score a last trick. This was the final lap of the Saturday night marathon for those people. But Dinah Coleman lived in a different sort of neighborhood. In a couple of hours, these people would be getting up and dressing for church.

"How about some breakfast?" Tom said. "I could pass from hunger."

"All right."

"If I don't get something to eat first thing, then I'm just *wrong* for the rest of the day."

We went to an all-night place called Ray's that served truckers, farmers, hunters, fishermen, and off-duty cops out by the interstate north of town. The unpaved parking lot was empty except for a couple of old pickups.

The air inside Ray's was warm and thick with the smell of greasy sausage cooked on a grill. The light hit my dilated eyes like a strobe.

"Umm," Pine said, "smells *good* in here."

Two men at the counter wearing hunters' camouflage looked at us for a moment, then went back to their coffee and eggs. Pine took a table near the back of the room, away from the counter, and faced the door. A short, stocky man wearing a white apron came from behind the counter, carrying an order pad and a pencil.

"Morning, Lieutenant," he said. "You need a menu?"

"Morning, Ray. No menu. Just coffee. Four over gentle, patty sausage, a pile of grits, and biscuits."

Ray wrote that down and looked at me.

"Coffee," I said. "Two, lightly scrambled."

"Toast?"

I shook my head.

"Grits? Ham? Bacon? Biscuits?"

"Ray makes some righteous biscuits," Pine said.

"Just the eggs, thanks."

Ray wrote that on his pad, turned our cups over, and went back to the counter for the coffeepot.

"You're going to waste away, starving yourself like that," Pine said. "What do they call it when teenaged girls do that? Start eating like a bird and get skinnier and skinnier until they just starve?"

"Anorexia."

"That's it. Man, I can understand all kinds of things people will do to screw themselves up, but that one just goes past me. How can you stop *eating*?"

Ray returned with the coffeepot and filled both cups. Steam rose from the cups and Pine took a careful taste.

"Whew. Now that will get you going. So what are you, worried about cholesterol or something? My wife stays after me about that all the time. 'Course eggs are supposed to be bad for that, too. Right?"

"That's what they say."

"Well," Pine said, "I have a hard time going along with that. I figure if it comes out of a chicken or a cow, then it's got to be good. If it hadn't been for chickens and cows when I was a kid, my whole family would have starved."

I nodded and took a sip of the scalding hot coffee.

"So what do you think about Dinah Coleman's story," Tom said.

"I think I need to talk to Nat Semmes about it. He goes to church with his family every Sunday morning, early. I'll call him after he gets back home. What do *you* think?"

Pine thought for a moment. He seldom did or said anything on impulse.

"I know for sure that she's not lying," he said. "If she says the man came by with that proposition, then it happened. I've known her all my life. She's straight as a string."

I'd thought the same, without having known her at all before we talked.

"What about the man with the proposition?" I said. "You think he was lying?"

Pine took a sip from his cup and drummed his big fingers on the Formica table. "Well, we know he wasn't lying about her boy being in jail. He had that right. Question is, how did he know? Jackson didn't make any calls."

Ray brought our plates and put them down in front of us. My eggs looked sparse compared to the portions piled on Tom's plate.

He sprinkled salt and pepper on everything, then covered the eggs with steak sauce and went to work with his fork, puncturing the yolks and mixing the eggs with his grits and sausage. He ate steadily and seriously, not saying a word until he had mopped up the last of the eggs and grits with a biscuit and Ray had returned with the coffeepot.

"How was it, Lieutenant?" he said as he poured.

"Just great, Ray. I'd like to do it again."

"Well, if you're buying, I'm frying."

"Nah," Tom said. "I'd better not. Phyllis wants me to lose some weight."

"Lot's of luck," Ray said on his way back to the grill.

Pine unbuttoned a pocket of his uniform shirt and took out a toothpick. He worked it around his molars carefully, then stuck it in the side of his mouth and said, "There's lots of ways, I suppose, that fellow could have found out that Jackson was in jail. He could know some cops or maybe just been at a bar where one of them was doing some loud talking."

"Or," I said, "he might be one of those people who listen to police calls on a scanner."

"Could be," Pine said. "There's enough of them. Sad, you know, how bored some people are. Sitting around listening to police calls just to give their lives a little juice.

"Anyway, let's skip over how our man found out about Jackson being picked up for murder and ask ourselves if he is really in a position to make Dinah Coleman a deal. That's the part that got me to call you."

I waited for him to explain that.

"I don't work for the prosecutor, exactly. And I ain't afraid of him, either. He's just another guy grubbing votes. He'll wind up a judge or a senator or in jail, like all of 'em. They come and they go.

"But I can't exactly investigate this thing without the prosecutor finding out about it. Even if I tried to do it on my own, it would likely get back to him. And if I did it official, then it would get back to him for sure."

"Which wouldn't be a problem," I said, "just as long as he's innocent."

"Exactly," Tom said. "But if he ain't, and he knows I'm sniffing around, then he can do whatever he needs to do.

"But I can't just ignore it. Wouldn't do it, even if I could. I can't see treating anyone like that. Especially not Dinah Coleman. I'd feel like I was growing slime for skin if I just dropped it and left her hanging."

"I understand," I said.

"I could go higher. To the FBI or something, I suppose. It might come to that. But it seems like right now that might be going too heavy when what you need to do is travel light. First FBI agent who came in and anyone looking close would see the tracks.

"But if Semmes is Jackson Coleman's lawyer and you're working for Semmes . . . your asking questions would seem like routine stuff."

"Right."

"That's why I got you out of bed," Pine said. It made sense, but he looked like there was still something on his mind, more he wanted to say. I waited but he said nothing. He drummed his big fingers on the table and looked away from me. Thinking, probably, about what he still had to say.

"Seems unlikely a prosecutor would make that deal in the first place," I said to fill the hole his silence had made.

Pine raised an eyebrow.

"You believe he would?"

Pine smiled slightly. "You heard the old joke about the fellow who was working on his Ph.D., doing research on peckerwood churches?"

"No."

"Well, he's going around some red dirt county like this one, asking people how they feel about sin and salvation and such and he's talking to this used-up old farmer, writing down the answers in his notebook. He's getting pretty good stuff and finally he says, 'Well, what about baptism by immersion? Do you believe in that?'

"The peckerwood gives him a look like he's wondering if the fellow was born dumb or had to go to college and work on it. Then he says, 'Believe in it? *Hell.* I seen it done.' "

Pine laughed at the joke and so did I.

"Well," Pine said taking the pick out of his mouth and studying it, "you'd be amazed at the things grown men will do to get some kid who can play ball to go to their old alma mater. Some of the stories would just water your eyes."

"You mean giving the kids cars and things like that?"

"A car isn't any big thing these days," Pine said. "Just the ante. Kids who won't ever get past the second team expect to be driving a nice car when they go off to school."

"I see."

"When you have a kid with William Coleman's talent, then you are talking about cars, houses, jobs, and lots of money. Cash money, trust funds, whatever works."

"That bad?"

"Oh yeah," Pine said and reached for the check that Ray had left face down on the table.

He studied it for a second, then stood and took out his wallet and selected a bill.

"Let's talk while we ride," he said. "I'd like to get home before everyone wakes up. Sunday is family day around the Pine house."

"Come back, Lieutenant," Ray said when we were at the door.

"Count on it," Tom said.

The sun had risen enough that thin clouds on the horizon glowed like the coals of a carefully banked fire. It felt strange to be driving home at this hour. Tom Pine kept his hands on the wheel and his eyes on the road and talked softly.

"It's television that's done it. That's what everyone says, and it makes sense to me. When I played ball a million years ago and came out of high school, a kid might get a little something under the table. But nothing like what he gets offered today. There just ain't any comparison."

Tom Pine had been an all-state football player at a high school a couple of miles from Ray's diner. He was a defensive lineman who had everything—size, speed, and hunger—and he went North on a football scholarship, because in those days black ballplayers could not play for the state university. "I hated it up nawth," Tom told me once. "It was so far from home. The food was different, the people talked funny and were about as friendly as guard dogs. Colder than a well-digger's ass, too. I'd never seen snow before and here I was, trying to play ball in the stuff."

He made the adjustment well enough to be an all-American in both his junior and senior years. He was *Sports Illustrated*'s player of the week after he made seventeen tackles against Ohio State and knocked them out of the number-one position in the polls just about single-handedly. After the game, someone took his picture. He was all brown mud, red blood, and coal-black skin. It was a picture to give children nightmares.

He could have played in the pros and made the big money except that, while he was in school, he had joined ROTC. He signed up for the money and then stayed because he liked it. He told me once that being an all-American football player hadn't meant anywhere near as much to him as wearing an officer's uniform.

"They expected big black men to play football," he said. "The gold braid, now, that was for white boys."

He could have gotten out of his contract with the army. His knees, after all the years of football, weren't good enough for the infantry. The Green Bay Packers, however, thought they were just fine.

But Pine turned the Packers down and took his commission. He even managed to sneak through jump school and wound up running a platoon in the Central Highlands, where he finally ruined the knees for good jumping out of a chopper to get to a firefight. That finished him for both his loves—the airborne and football. So he became a cop, and as far as I know nobody has ever heard him bitch about his luck.

He talked in a soft, detached tone as the big cruiser settled on the shocks through a wide, banked turn in the highway. "Football was big back when I played. So big that I couldn't have imagined it would get any bigger. Strangers would come up and just touch you, like there was something that would rub off, you know, something magic that would stick to their fingers. These studs in suits would come into the locker room after a game, going around and shaking hands with anyone who'd had a big game. You'd look in your hand after the guy was gone and there'd be a bill. A fifty, usually, or sometimes a hundred. More money than my old man would see after a week of busting his ass, and this guy in a suit, whose name I didn't even know, was just giving it to me. I figured they did it so they could tell all their buddies about it and because it made them feel good, like they were part of it. I always sent the money home."

He shook his head and chewed on his pick for a minute or two. "We went to the Rose Bowl my senior year. Seems like we were in the top ten all three years I was on the varsity. And you know what? I think we were on television maybe four times, including that Rose Bowl game. These days, any second-rate school from a good conference expects to be on the tube four times. One good bowl game brings in more than a million dollars for a school.

"Basketball—William Coleman's game—is just as big. You get into that sixty-four-team playoff system they've got and the money starts rolling in. By the time you get to the finals, you're talking millions. And in basketball, one player like William can make all the difference. One man with his talent can change a team from five ordinary guys into a championship contender. One player can take you from barely breaking even to making five million dollars in TV money. For someone like that, people are willing to go a lot further than a few hundred-dollar handshakes.

"Take a whole lot to surprise me when it comes to what some people will do to acquire that kid's services on a basketball court."

"Even a DA selling his office?"

"Yeah," Pine said, "that sounds kind of rank, don't it? Depends on how bad the DA wants to see the U win a championship, you know."

"Do you know this DA?"

"Not enough to say he's a booster."

"Well," I said, "we'll find out soon enough."

"Yeah," Tom said softly with a note of uncertainty in his voice. He said nothing after that. Kept his eyes firmly on the road until we had eased up my drive and parked under the live oak next to

my truck. He cut the engine and stared through the windshield.
The sun was up enough to have cleared the tree line. It looked like
another clear winter day.

"What's troubling you, Tom?" I said.

He sighed and said, "Two things. One small. The other . . .
maybe not so small."

"Okay," I said. "Want to tell?"

"First, I don't want to be derelict in my duty. That's small. I
know I'm doing the right thing even if it ain't the *official* right
thing, you know. Bringing in somebody from outside when I have
reason to believe a crime may have been committed . . . that might
not look too good. But I won't starve if I lose this job. And I don't
want to keep it just because I'm scared of losing it. But I don't want
to lose it just for being stupid."

"Okay."

"When you talk to Semmes, if he tells you that I'm way out of
line here, I'd like to hear it."

"All right," I said. "What's the big thing?"

"I don't want to be shut out, you understand. Doing it this
way . . . that doesn't mean I'm washing my hands of it."

He was scowling and I understood his frustration for the first
time. What he wanted to do was go out and break some heads.
Instead, he was asking for help and sitting on the sidelines.

"I won't shut you out, Tom," I said. "But I won't involve you
in anything that isn't straight up, either."

"What's that mean?"

"You're going to have to trust me."

"You and Semmes?"

"Yes," I said. "Me and Semmes."

Pine thought for a moment, then said, "All right. I can live
with that."

Semmes's name had that effect on people.

"Good night, Tom," I said, getting out of the cruiser.

"More like good morning, I'd say. And listen, Morgan . . ."

"Yes."

"Thanks. I appreciate your going to the trouble."

"No trouble, Tom. No trouble at all."

I went into the house feeling wide awake and more alive than
I had in what seemed like a long time. It was the prospect of action.
Does it for me every time.

5

Nat Semmes lived by a number of rules, all of which he followed strictly. One of them was that he never took his work home with him. He'd told me once that he'd rather sweep streets and haul trash than turn into one of those people who sell themselves to their jobs.

So when I called him at home, at an hour when I guessed he would just be getting home from church, I expected him to tell me it would wait until Monday morning. But I called just the same, so I could tell Dinah Coleman and Tom Pine that I had talked to Semmes. That would be enough to reassure them, for the moment, anyway.

"Sorry to be calling today," I said. "But it's important."

"It always is," Semmes said. "No matter what it is, it's always important. You ever notice that, Morgan?"

"I don't want to take you away from your family—"

"Well, as a matter of fact," he interrupted, "you aren't. I took Bobbie and Maggie to the airport after church. They're flying up to North Carolina to look at colleges. And Brad is spending the day with friends. It's just me and the dogs here today. I was thinking about working on the boat."

"Something came up last night," I said. "It involves Dinah Coleman and Tom Pine."

"A case."

"Potentially."

"I see. Are you free in an hour?" Semmes almost never neglected the courtesies. He could have said, "Meet me in an hour," in the manner most busy, successful lawyers employ, but then he wouldn't have been Nat Semmes if he had, and I wouldn't be working for him.

"Matter of fact," I said, "I'm free all day."

"I'll see you at the office," he said and hung up.

Semmes's office was on the top floor of an old quarrystone building in downtown Pensacola. The building had once been the headquarters of a bank that had left for a more modern and imposing place, the kind with tinted glass windows that do not open and some kind of central "climate-control" apparatus that works twenty-four hours a day, every day of the year. The old bank building was too sturdy to knock down with anything less than dynamite, but in a good month fewer than half its offices were rented out, and on a Sunday in January only the one leased by Nat Semmes was occupied.

"Come on in," he said when I knocked.

He was sitting behind his big oak partner's desk, still wearing his church clothes, and reading the Sunday *New York Times*. Semmes followed the news as faithfully as he attended church.

He laid the front section of the paper down on a corner of his desk, stood up, and shook my hand.

"Thanks for coming in," he said, even though it had been my idea.

"And thank you for taking the time."

"Well, the only thing you are interrupting is my reading. And that gets to be more of a burden every day. You wonder, sometimes, if the world will make it to next week."

He shook his head, then smiled slightly and said, "You want something to drink? I made some coffee."

"Coffee would be good."

He walked over to a small table in the corner of the large room and filled two mugs from a stainless-steel percolator. I took my usual chair in front of his desk and looked around the room. It always struck me how accurately this room reflected the personality of its occupant. There were bookshelves on two walls, filled with all the soberly bound legal volumes, except for one small shelf, easily reached, that was lined with the books that Semmes read for pleasure, and something a little more than that. A sense of the civilized man's obligation, perhaps. Shelby Foote's Civil War trilogy was there. The letters and speeches of Lincoln. Shakespeare and Dante. Other classics. Semmes's framed law degree hung on the wall that was not taken up with bookshelves, along with portraits of his wife, son, and daughter. Some photographs of his sailboat, a thirty-foot sloop that he'd brought down from the Chesapeake and spent a year rebuilding.

What struck you about that wall, if you knew Nat Semmes, was what was *not* framed and hanging there. He had all sorts of certificates for achievement and citations as one organization or another's Man of the Year. He'd been written up in national magazines and his picture had been in some of the big-circulation newspapers. He was an important man who had accomplished a lot but you would never know it to look at that wall. Nat Semmes did not put his trophies on display and he didn't do what he did for recognition.

He came back across the room, handed me my mug, and went around his desk to sit down. Through the window behind him, I could see the level blue surface of Pensacola Bay and, beyond, a well-developed barrier island, and then the vast green expanse of the Gulf of Mexico. It was a view to take your mind off your work or, if you were one of Nat's clients, your troubles. I'd spent many hours listening to him talk with the dreary, fact-processing part of my brain while the other half soared out over the Gulf like a prowling seabird.

"One of those days when it seems just a shame not to be sailing," Nat said. "Or doing something outside."

"Absolutely."

"Well," he said, sitting up straight behind the desk and pulling a notepad and pencil within reach, "no point in thinking that way. Let's get down to it."

I told him the story. How I'd gone out to see Dinah Coleman with Tom Pine; what she'd told me about the man who came to see her; my conversation with Tom Pine after we'd left the Coleman house. He listened without interrupting and without ever changing expression. He took one or two notes, and when I'd finished he leaned back in his chair and looked at the ceiling.

After a minute or two, he said, "Tom Pine takes it seriously?"

It wasn't really a question; more like a starting point. When he was working, Nat Semmes moved logically from point A to point B. No shortcuts.

"Yes," I said.

"Well, he should," Semmes said. "No question about that."

I waited for him to move on to point B.

"I can't represent both Tom Pine and Jackson Coleman. Not to mention Dinah Coleman."

I nodded.

"I'm sure that Tom can get a good legal opinion regarding his duties from inside the department. Or, if that isn't satisfactory to him, then he could talk to some outside counsel on his own. There are a number of people I could recommend."

And now, to point C.

"Of course, if I'm representing Dinah and Jackson Coleman, then I have to think that it is to my advantage—*their advantage*—that Pine not investigate this matter. Not yet, anyway. It would be better—a hell of a lot better—for him to treat it as something other than an official complaint. If there has been any official misconduct by the prosecution, then that would prejudice a case against Jackson Coleman. But it has to be proven and a premature investigation might make that very difficult."

I nodded.

"Police officers," he went on, "hear all sorts of things from family and friends and they have to use their discretion."

"Absolutely," I said. And Semmes moved on to point D.

"As of the moment, I have not been retained by Jackson Coleman or his mother. So I suppose we need a client."

He flipped through a Rolodex and when he found the number, picked up the phone and punched the buttons. He put the receiver to his ear and waited.

"Hello," he said, speaking formally, "may I please speak with Mrs. Coleman."

After a pause, he said, in a more familiar tone, "Hello, Mrs. Coleman. This is Nat Semmes calling. You probably remember me. I represented your son Jackson in a legal matter a while back."

Pause.

"I'm just fine, thank you. How are you?"

Pause.

"Yes. I understand. I've just been speaking with my associate,

Morgan Hunt, about it. Mr. Hunt has been telling me about your conversation."

There was another pause, longer this time, during which Semmes's expression changed just slightly. The look, I knew, was one of sympathy, the helpless sort of sympathy you feel for someone whose pain is undeserved and, in the end, beyond your ability to ease. Semmes tended to be that way about his clients. He empathized, as they say, and he considered it a weakness.

"Yes ma'am," Semmes said soothingly, "I would be happy to look into it and represent Jackson if it comes to that."

The pause was shorter this time.

"I don't think you need to worry about my fee at this time, Mrs. Coleman. We can discuss that later but it won't be a problem."

Pause.

"I wasn't worried about the money then, either, Mrs. Coleman. I was very amply compensated. Let's worry about Jackson and his difficulties for the moment."

Pause.

"God bless you, too."

Semmes hung up and stared at the phone for a moment. "Sharper than a serpent's tooth, you know, Morgan," he said, "after all that woman has been through, her own sorry-assed kid bites her in the foot. Whatever else he did, that's the real crime."

I nodded and said, "So you want me to go talk to the punk?"

"The *client*," he smiled. "Yes. Go speak to Mr. Jackson Coleman and get his side of the story. I'm sure he was framed. No doubt he was in bed at the time the crime was committed. Or maybe he was studying for his remedial reading class so he can get a job and better himself."

"Or at church."

"No. That would require eyewitnesses."

"I'll be at the jail when they open."

Semmes nodded and turned and looked out the window at all that clean, uncluttered water.

After a moment, he said, "Whatever Jackson Coleman says, it won't make a lot of difference to the case."

"Why's that?" I said. I didn't understand the law's distinctions and never saw the point in trying to unravel them except when they applied to me directly.

"The State Supreme Court has ruled on it again and again,

Morgan. Every year, they get three or four cases involving a murder that is committed during the course of a drug deal and even when it looks like self-defense, it still comes out felony murder."

"Which is?"

"When you went into the park to buy or sell drugs, you were engaging in the commission of a felony. And when a murder is committed in the course of the commission of a felony, the technical term for that is felony murder. And that is always homicide in the first degree. They are electrocuting people on a semiregular basis for that over at Raiford."

"You think he'll get the death penalty?"

Semmes shrugged. "It doesn't help that he's still on probation from the last time he was in trouble."

"No. I could see how that would work against him."

"I don't much care about Jackson Coleman, myself. He's not worth a morning of my time. He could get all the legal counsel he's entitled to and deserves from the public defender. I'll be representing him, but my real client is Dinah Coleman. I'd like to keep her from having to see one of her children go to the electric chair. I've known her a long time, and I'd like to spare her that.

"Of course," Semmes went on in a tone I recognized, the one he used when his combative juices were beginning to surge, "it could be that this is just what you've been needing. A gift to help you break out from your boredom."

"You and me both," I said.

Semmes liked that. He smiled and said, "You remember what Robert E. Lee said when he was up on the ridge at Fredericksburg, watching a Union attack and then a counterattack by Stonewall Jackson?"

"No, Nat. I wasn't there that day."

He ignored that and went on. "Lee was looking over the battlefield, at the one line moving forward and the other giving way, slowly at first, and then faster until finally it just broke altogether and the retreat was on. Lee watched and turned to one of his aides and said, 'It is good that war is so terrible. Else we would grow too fond of it.' "

"He had that right."

"That's the worm in the heart of the law, Morgan. Lawyers have a wonderful time. Just like generals. A good case is like a great battle. But it takes clients and witnesses and jurors and they don't have much fun. I don't expect there's any chance Dinah

Coleman will share my sense of exhilaration and glory any more than some butternut who got his leg smashed by a minié ball could share Lee's feelings about the battle of Fredericksburg."

"No, Nat," I said, "I don't suppose so. And I don't suppose there is a hell of a lot you can do about it either."

"No. I just try to take good cases and then win them."

"I'd say that's a good start."

"And try not to love it too much."

"That too."

"Call me after you've talked to Jackson Coleman."

"I'll do it."

"I appreciate your help, Morgan."

"Any time, Nat. Any time at all."

6

The interrogation room where I waited for Jackson Coleman was small, glaringly bright, and unventilated. The acoustical tile was yellowed from nicotine, like a smoker's teeth, and the floor was smeared with the streaks of a trustee's filthy mop. I sat behind a bare steel table and waited. They like to make you wait.

After ten minutes, the door opened and a man in police blues brought Jackson Coleman in, holding him just above the elbow, the way you would lead a blind man through a crowded lobby. Coleman's hands were secured to a chain that hung from a belt at his waist.

"Okay," the man in blue said, "sit there and do your talking."

Coleman shuffled across the room. Another chain ran between his ankles and dragged listlessly along the floor.

He sat down and looked at me.

"How about unlocking him?" I said.

"Can't do it," the guard said. His lips hardly moved under his brush mustache.

"He's not going anywhere," I said. "Just unlock him, close the door, and leave us here. I won't let him get away."

The guard looked at me, then at Coleman, who stared at the floor.

"You don't have to hard-ass him full time," I said. "It'll be on me."

He shook his head.

"Look," I said, "if you want to push it, I'll leave and go call Nat Semmes. That's who I'm working for. Semmes will listen to what I have to say and he'll call your chief and raise a stink. You don't need that on Monday morning, so why don't you just unlock him?"

The guard thought for another moment and then slowly took a ring of keys off his wide, polished leather belt. He spent some time looking for the right key and when he'd found it, used it on one of the bracelets on Coleman's wrists. Then the other.

He turned to me and said, "The legs stay locked," then left the room.

When the door closed, I looked across at Jackson Coleman, whose eyes were still lowered. He was thin, like his brother, but not quite as tall, with the same long limbs that looked almost unjointed. His hair was longer and he had a rough, three- or four-day beard over some old acne pits and a pink, four-inch scar that would have been made by a knife or straight razor. The little air-less room was full of his smell, the jailhouse stink of old sweat, trapped smoke, and a kind of rank, glandular desperation. It was a sickeningly familiar smell that had me sweating, even though the room wasn't especially hot.

"My name," I said, "is Morgan Hunt. I'm working for Nathaniel Semmes. He was your lawyer on another case. I'm sure you remember. Yesterday, Semmes told your mother he'd try to help you again, now that you're back in trouble. That's why I'm here."

Coleman said nothing. Did not move. Kept his eyes on the floor.

"Nat Semmes is the best shot you've got at staying out of the electric chair," I said, "so I'd suggest you straighten up, look at me, and answer my questions."

He raised his head. His eyes were wide and seemed to glitter in the glare of the little room. "*Electric chair*," he said. "No way man. I didn't kill nobody."

"You'd also be doing yourself a favor if you told the truth. Lying won't help you and lying to *me* might *hurt* you."

"I'll talk to Mr. Semmes."

"Eventually," I said. "But right now, you're talking to me.

And talking to me is the same as talking to Mr. Semmes. It's privileged, same as if you were talking to him."

"Privileged?" he said, mocking me.

"That's right," I said. "It means that I can't be compelled to reveal anything you tell me. And if I do, it can't be used against you and, furthermore, I'll get my ass in a crack for violating the confidentiality of our conversation. You understand all that?"

"Sure, man."

"Then answer my questions and tell me the truth. Leave the thinking to Semmes. He's got a lot more experience and a lot better equipment than you or me."

Coleman sneered at me and said, "All right, man, I'll answer your fucking questions. But what's this bullshit about the electric chair. Even if they can prove I did kill the dude, it was self-defense. Him or me. He pulled on me and I did what I had to do. I ain't supposed to go ahead and die, am I?"

"No," I said. "But when you volunteer for drug duty—buying or selling—you are engaged in the commission of a felony. And if somebody gets killed during the commission of a felony, even if it's self-defense or just an accident, then what they call it is felony murder. And that is first degree. Every time."

Coleman stiffened and his eyes went quickly from side to side so that he looked, for a moment, like a small, trapped animal.

"Bullshit, man. That's bullshit."

"No," I said, a little sorrowfully, trying to make myself sound sympathetic. "I'm afraid not. Nat Semmes explained it to me. Better than I explained it to you, probably. Ask him when you see him."

"Bullshit. Guy pulled on me. I didn't have no choice."

"I understand. But the law is the law. You didn't leave the law any choice, either." If I managed to sound sincere to him, then it was because I was. Something like the same thing had happened to me. My sister had been beaten by a man she was married to. She was hiding out in my house and he came looking for her. Once I'd started on him, I didn't stop until he was a puddle. I'd had my reasons and I was awfully sorry about the whole thing. But the law was obliged to do what it did.

"Listen, Jackson. You aren't going to get anywhere arguing with *me*. I'm working for Semmes and he knows what he's doing, right?"

"Yeah, man. I suppose so."

"Semmes is your lifeline right now. Before he can help you, you've got to help me. You understand that, don't you."

"Yeah."

"So how about answering some questions."

"Okay, man," he said, licking his lips as though he were suddenly very thirsty. "Ask your questions."

"All right. But one more thing."

He looked at me and blinked.

"Don't call me 'man.'"

He gave me a bewildered look but I didn't give him time to say anything.

"I'm not your cellmate or one of your street buddies," I said. "If you have to call me something, call me Mr. Hunt. Now let's get down to business."

I wanted to establish a relationship with Jackson and it was not one based on friendship. I wanted him to tell me the truth— and be too afraid of me not to.

He nodded and straightened up in his chair. I knew I had his attention.

"You think Mr. Semmes can get me off?" he said while I was taking out my notebook. "Get it down from first degree, I mean?"

"I don't know. But if he can't, then nobody can."

"I mean, it ain't like I met the dude so I could kill him. He called *me*."

"And you agreed to meet him, right? To sell him some rock?"

"Yeah, but right away I knew it was wrong. He was either fixing to rip me off or he was a narc. Something."

"Did he *say* he was a cop?"

Jackson Coleman stared at me for a moment. "You think he's gonna introduce himself or something? 'My name is Officer Jones. Nice to meet you. Now why don't you sell me some rock and then please accept these marked bills I'm carrying so that we can use them in evidence and send your ass to prison.' Sheeeit."

"He did not say you were under arrest? Show you any identification?"

"He never *said* nothing about being a narc. And I ain't dead sure he was. He could have been just wanting to rip me off or he could have been some kind of scum informer. I wasn't waiting around to run no investigation."

"Known him long?"

"Not to talk to. Seen him around, though. He was just another dude until a couple of weeks ago, then he started bumping into me at bars. Making conversation and buying beers. Eventually, he got around to saying what was really on his mind. We set up a meeting. I'd bring the stuff and he'd bring his money."

I asked Jackson Coleman for the details. Time, place, how much stuff, and how much money. He answered in the bored fashion of someone who had done it hundreds of times. And he probably had. A drug deal was no big thing in his life. Nothing much was.

"Except when we finally had our meeting this dude was in too big a hurry, you know. Coming on *very* hard. Like he just could not wait to get his money into my hands. Seemed like he wanted to get rid of the money more than he wanted to get ahold of the drugs. Seemed like it was more important for him to get the deal done than it was for him to have some coke to put inside of him, you know what I mean?"

"So what did you do?"

"Well, when I saw how strong he's coming on, I decide I don't want to play. It's a seller's market. I don't have no trouble moving merchandise. I did what all those straight folks tell you to do, I just said no."

He looked at me and smiled. But there wasn't that much relief for him in this feeble stab at wit. His face glistened with a film of greasy sweat, his hands trembled, and he chewed nervously at his lower lip.

"What did he do?"

"He grabbed at me, said something about how he wasn't going to be fucked around. He'd met me 'cause I told him I was going to sell him some drugs and now, by God, I was going to sell him some drugs."

"Uh-huh."

"Came out with a lot of that. Got right in my face until I pushed him away. That's when he went for something in his coat. Well, I don't go undressed to a party like that. I had my own piece and I got to it before he could get to his."

"Shot him?"

"Two times."

"Then?"

"I beat feet out of there."

"Anybody see you?"

"Could have been somebody in the parking lot across the street, but I didn't see no one. And if they saw me, they didn't get a close look because I wasn't standing still."

"Where did you go?"

"Bar."

"Which one."

"Midnight Rose. Kind of a dump."

"And the cops came for you there?"

"That's right."

"How long after you got there."

"I don't know. Half an hour."

"And took you downtown?"

"Just as soon as they'd read me my rights."

"They put you in a lineup?"

"Yeah."

"And somebody identified you?"

"Yeah."

"They give you a paraffin test?"

"The thing where they put the stuff on your hand? Yeah, they done that too."

"You still carrying the gun when they picked you up?"

He shook his head slowly and his voice dropped into a register of disappointment, probably at his own stupidity. "Yeah. I still had it."

"Probably still had the cocaine, too, right?"

He slumped a little more in the chair and lowered his head closer to the floor.

I let him sit there like that for a minute so it would all sink in. I wanted him to listen to me like I was his last hope.

"Okay, Jackson," I said, "now I want you to listen to me very carefully. You may be slick on the streets but there is no way you can slide out of this one on your own. You've got a way of doing exactly the wrong thing and if you keep it up, you are going over to Raiford and ride the lightning. You understand?"

He looked up and said, almost in a whisper, "Yessir. I understand."

"All right. Do not—I repeat, do *not*—say anything to anyone about any of this. Not to one of your keepers and not to any of the other studs they're holding in this jail. One of them would be only too happy to talk to the prosecutor if he thought he could cut a

deal. You talk about this with two people—and only two people—
me and Mr. Semmes. You got that?"

"Yessir," he said in the same strained voice and nodded.

"Okay. Now, one last thing—do you get a lot of people coming
up and talking to you about your brother?"

"William? He's not in this. Not in none of it. Not the drugs or
any of the rest. We keep him out."

"Yes," I said. "We do. But I need to know."

"How come?"

"Let me worry about that. Just answer the question."

He pinched his chin and looked past me. "People are always
coming up to me to talk about William. Seen him in a game, you
know, and want to tell me how good he is. Ask where he's going
to school and if they can buy a piece of him, like a stud horse. Stuff
like that."

"Anybody ever ask you if you had any influence with him?"

Coleman studied me for a minute, plainly trying to figure
out where this line was coming from and wondering if there was
something in it he could use.

"Anybody at all?"

"Most folks ain't that stupid. What sort of influence could I
have with William?"

"What about the man you met in the parking lot, Jackson? You
said he came up to you at bars, making conversation. Did he want
to talk about William?"

"I suppose," he sighed, like a man weary of being hassled. "I
don't remember."

"Okay," I said. "No skin off my ass. You're the one looking at
a fast first-degree verdict. If it's too much trouble . . ."

"Okay. Okay. Gimme a second." He put his fingers to his
temples. "Hard to think when you got something this heavy on the
brain."

I waited, and after a minute he said, "Yeah, I remember a
week ago, just about, when the dude found me at a bar and bought
a couple of malts. He was talking about William and how a man
could get well for life just being his agent. I told him it wouldn't
be happening soon since William promised our mama he'd go to
college and finish. He's good for keeping promises."

"And that was it?"

"Yeah, just about. Guy said something about how when you

started talking really big money, even the straight ones started bending. Then he paid for a couple of more malts and we talked about something else."

I closed the notebook, stood up, and walked to the door. Before I opened it, I looked back at Jackson Coleman and said, "All right, remember what I said."

"No talking."

"That's right."

"Okay. But tell me something."

"I'll try."

"Mr. Semmes going to be able to help me?"

"I don't know. Maybe. If he can't, then probably nobody can. For now, help yourself by keeping your mouth shut."

"I understand," he said. He was shivering now, even in the warmth of the stuffy little room. "Do something for me, will you?"

"What?"

"If you see my mama, tell her I'm okay and to please come see me."

The man in blue came back in the room, shackled Jackson's wrists, and, holding him by the upper arm, led him out of the room and back to his cell. He'd been bad on the streets but now he was just another sick, scared convict who had dug himself a hole deeper than he could ever bullshit or hustle his way out of. And he knew it.

7

It felt good to leave the police station, with its little, unventilated rooms and constant, metallic din, its oppressive closeness. Relief was the word, I suppose. That, and a sense that you could finally breathe deep. In jail, you always feel starved for air.

I walked up the street for a block or two and then turned around and walked back the way I had come, filling my lungs with new air every three or four steps.

This little walk took me by the oldest graveyard in town, a ten-acre plot that is full of big crypts and ornate statues marking the mortal remains of people nobody remembers. It has been years since anyone was buried here so the maintenance tends to be hit or miss. The place was just crying to be bush-hogged. The weeds were knee high everywhere and vines were coiled like snakes around some of the dirty granite obelisks. This place, I thought, had the right look. No one would ever mistake it for a golf course.

Before I made it back to the lot where I'd parked my truck, I found a pay phone and called Tom Pine.

"Pine," he said. If bears could talk, they would sound like Tom Pine.

"Morning."

"How yew, Morgan."

"Fine. You busy?"

57

"Well, you know, it *is* Monday morning and folks do like to weekend hard. We've got to count the bodies, round up the prisoners, and write the after-action reports. But I've seen it worse."

"You got a few minutes to talk about that business we were on yesterday?"

"Yeah," he said cautiously. "I believe I can manage that. You want to meet at Ray's? About thirty minutes?"

"That would be fine," I said.

I drank black coffee and so did Tom Pine. The difference was, he had two slices of pecan pie to go with the coffee, and even so, that was just nibbling. I watched him eat and wondered what one of those evangelists of good nutrition would think after a day or two in Tom's company. That he was sunk in the muck of sin too deep ever to pull himself out, probably. But you just couldn't imagine Tom ever standing up to the temptations of fried chicken, pecan pie, and barbecued ribs for the righteousness of green salads and soda water. That kind of conversion wouldn't accomplish Pine's deliverance, anyway. It would just make him thinner and, probably, irritable as a nest of moccasins. Food seemed to quiet the beast in him.

"Now that is some fine pie," he said, cleaning the second plate. "You don't usually find pie of that *quality* in no restaurant."

"Proud to see you are getting your nourishment, Tom."

"Yeah," he said contentedly, "this time of morning, I'll have a little sinking spell unless I can get something in my stomach. But now, I'm good."

"Ready to talk about Jackson Coleman?"

"Ready as I'm likely to get. You talked with Semmes?"

"Yesterday afternoon."

"And . . ."

"He can't work for you and Jackson Coleman both. You can see why."

Pine nodded slowly. He knew there was more and he would wait for it before he committed himself.

"He did tell me that it would be better for Jackson Coleman and his mother if there was no official investigation of her charges. For the time being, anyway."

Pine nodded again. He knew that Semmes would not leave him hanging.

"Nat says there are people he could recommend if you want some outside legal advice. A thing like this, it seems like nobody really knows. You hear something from a neighbor or a friend. Do you launch an official investigation, or do you just poke around informally?"

Pine thought for a minute, picked at a last crumb of pie crust on one of the plates in front of him, then said, "I don't need any outside advice. If Semmes says its a judgment call—and that's what I hear you saying—then I'll use my own judgment instead of some lawyer's. It's carried me this far."

"What's your judgment tell you right now?"

"Little early yet, I think, to start any kind of formal investigation. Probably just scare off the folks we'd be trying to catch. I suspect the best thing I could do right now is hide in the weeds and watch who comes down the trail. That, and keep talking to you. You are still talking to me, ain't you, Morgan?"

"Absolutely."

"So"—Tom smiled and his big, straight teeth showed bright as bleached porcelain—"what can you tell me?"

I waited while the counterman filled our cups, then I told him about my visit to the city jail that morning and my conversation there with Jackson Coleman. It took a while and once or twice I had to look at my notes. Tom listened impassively until I was finished, sipping at his coffee and reaching in his shirt pocket for a toothpick, but showing nothing at all in his face.

"Now *that*," he said a moment or two after I'd finished, "is one dumb sumbitch. Still packing the gun *and* the drugs. Wonder he didn't paint up a sign, wear it around his neck, saying, 'I'm the one, Come on and bust my dumb ass.' "

"I expect he was flying pretty high."

"Sure he was," Pine said. The sleepy, passive voice was gone. The one that had replaced it was hard, blunt, and full of contempt. "Like that is some kind of goddamned excuse. Dumb shit like that . . . he's got an excuse for everything. 'Sheeeut man, let me tell you,' " Pine said, dropping into a broad, contemptuous parody of street dialect, 'I cayunt get me no good job cause I ain't got no education. Reason I'm dealing, you see, is the only other job I could get is flipping burgers at the McDonalds.' "

Pine hit the table with the flat of his massive hand. The counterman jumped a foot.

"You've heard that old bullshit, haven't you," he said. His face was alive now, and his eyes were hot. "About how these kids are dealing drugs because it's the only open path they got?"

"Yeah," I said, without committing myself. I didn't want Tom to take it out—whatever it was—on me.

"Well, you know, they're giving out educations free all over town and with what these dudes make dealing in a couple of months, they could go out and buy themselves a year at Harvard. So I ain't buying. Jackson Coleman is a sorry-assed, no-good, low-rent punk. He's got an excuse for everything. For why he couldn't finish school, why he can't hold a job, why he sells drugs and smokes up all the profits, why he found himself in the wrong alley with the wrong man. 'Wasn't my fault, man,' " Pine said, mimicking broadly again, " 'dude was *packing*. He pulled on *me*.' "

"That's just about exactly what he told me," I said.

"No surprise," Pine said. "Shame you can't just let him sink like a stone. You hate to see someone like Semmes wasting his time on such jailhouse trash."

"Maybe so," I said, "but where would jailhouse trash like me be if it wasn't for Nat Semmes?"

Pine broke out into laughter that rolled through the little closed spaces of Ray's like summer thunder. The counterman looked for a moment like he might be about to run for it. Pine leaned back in his chair and laughed for a full minute and when he had finally laughed himself out, he pulled a blue bandanna from his back pocket and wiped his wet cheeks, then blew his nose. He looked up at me and smiled. "Morgan, you might be a lot of things but one thing you most surely *ain't*, and that is jailhouse trash." Pine laughed again, more softly this time.

I smiled and took it as a compliment.

Tom drank a couple of glasses of water to cool his throat and was ready to get back to business.

"Can't stay away *all* morning," he said, looking at his watch.

"Okay. I won't keep you. But what about the victim? Any chance he was a cop, like Jackson said?"

"Nah."

"Why not?"

"In the first place, it just sounds like another excuse. Jackson probably shot the guy because he was getting ripped off—or he was trying to rip the guy off—and he's such a fuckup he couldn't handle it without shooting. But it sounds better if he says the guy was heat. Makes him bad, instead of just dumb."

"Any other possibilities?"

"Well, I suppose the guy *could* have been some kind of pissant junkie informer. Street slime that gets left alone just as long as it keeps coming up with names and information. But that's a long way from an undercover cop."

"Okay," I said, "then let's assume for a minute that Jackson's razor-sharp instincts were correct and the guy was some kind of street informer."

Pine snorted.

"Then," I went on, "wouldn't somebody have known about the meeting?"

Pine thought for a moment. "Probably."

"I mean, it does seem like they picked him up awful quick. And Jackson says there was nobody around to witness the killing, but then he got put in a lineup and identified."

"Well, I doubt Jackson had real good flank security. Just because he didn't see nobody doesn't mean there wasn't somebody there."

"Still, they came for him awfully quick. Soon enough that he still hadn't ditched the gun and the dope."

Pine sighed. "That dumb-ass might still be holding on to that gun and that coke today."

"Maybe. But I think I'll go out to that bar—what did he call it?" I checked my notes.

"The Midnight Rose."

"A real gutbucket," Pine said.

"I'd like to talk to the help. Get some idea about how the arrest went down. See if the boys in blue just walked up to Jackson like they had him in their sights all along."

Pine looked at his watch. "You don't want to be going out there for a while yet. Five or six hours. This time of morning, they haven't even cleaned up the blood from last night."

"Three o'clock?"

"Yeah. They ought to be opening up around then."

That would give me time to ask my questions at the bar and still get back to Semmes's office before he went home for the day, I thought. It left me with a lot of time to kill, but not quite enough to drive back to the river house and then back into town.

Tom looked at his watch again and said, "I got to get back, Morgan. Stay in touch. And be careful when you go out to that bar, now."

"I will, Tom. Promise."

"No fooling. That joint is in a bad part of town, for one thing. And for another, you are the wrong color. Be careful and be polite. It's early in this thing. Too soon for you to be getting cut."

8

When I pulled out of the lot in front of Ray's, I turned on the radio. It was too late, by hours, for the farm report so I thought I'd listen to an oldies station while I considered what to do next.

I got sports instead of oldies, with the urgent, sandpapered voice of Mike Grantham reading the weekend's basketball scores like they were hot dispatches from some combat zone.

"The Wolfpack," Grantham was saying, "went out on the road this weekend. It was a short march down Interstate Forty into hostile territory where the Blue Devils take no prisoners. . . ." And so on and so forth. You'd never know, sometimes, that these people were talking about games played by adolescents wearing short pants.

Actually, I enjoyed listening to Grantham. He was sort of a local institution. I suppose every fairly large town has someone like him, especially in the South. The man for whom sports is Truth, Beauty, and the Spheres in their orbits. The transcendent jock-strap. His was probably one of the most popular—or at least recognizable—figures in town and people would miss dinner to listen to his nightly call-in show. I'd met him once when Tom Pine and I were out eating ribs. Grantham came over to the table and put his hand on Pine's shoulder. He called him stud and big fellow and generally laid it on thick. He was mildly, convivially drunk. Pine seemed to tolerate him and, when he had an opening, introduced me. Since I'd never been an all-American, Grantham merely shook my hand politely, then turned back to Tom and asked him how he thought the Sugar Bowl would turn out. Pine told him he figured the more physical team would win. Grantham seemed satisfied with that and let us get back to our ribs.

When Grantham had finished with the scores and signed off until drive time, I stopped at a convenience store and used the pay phone to call him at station WZZA. I had some questions that he might be able to answer. It was his territory I was walking, after all, even if he didn't see the terrain quite the way I did. The switchboard put me through.

"Yeah," he said in a voice had been roughed up by whiskey.

I told him my name and reminded him that Tom Pine had introduced us.

"Sure," he lied. "I remember."

"Well, Tom said you might be able to help me with something." If he could lie, so could I.

"This some kind of police business?"

Sort of, I explained.

"Well, as long as it's for Tom and I ain't a suspect."

"Strictly unofficial," I said.

"Come on out, then. I'm just sitting here drinking coffee, eating aspirin, and reading the funny papers to get ready for my next show."

I told him I'd be right there.

Grantham met me in the lobby of the studio. He was short and thick, with a melon for a belly, and a face full of fine red fissures where the veins had broken under the strain of the booze. He wore wrinkled khaki pants, a blue cotton shirt that was unbuttoned at the collar and rolled up at the sleeves, and a tie that was loosened and looked like it stayed that way.

"Come on back," he said after we'd shaken hands and he'd studied my face, trying to remember where and when he'd met me and then giving it up, most likely, as something lost, like a lot that had happened in his evenings.

"Thanks," I said. "I know you're busy. Damned if I can see how you keep up with all of it the way you do." Nobody needs flattery like someone in show business.

He smiled with gratitude and led the way through a door and down a line of cubicles. His was at the end, small and cluttered,

with the day's papers spread over the surface of his desk and magazines piled uncertainly on the floor. The cork bulletin board was
covered with news clips and pictures, most of which showed him
holding a microphone in front of some athlete who looked large
and fit next to him.

He pulled a small chair out from the wall and said, "Have a
seat. So Tom Pine sent you?"

I nodded.

"Tom is much man," he said, with something approaching
reverence. "Much man."

"Yes."

"There are a lot of good athletes. Millions of them. You go
around these schools like I have, and you get to where good athletes
don't really impress you much anymore. A lot of them are fast, can
jump over my head, and lift four hundred pounds. But not many
have what Tom Pine had. You know what that is?"

"What's that?"

"Heart. That sumbitch was a *player*. You know what I mean?"

I said I did.

"He could have been another Butkus if he'd played pro."

I agreed.

"He's still that way, from what I hear. I wouldn't like to be
the poor sumbitch he busted."

"No," I said. "Me neither."

"His kind just doesn't come along every day."

"No."

He rocked back in his chair and looked around the little office
for a moment. His eyes fell on his computer screen. He studied it
for a second and tapped a couple of keys.

"My commentary for tonight," he said. "Hard-hitting stuff
about steroids. Want to make sure it's saved. I've lost more good
stuff trying to learn how to use this computer."

I nodded.

"Well, what can I do for you?"

I told him I was working for a lawyer and his face went solemn.

"Not my favorite class of people. But that's probably because
I've paid so many of them for divorce work and wasn't happy with
the results."

"This is a little different. We're trying to help a kid who might
be getting a bad deal from college recruiters."

His mouth tightened and his eyes narrowed so that he looked

less like a harmless bullshitter and more like a man with some serious business on his mind.

"Well, there's plenty of that. It's a rotten system and it's been so rotten for so long that people don't pay any attention anymore."

I waited for more. "Do you remember the Davis kid, a few years back?"

I nodded, even though I hadn't heard of any Davis kid.

"Well, when he was a sophomore in high school and still just a growing boy, people were already talking about how he'd be a sure Heisman winner one day if he didn't get hurt. He was that good.

"One of the big hogs in town, man named Griggs who made a pile in insurance and who is a big university man—bled with the Gators every Saturday and worried about them all year long, even had him a vanity plate on his car that said B L G T R, for Bull Gator, you know—well, this Griggs decided that he was, by God, going to do whatever it took to get Davis to Gainesville.

"What he did," Grantham said, shaking his head at the memory, "was, without even letting on what was on his mind, he hired the Davis kid's parents to work for him. The daddy was some kind of grease monkey at a muffler shop. Griggs made him a 'building engineer' and paid him about five times what he'd been making. The mother was a school secretary. He gave her a job, too, and kept promoting her until she was just about running things in the office. He got to know them both and told them what a fine son they had. He went to all the games and when the team played out of town, a long way from home, he'd take them to the game with him in his airplane.

"When it was time for the kid to decide where to go to college, Griggs told the parents he'd use his influence to help the kid get into Gainesville. That was a joke. That kid didn't need any help from Griggs to get in Gainesville or anywhere else. He could have gone to Notre Dame if he'd wanted to, except I heard he couldn't read so good, so maybe the Irish couldn't have taken him since they're still fussy that way. But they would have tried. And any other school in the country would have found a way. Hired full-time tutors and made the kid into a phys ed major so he could take courses in Playground Dynamics until he'd used up his eligibility. Happens all the time."

I nodded and said something about how it was a shame the way the kids got used.

Grantham sighed and shook his head.

"I'm not as pure as I used to be on that. You go around to these schools and you see a lot of kids who aren't there for pre-med and poetry. The fraternity houses are full of them. But if some party boy gets hepatitis and has to quit drinking beer . . . what happens then?"

I looked at Grantham and blinked. I wasn't following him.

"You think they throw him out of school because he's taking up space and they got a line on some other hell raiser with real potential?"

I still didn't get it.

"The Davis kid went to the U. His parents had already moved into a nice new house on what Griggs was paying them. Second game of his freshman year, he broke his leg. At first, it looked like no big deal. The doctors could fix it and since he hadn't played but four or five quarters, they might even be able to red-shirt him so he'd still have four years of eligibility left. But he got some kind of infection. Staph, I think. And the doctors had to go in and take out about this much bone." Grantham held his hands four or five inches apart and shook his head sadly.

"Kid will be limping the rest of his life. I can run the forty faster than he can now."

"That's a tough one," I said.

"What do you think the U did for the kid?"

"I don't know."

"Flunked him out of school, that's what. And what do you think Mr. Bull Gator Griggs did for him and his family?"

I could see it coming but he was on a roll so I let him tell it.

"He had a shakeup at the office. Didn't need the Davis mother or father anymore. Computer took her job. New machinery handled his. They don't travel with him in his airplane anymore, either. And they had to sell the house.

"What we're talking here is some kind of strange combination of servitude and the lottery. The U makes millions on a kid like Davis if he stays healthy. What it gives him is a free education if he's smart enough and tough enough to take advantage of it. But his coaches don't exactly encourage him to sign up for the toughest courses in school. They want him concentrating on what he's there for . . . and that's not calculus.

"But okay, say the kid doesn't get an education. At least he plays ball and gets a shot at the pros and big money. That's what a lot of people would tell you, anyway." Grantham shook his head at the folly of that notion.

"But how many kids make the pros?" he said, wearily.

I shrugged.

"Say a hundred a year, and that's probably high. Every big-time school has that many on scholarship. Every single one. So what happens is, most of these kids play real hard for four years, make the school a lot of money, and then they go back home, just as poor and dumb as they were when they left. Those schools use 'em and throw 'em on the scrap heap.

"Now these kids aren't stupid. They may not set the classroom on fire but they can smell bullshit when they're standing in it. It's their bodies these schools are using to make money, so when some coach or rich alum like Griggs comes around saying, 'Come play for us,' what a lot of these kids want to know is, 'How much are you paying?'

"There's a grant-in-aid—that's what's on the table. But that's just the frosting. What the kids—and their parents—want to know is . . . what's passing *under* the table? They're thinking cars and cash. And Griggs, or somebody like him, will always be there to come up with the package. Even so, the kids are selling cheap."

Grantham was sagging a little now, as though explaining all of this might have worn him out. His face had gone gray and moist and I could smell the alcoholic residue of last night's drinking as it seeped from his pores.

He looked at his watch. "Listen, it's getting close to noon and I need a bottle of lunch before I come back and gear up for the show. You up to that?"

"Sure."

"There's a little place I go. Pepper's, it's called. They're trying to make it into a real, big-city sports bar. You want to follow me there and grab a bite?"

"Fine."

He stood up, put on his Seminoles hat and one of those satin warm-up jackets, checked to make sure he had his wallet and that his answering machine was turned on, then said, "Okay, let's travel. We can keep on talking when we get there."

Pepper's was just inside the main entrance of the newest, state-of-the-art shopping mall, with a jewelry store on one side and a jeans and T-shirt shop on the other. It was dark, with a long bar and a couple of dozen heavy-looking tables, all of them empty. Television sets, with screens large enough to make a table for four, sat on raised platforms along each wall. The remainder of the decor consisted of posters showing basketball players dunking or dribbling and football players throwing, catching, running, or tackling.

"Hey, Bo," Grantham said to the man behind the bar. "How you making it?"

"Hanging in, Mike. Hanging in. How about you?"

"I'll be better soon as you open me a beer."

"You got it," the man said.

With the bottle and a frosted mug in front of him, Grantham ignored the glass and took a long pull from the damp bottle. The bartender shrugged and looked at me. "What's yours?" he said.

"Got any coffee?"

"Just made a pot. How do you like it?"

"Black, please."

When I had my mug of coffee, Grantham said, "You getting much lunch business?"

"A little," the bartender said mournfully, "but Monday's bad."

"Well, hang in there. It'll catch on, takes time."

He turned to me and said, "You go to any city bigger than this one, and there'll be at least one of these places going gangbusters. People come in, watch the games on these big screens, drink beer, yell and scream for their team. I do some of my shows from down here. Bo here is going to make this thing work, right?"

The bartender, who was young and plainly working at keeping his spirits up, said, "It's hard, Mike. Town this size. If they had Monday night football every night, it would be easy."

"You'll make it. You got plenty of the old want to. And I'm going to keep talking it up on the show until people come in just to see what all the noise is about. You get 'em in once, and they'll come back. You watch."

The bartender nodded and gave Grantham a tepid, professional smile.

"Nothing worth watching this time of day, is there?" Grantham said, "Not even on ESPN?"

"Just soaps and some golf tournament."

"Well, how about putting on one of those game tapes? Maybe that Duke/Carolina game from a couple of years back. You know the one."

"Sure."

"And give me another one of these." Grantham tilted his empty bottle in the bartender's direction.

When he had his fresh beer, Grantham led the way across the room to a table. The televisions came to life with the tip-off of a basketball game.

"That was my idea," he said, once we were seated. "I told Bo there to get tapes of some of those old games and show them. People remember the great ones."

I didn't think so, but I merely said, "Did it work?"

"It's catching on," Grantham said, as though success wasn't really the proper test of an inspired idea. "You know, people over in Louisiana still listen to the radio replay of the punt return Billy Cannon made against Mississippi more than thirty years ago."

I wasn't sure what he was talking about and it must have showed.

"You're not a big fan, are you? You must have played ball, then. Like Tom Pine. Nobody who played really follows the game unless he goes into broadcasting. Even most of those guys need help."

I nodded.

"Billy Cannon was one of the great ones. A hero in Louisiana and all over the South. I was just a kid when he played and I thought he was a god."

Grantham drank some beer and shook his head. "No . . . not a god. One of those epic heroes, carved out of marble and *touched* by the gods. He was Hector *and* Achilles."

He saw my look and smiled.

"I might have grown up in a sawmill town," he said, "but I went off to college and studied literature."

He pronounced it *liht*-rha-tuah.

"I was going to write the epics of our times. The heroes would be ballplayers. I didn't realize I'd be working for the funny papers and then running my mouth for the radio. . . ."

He shook his head and swallowed some more beer.

"Anyway . . . Billy Cannon. One night, LSU was playing Old Miss at the Tiger Pit in Baton Rouge. Ole Miss had 'em on the ropes all night long, playing defense like their end zone was sacred soil. Got a field goal and sat on it for three quarters.

"Then they punted to Cannon like they were just *daring* him to take his best shot. He took the ball and started upfield. I remember listening to it on the radio in my room. When the announcer described how Cannon took the ball and cut around the first man downfield to cover, the crowd noise just started rising, like the wind. The announcer was shouting over it, telling how Cannon faked another tackler and then how another one just about had him but he broke out of it. And then how he ran over another one of those Mississippi kids and put him on his back. Every Mississippi kid had a shot at him but he made it all the way. None of them could bring him down. By the time he made it to the end zone, the announcer was sobbing.

"It was the goddamnedest run ever," Grantham said, shaking his head. "I swear it was."

"I don't know why I'd never heard of it," I said. The way Grantham had told it, I was actually sorry I hadn't.

"Come by my office sometime," he said, "and I'll loan you my tape."

"All right."

He sat back and drank the rest of his beer, then stood up to get another.

"More coffee?"

"No thanks."

He took very deliberate steps to the bar.

"If you've never heard about that run," he said when he was back and had taken a long, thirsty swallow from his new bottle, "then you probably don't know what happened to Cannon later."

"No."

"Well, that run was the apotheosis. There's a good five-dollar word for you. Afterwards, it was never as good. Not for a lot of people who saw the game or listened to it on the radio, and not for Cannon, either. He played in the pros but it was never the same; no way it could have been. Then he retired and you know what he did?"

I shook my head.

"Fixed teeth. He was a dentist. Talk about coming down. That must have been a hard landing. But it got worse. The last newspaper story I ever wrote was about Billy Cannon going into federal court and getting sentenced to jail. Conspiracy to defraud. Some kind of real estate scam.

"I went to the courthouse and stood around with the other reporters. They were all young guys who didn't know anything about that punt return. To them, Cannon was just an ex-ballplayer who'd gotten in with some hoods. They saw it as a crime story.

Strictly straight news. They were talking about pleas and deals and sentencing guidelines but I couldn't follow any of it because I was thinking about how the Greeks would have played the story. To me, it was hubris and the gods of measure and all that. One minute of glory that came with a heavy pricetag in woe.

"When I saw Cannon, I couldn't believe it. It was like seeing an old friend who's been on chemo and radiation for some kind of hopeless cancer. He wasn't just overweight and out of shape, like a lot of them get. His flesh was all doughy and shapeless and his skin was a mix of yellow and gray, a really horrible color, and his eyes were just dead. You couldn't believe anything great had ever happened to him. He looked like a man who had run a pool hall all his life and had debts and ulcers. I could hardly take notes, my hands were shaking so bad.

"Cannon was sentenced to a couple of years and they led him out of the courtroom in cuffs. I went back to the paper and tried to write the story. I put in all kinds of stuff—Icarus and Houseman and such—along with a description of that punt return under the lights all those years ago.

"My editor called it drivel. Spiked it and ran the wire story instead. That's when I quit the funny papers and went over to radio. I remember thinking I would have traded places with Cannon. At least he'd had his moment."

He took another swallow from his beer and looked up again at the television where the boys in Carolina blue passed the ball from corner to corner, working for the open shot.

"They shouldn't mix it all up with money," Grantham said quietly, after a minute or two. "That's the problem. The money is like some virus that gets in there and latches onto the strongest cells so you can't fight it without killing everything."

Grantham stood up unsteadily and started for the bar for another beer, drunk as much on sentiment as anything else.

9

When Grantham was back at the table, slumped in his seat and damp with beer and self-pity, I said, "Why don't you skip that brew and have some lunch instead. A bowl of chili, maybe. None of my business, but you've got a show this evening."

He looked at me and I expected some variation on the old "I can handle it" line. As much time as he'd spent around jocks, he would have heard that a lot.

But he wasn't a jock. He was some kind of failed artist. Had the soft side of it, but not the hard one. The feeling, but not the discipline. So he'd become what he was and instead of arguing with me, he was grateful.

"You're right," he said, pushing the beer bottle away, as though out of reach would be out of mind. "I got started on Cannon . . ."

They always need an excuse.

"Chili all right?" I said.

"Yeah, fine. And some coffee."

I went to the bar and asked Bo for two bowls of chili and two coffees. He gave me a sympathetic nod.

"Listen," Grantham said when I got back to the table, "I didn't mean to go off on a ramble like that. Mondays are hard. What was it you wanted to talk to me about? I'm sure it wasn't the way my destiny converged with Billy Cannon's, fascinating as that story might be."

He smiled and so did I.

"It's a good story," I said. "I always thought it was probably hard on these kids who are stars and washed up before they really know anything."

"Yeah. Well, some handle it and some don't. Consider Tom Pine."

I nodded.

"Anyway . . . Tom told you I might be able to help you with something."

"I'm working for a lawyer. He's handling a case that involves college recruiting." I'd told him that earlier, before he started with the beer.

"Want to tell me who the kid is?"

I shook my head.

"Okay. I understand. This is a small town. I'll probably find out anyway. You want to know what is legal and what's not."

"No. I'm trying to identify a man who has been making some . . . well, call them *unusual* offers."

"A scout? I wouldn't know most of the people the schools would be sending here. Unless it was a big-name coach."

"I think this guy is local."

"Do you know his name?"

"That's what I'm trying to find out. I only know what he looks like."

Grantham sipped his coffee while I described the man who had been to see Dinah Coleman. I described him the way she had described him to me. It seemed unlikely that Grantham could do much with that kind of second-hand information and I thought, as I was talking, that all I'd have to show for this meeting was the Cannon story. But I had come away from a lot of these kinds of meetings with less than that.

"Well," Grantham said when I'd finished, "you may be lucky. I have a good memory, most of the time." He cut his eyes in the direction of the still-full beer bottle. "I remember a guy who looked like that. He was a basketball player who did pretty good in high school a few years back. Went to the U and rode the pine, mostly. Not fast enough or quick enough for that level of competition. Bad case of white man's disease."

He saw my look.

"That's jock talk for a guy who can't run fast or jump over his own shadow."

I nodded.

"This fellow graduated and tried his hand at high-school coaching for a while over at Carver High. He only lasted one year. He wasn't cut out for it. Too much yelling and screaming and not enough real coaching. I don't think he knew the game as well as he thought he did and he didn't like the black kids at all. Carried a sackful of resentment, you know, from when he'd been at the U and all the black players were so much better than he was.

"There was a rumor, after he got fired, that somebody reported him for making bets on his own team with a local bookie."

I straightened up in my chair when he said this. But before I could say anything, Bo arrived at the table with two bowls of thick, chocolate-colored chili. Grantham went at his like a man who hadn't eaten in three days. I took a spoonful. It was thick, tasteless, and nowhere near spicy enough. Chili for the masses.

"Did anything come of it?"

"No."

"Did you look into it?"

He finished chewing a mouthful of the tasteless beef and said, "We are not living in a hotbed of investigative journalism."

"Right."

"It was a rumor. Whenever some team loses a game people think it should have won, you'll hear that stuff. They tanked it. Somebody was on the take. Coach was betting the other side. People gamble on sports, and when they lose they think the fix was in. It's the money again. I never believed that coach was betting on his own team's games and you know why?"

"Why?"

"Because there isn't any action on high-school games. You might get a pool down at the office or make a bet with your fishing buddy, but no bookie is going to handle high-school stuff. If he comes up heavy on one side, there is no way he can go to a bigger bookie out of town and lay off some of the action. There's plenty of college and pro stuff to keep the dedicated bettors happy and the bookies' sheets balanced. There just isn't any action in high-school sports."

It made sense.

"The fellow may have been a gambler. A lot of them are. They get used to easy money and that starts to look like the easiest there is. So he might have been betting on college games or the pros, and some people knew about it and started the rumor that he was getting down on his own team. Or *against* his own team, which would have been a lot sexier rumor. Anyway, he lost his job and the rumor died. Folks found something else to talk about."

"I see."

Grantham had finished his chili and his coffee and there was some color in his face, now.

"I suppose I ought to check this man out," I said. "Do you remember his name."

"His last name was Folsome. They called him Stitch for some reason. I don't remember ever hearing his first name."

"Carver High?"

"Five years ago."

"Thanks."

"Sure. Anything else I can do, just call. And when you see Tom, tell him I said hello. He's one of the good ones. One of the best."

The afternoon light outside the bar hit my eyes like a strobe, and for a second or two I felt a touch of something like vertigo. Enough to make me wonder how afternoon drinkers like Grantham could take it.

Practice, practice, practice, I thought. Just like they always say.

I got in the truck and put on a pair of sunglasses, then eased my way out of the mall parking lot and into traffic. It was midafternoon, time to drop in at the Midnight Rose.

It was only a ten-minute drive, just two or three miles, but in that distance I crossed over from a world of urgent prosperity to a neighborhood of run-down buildings and defeated people. Most of the buildings were so far past the possibility of repair that they had been boarded over with raw plywood that had then been spray-painted in pointless graffiti. And the people you saw on the streets no longer moved with any purpose from one place to the next but lounged, instead, with a kind of heavy apathy as though there were no place worth going to and nothing worth doing.

The projects here were small, single-story structures made of new red brick that looked, with age, like rusted iron or dried blood. The little yards were both untended and cluttered. Some of the glass in the windows had been broken out and replaced with cardboard, giving the buildings a mottled, pocked look, as though they had been infected by some fungus. Every third or fourth car in the street was abandoned and stripped to the carcass. A few had been burned.

The Midnight Rose was in the middle of the block, a squat, windowless, cinder-block building the color of charcoal with a parking lot on one side and a vacant lot full of trash on the other.

I parked close to the front door of the Midnight Rose. Better for a fast getaway, I suppose. I locked up and wondered if the factory radio and tape deck were valuable enough to make it worth breaking one of my windows in order to steal it. In New York, I'd read, people put hand-lettered signs in the back glass of their cars. *Radio already stolen.* Crime-fighting in late twentieth-century America. Don't rob me, bud. I've already been robbed once today.

I pushed open the heavy door to the Midnight Rose and stepped inside. It was dark, the only light coming from a jukebox and several gaudy beer signs behind the door. The air was damp and foul with the scent of sour beer and old, trapped smoke. My physical instinct was to back out, even before the door closed behind me. But I walked, instead, across the room to the bar.

Five or six men sat on the stools, indistinct black faces in the bad light. But while I could not make out the features on any of those faces, I could see they were all turned on me and I felt the alarms going off in my head and down the length of my spine, which tingled like a hot wire.

You don't go in some places if you don't want trouble, which was something the men in this bar had known all their lives. No matter what the law said about equal access and the rest, they knew better than to drop in at some redneck roadhouse on the highway outside of town. Do that and you were asking to have your ass handed to you. You'd get the same look that I knew I was getting, even though I was still too night-blind to make out the eyes in any of the faces. And eventually you'd hear somebody at your elbow saying, "Just what is it brings you here, nigger?" Or "white-eyes."

I took a place at the bar, directly in front of the bartender.

He looked at me and I could make out his hooded, impassive eyes in the light of one of the beer signs. He said nothing. Did not nod or acknowledge my presence in any perceptible way. The other men stayed where they were and watched.

I didn't know exactly how to proceed or even if there was any good way to go about asking my questions. But I knew that the very worst way was to be cute. I was not going to bullshit these citizens.

"Good afternoon," I said to the bartender.

"You don't say."

"I wonder if you'd mind helping me out?"

"Car break down or something?"

"No," I said, "I'd like to ask you a few questions."

"He's a cop," a voice said, coming from my right out of the gloom.

"That true?" the bartender said. "Are you with the police?"

"No," I said. "I work for a lawyer."

"Doing what?"

"I'm an investigator." There was no reason for that to make him suddenly decide I was okay. I could have been with a lot of different agencies, none of them on his side. The bartenders and the drinkers down the bar did not hold authority in great esteem. And since I was white, I was most likely authority. No matter what I said.

"Investigating what?" another voice said.

"A crime."

A few snickers came out of the gloom and a single, deep voice saying, "Sheeeit."

I did not look at the other men in the room but kept them located by feel so I would know if any of them moved.

"Were you here on Saturday night?" I said to the bartender.

He shrugged. "Could be. Why do you need to know?"

"Tell him to stroll on, Herk," one of the voices said. "We trying to do some drinking here. Hard when there's white boys about."

"Shut up," the bartender said.

"Sheeeit," the voice came back.

The bartender turned toward the voice. His expression did not change but the other man did not say anything more.

The bartender turned back to me.

"You drink?" he said. "I talk to customers."

"Then I'll have a beer."

"He ain't on duty," one of the voices said. "That, or he ain't no cop."

"What kind of beer."

"Cold."

He opened a bottle and put it on the bar in front of me. I got

a better look at his face. It was gaunt and immobile, the kind of
face a fighter puts on before the first round.

I gave him a bill and he brought me my change. None of the
other men at the bar moved or said anything.

"Investigating a crime, you say," the bartender said as though
that were a novel idea and he needed time to consider it.

"That's right."

"When did this alleged crime you investigating take place?"
He knew the vernacular. Probably learned it in court or in jail.

"Saturday night."

"Saturday night?" he said softly. "What went down on Saturday night?"

"Man got picked up and cuffed in here."

"Why are you interested?"

"I'm working for the man who got arrested," I said. "His
lawyer, actually."

"Coleman," the bartender said, almost pensively. "You working for Coleman's lawyer?"

"Yes."

"Same lawyer he had on his last beef? Fancy white lawyer with
the fancy white name?"

"Semmes," I said. "Nathaniel Semmes."

"Yeah, I know. I read about him in the papers all the time.
What's a fancy white lawyer like him doing on a spade killing like
this?"

"Semmes takes all kinds of cases," I said. "I'm just the investigator."

"I see," the bartender said and fell back into a deep silence.
Nobody at the bar moved or said anything but I could feel their
eyes, their suspicion, and their hate.

It was like being back inside and suddenly finding yourself
alone in a space taken up by Five Percenters, the black answer to
the Aryan Brotherhood. The only thing was to hold your ground
and hope that the moment would pass without a hand going for a
shank. It was all posture, gesture, and slight, almost imperceptible
signals, like the kind that go down between territorial animals to
establish dominance and keep them from killing each other. Most
of the time it worked, but even wolves sometimes kill each other
when the signals are not right.

I'd known the Five Percenters might kill me. I had stepped
into a small, gloomy tool shed at the wrong time, returning a shovel.

There wasn't a guard within five hundred yards—might as well have been an ocean—and I was alone with five of them. They had a needle and were shooting up. I had invaded their space about as decisively as possible.

The man holding the needle looked at me, his black skin glittering with small blisters of sweat from whatever opiate it was.

"Now look at here."

I held my ground, nodded.

"What you doing here?" another one said.

"Shovel," I said.

"Yes. It sure is," a third one said and came close.

I kept the shovel in my hands and my eyes on him.

"You spying, white eyes?"

"I'm blind, can't see a thing. Too dark."

The fourth man came up a little to the side and behind. "But I can swing a shovel," I said.

We held that little formation for what seemed like minutes, with the air still and full of the smell of our mutual fear. We were like wolves, lacking only the nose. So we tested something else. Signals that no free-worlder would have recognized. Finally, the one with the needle said, "Back on out."

"One more hole to fill," I said. "I'll keep the shovel."

My knees were liquid when I stepped out into the light. But the signals had been right.

The odds in the Midnight Rose were lower, but I was still clammy with sweat. That was another signal between animals, but in here it would be lost. The stink of the bar overpowered the stink of my fear.

I took another drink from my beer and waited for the bartender to say something, even if it was to tell me to get out.

"Whatever they got Coleman for," the bartender said, "it didn't go down here. Got nothing to do with this place and I ain't no witness to nothing."

"All right," I said. "I'll buy that. But he was picked up here, right?"

"Truth."

"Well, then, how about telling me just how that went down."

The bartender thought for a moment, then shrugged. "No harm, I suppose. I believe I know about you, anyway. Read about you in the papers, in one of those stories about your lawyer boss.

You'd be the old Sneaky Pete he got out of the joint, right? Got pardoned and went to work for the lawyer."

"That's me."

He nodded approvingly. "Then I could talk to you, I suppose. We've been in some of the same places. If you was a rat, you'd probably be dead by now."

This time, I nodded.

"But it'll cost you another beer."

I put the money on the bar. The signals had been right.

10

I could see light coming from the river house when I turned up the drive. I made it a habit to hit the switches any time I left for more than a few minutes, so I wondered, for a moment, if I was being visited by some second-story man. Or someone who had come out to remedy an old grievance. I turned off the headlights and the radio, rolled down the window, and eased up the drive, trying to pick up sounds over the soft crunch of oyster shell under the tires.

I was halfway up the drive, feeling the electricity along the back of my neck and thinking about the shotgun I kept behind the seat, when I made out the shape of Jessie Beaudreaux's Alpha, parked next to my spot under the big, spreading live oak.

She was back early. I hadn't expected her for another day or two.

I parked and walked across the deep centipede grass in the front yard, then up the front steps, heavily enough that she could hear me. I didn't want to startle her.

"Morgan? That you?" Her voice was clear and welcome.

"None other."

"Where have you been?" she said, coming across the living room to meet me at the front door. "I've been missing you, man. Missing you *bad*. Been waiting here, must be four or three hours now."

She looked good in a pair of old jeans and a faded red flannel shirt with the sleeves and collar turned up. Her long, raven-black hair framed her fine, angular, slightly lopsided face, and she was smiling so that thin creases bracketed her mouth. She put her arms around my neck and said, "Give us a kiss."

That took a while. When she'd had enough, she leaned back and studied my face. "You always look good to me, Morgan, but you look most specially good when I've been gone away from you for a while. I guess that makes it worth the going away."

"You look pretty good yourself," I said.

"*Pretty* good?"

"Better than that."

"How you been? You hungry? I hope you didn't eat yet because I brought along a sack full of good things to eat and I feel like cooking for a man."

"I haven't eaten," I said.

"Outstanding. Come on back in the kitchen and shuck us some oysters. I got some fresh from Suzy down at the canal bridge. I believe this is the absolute best time of year for oysters, don't you?"

"No question about it."

I smelled the oysters before I saw them, three or four dozen of them piled in the sink, so fresh they were still coated with bottom mud and smelled like low water. I rinsed them, then found a rubber glove like the commercial fishermen use to tend crab traps and a thick-handled oyster knife. I knocked the crust of barnacles off the first oyster, then laid it on the oak bar I'd built next to the sink for just this reason. I worked the blunt end of the knife into the joint, and when the shell parted, I torqued the knife slightly so the blade slid under the connecting muscle and severed it without pulping the swollen flesh of the oyster.

"You eat this one," I said. "It'll give you an appetite."

She lifted the shell to her lips and poured the oyster into her mouth. "Ummmmm. That's just right, Morgan. Open the rest of them while I get everything ready."

I opened two dozen or so, enough to cover two plates, while she sliced lemon, opened a jar of horseradish, and poured wine from a bottle she'd brought along. If I'd been alone, I would have had a glass of beer, but Jessie studies wine and tries to get me interested.

We sat at the table, facing each other across the two plates of fresh oysters and the tall, clear glasses full of faintly amber wine.

She held her glass up and said, "This is how it ought to be when you come home from the road. Fresh oysters, cold wine, and a man. Let's drink wine to us, Morgan."

We touched glasses and drank. The wine tasted clean and, I suppose, dry. Better than a beer.

And the oysters were even better. They seem to firm up a little in the winter when the water is colder, and there is more of the salty, metallic taste that isn't like anything else in the world. I squeezed a little lemon over each oyster, then put on some horse-radish. We talked and sipped wine while we ate.

"How come you're getting home so late, Morgan? Been out at a party without me?"

"Been working," I said. "For Nat Semmes."

Her face darkened slightly. Jessie had worked hard to help Nat Semmes get me out of prison. She'd written letters to the governor and the newspapers and sent me copies while I was still inside to keep my spirits up. She had never come to visit me while I was inside; had said that since she didn't think of me as a convict in the first place, she didn't want to see me dressed up like one. She didn't entirely approve of my doing work for Semmes. Thought it put me back on dangerous turf among people who, at best, could do me no good. It was a needless risk, the way she saw it.

I saw it as a way to satisfy an abiding appetite for action. We tried not to argue about it.

"What's he got you doing?" she said.

I told her about William Coleman and made it about halfway through my day before we finished the oysters.

"You want me to open the rest of them?" I said.

"No. Let's do them on the grill. Steam them open and eat them with melted butter. You can finish your story while the coals burn down. I said I felt like cooking for a man but it looks like you're doing the cooking."

"Fine with me," I said.

"Then I don't mind either."

We poured the empty shells into a bucket which I would dump onto the driveway in the morning. Then we went out on the back lawn where I laid a mound of coals in a small grill I'd built from scraps off a pile of old, home-kilned brick that I'd found in the woods just inside my property line.

The night had turned very cool, and the sky was the deep

black color of a gun barrel with the stars looking like tiny pits in its smooth surface. I felt Jessie next to me, shivering a little as we looked up at the sky.

"Cold?" I said. "Want me to get you a jacket?"

"No," she said. "I like it. I've been inside at stuffy meetings for three days. Being out in the air, even cold, feels good."

"How was the trip?" I said. "Did it pay off?" It would be better, I thought, if we talked about her work instead of mine since I did not disapprove of what she did.

She got rich in the Louisiana oil boom and had the good sense to sell out when the price was close to forty dollars a barrel and most of the people she did business with believed it would never stop anywhere south of a hundred. They all thought she was acting like a scared woman. Turned out they were behaving like greedy men. She was retired now, and they were talking to bankruptcy lawyers.

But she was too young to just sit still and she didn't have the temperament of a full-time shopper and tennis player. So she worked in conservation causes these days. Land trusts, mostly, trying to preserve what was left of this coast. She worked hard at it. Putting her money and her time where her mouth was.

"Oh, yeah. It was a great meeting. I saw a lot of smart people and learned a lot. We got a new project lined up, looking at some of what the government owns up and down this coast. The navy and the air force have got *miles* of beach that they've been using for bombing practice since World War II. We're thinking that since they don't have so many people in the world who need bombing anymore and the government doesn't have any money, we might be able to cut some deals. We came up with some good ideas. We're going to lean on a couple of congressmen who owe us and hit some of the fat cats we know we can count on. I think we're going to do good things.

"But it went on too long. Meetings like that always do. You see people you need to see, been counting on seeing, but after a while, you've had enough of them. Probably they feel the same way. But I'm glad I went and real glad to be home. You know how it is."

I didn't, actually. Couldn't remember ever going to a conference on anything and felt like I'd missed something, though I couldn't say exactly what. Just another component of normal life, I suppose, the life of business meetings, hotels, airports, rental cars, restaurants, and homecomings. Life in the groove.

The charcoal had become a single glowing orange mass which I broke apart with an old tire iron until it was an even layer of coals, so hot that it hurt when your hand was still half a foot away, where I set the grill.

I spread oysters on the grill, and in a minute or two they began steaming and popping open just slightly to bleed off the pressure. As they opened, I lifted them off the grill with a glove and put them on a tray. When the last one came off, we took them inside where Jessie melted some butter in a small saucepan, then squeezed in a little lemon. We sat at the table with more wine and dredged the oysters, which were barely cool enough to handle, in the butter and ate them.

When they were gone, Jessie said, "That was some kind of good, Morgan. Tell me again where you learned to do that to an oyster."

"North Carolina," I said.

"Well, they know something about cooking up there, then." Jessie was from Louisiana and not altogether sure that people anywhere else in America knew how to cook.

"But you know what?" she said.

"What's that?"

"I'm still hungry. I probably ought to be ashamed of myself."

She looked at me from across the table, with her chin resting in one hand. She looked serious but I couldn't be sure. She took a sip of wine.

"Do you think I'm fat?"

"You must be kidding."

Jessie was a lot of things, but fat was not one of them. She played tennis and swam the same way she ate—enthusiastically. She wasn't fashion-model thin—gaunt, in other words—but she sure wasn't fat. And for some reason, I loved to watch her eat. There was something erotic about the pleasure she took from food.

"Are you sure?"

"Give me a break," I said.

"Hardly any women like the way they look."

"I've heard that."

"And most of them—ninety or eighty percent, I'll bet you anything—think they are fat."

"I like the way *you* look," I said. "For what that's worth."

"Worth a whole bunch," she smiled. "If you're telling the truth."

"If I'm lying, then I'm dying."

"Good," she said. "Wonderful. That means I can have some more to eat, right? Let's finish off the oysters before your fire burns down."

"I can do better than that," I said.

"Nothing's better than oysters."

"Quail?"

"*That's* better than oysters."

So while she cleared the table and cleaned off the dishes, I worked at the sink, splitting the little birds, covering them with salt, pepper, and thin strips of bacon fat. When they went on the grill, the bacon sizzled and the rendered oil ran clear and popped when it hit the hot coals. When the tiny ends of exposed bone began to char, I turned the birds, left them another minute or two so they would be cooked through but still pink and moist on the inside, then took them inside to the table.

Jessie had poured wine from a second bottle. "Now *this* is real eating, Morgan," she said.

I was feeling a little light-headed with the wine. Not drunk but not entirely sober, either. It was the feeling, I suppose, of being entirely satisfied with everything at that moment and unconcerned with anything outside of it. I drank and ate and watched the woman sitting across from me while she did the same. The little birds were cooked just right, so you had to bite with force, and when the flesh parted between your teeth, you could hear a faint ripping sound like the tearing of an old sheet. The meat tasted faintly rank and wild.

"Oh man," Jessie said between bites. "This is worth coming home to all by itself." There was a faint spot of grease at one corner of her mouth. She licked it with her tongue.

When there were only picked-over bones left on our plates, we took the wine bottle and our glasses and went into the bedroom.

"You know how to make it good to come home, Morgan," Jessie said, some time later. The room was dark except for the thin light of the moon, enough that I could make out her face and the shape of her shoulder. She was propped up on one arm, wineglass in her other hand, looking down at me. "You must have missed me."

"I did."

"I'm going to have to make a regular thing out of this going away."

"Not too often," I said.

"No," she said. "Not too often." She dipped a finger in the wine, sprinkled a few drops on my bare chest, then kissed it away. For a moment, her hair covered her face, then she was looking at me again in the weak light, her face composed and vaguely concerned.

"You're not troubled about something, are you, Morgan?"

"Me?"

"No," she said. "The other Morgan here in bed with us."

"What would I be troubled about?"

"That's what I'm asking."

"Everything is fine. Right now, in fact, I think I can report that things have never been better."

"You're not worried about this job you got for Semmes? You never did finish telling me about it."

"No," I said. "I'm not worried about it. I'm glad it came up."

"What is it then?"

"Maybe I'm worried that you won't like it."

"I never *like* it when you work for Semmes. You know how that is. But I try to understand how you feel about it. You can't blame me for worrying, though."

"No," I said. There was the paradox and the trick was to live with it, maneuver around it.

"It's not just some wild thing," she said. "Not with Semmes in it?"

"It's a good job," I said. "Worth doing."

"Safe?"

"Yes. I think so."

"I don't like to worry about you," she said.

"Nothing to worry about."

She smiled and put the wineglass, still nearly full, on the floor next to the bed and tucked her head into the hollow part of my shoulder. "All right," she said. "But tell me about it in the morning, will you? I want to know, but right now I'm too tired to listen."

"All right," I said. "Good night."

"Night."

She was asleep in seconds, and for half an hour or so I lay very still, listening to her breathe and watching the bare, silhouetted branches outside the window as they moved with the slowly rising wind. It seemed a shame to let go and drop into sleep.

11

Jessie was still asleep when I came back to the house, sweating and breathing hard after what felt like a three-or four-mile run. The sun had been up for less than an hour so it was still a cold January morning. But even so, I took my shower outside, under a faucet I had jury-rigged out of some salvage. I didn't want to wake her up using the inside bathroom where I had hot water and, anyway, the cold water, which seemed to shrink every muscle in my body, felt good. By the time I'd dried off and started some coffee, I was no longer feeling the wine.

I was sitting at the table, wearing an old bathrobe and into my second cup of coffee, when Jessie walked into the kitchen, wearing her clothes from last night and no makeup, her hair pulled back tight against the sides of her head. She smiled and said, "Morning, sailor."

"Good morning," I said. "Sit down, I'll pour you some coffee."

"What a man."

She took a careful sip from her cup, then another, looked up at me and smiled again. "You are a bad influence on me, Morgan Hunt."

"Pretend you don't remember a thing."

"Nah. I remember *everything*. Wouldn't have it any other

way. I even remember drinking that last, extra glass of wine. And now I've got to do something about it."

I told her that a long run and a cold shower had worked for me. She shook her head. "Sounds too much like pain to me. Mortification, or something religious like that. I believe I'll go home and sit in a warm tub. Then later, I'll play some tennis."

"You want some breakfast first?"

"No. I didn't just drink too much wine. I ate like a fool, too. So what are you going to do today?" she said. "Keep on working this thing for Nat Semmes?"

"I'm going to a funeral," I said.

"Some people have all the fun."

"You want to go?"

"I'd love to . . . but I don't have a thing to wear. Who they burying? The one the Coleman kid killed?"

"That's right."

"How come you're going?"

"I want to see who else is there. And maybe talk to his family, find out if he was working for the cops or somebody who was trying to set Coleman up."

She shook her head a little gravely. "Well, I don't want to keep you, Morgan. I guess I ought to get on home and see what I can make of this day. Call me later. After the funeral."

"I will."

"And be careful, will you?"

"Absolutely."

She kissed me in a chaste, sisterly sort of way. A sign, I suppose, of just how she felt about the way I'd be spending my day. I watched until her car reached the end of the drive and then turned onto the blacktop. I rinsed out the coffee cups and the pot, shaved and dressed, then went out to the truck and left for the services.

I stopped for a cup of coffee at a convenience store and did not open it until I was parked across the street from Reyland's Funeral Home, which occupied the most substantial building on a block of small frame houses a lot like the one where Dinah Coleman lived. Reyland's was a two-story building with a kind of porch grafted onto the front for the sole purpose of providing a place for three feeble columns which had been added, no doubt, in order to give the building some gravity. Burying people was serious business, after all, like banking. Hardly any funeral homes went broke, though, bodies being more abundant these days than money.

I peeled the cap off the Styrofoam cup and sipped the coffee. It tasted faintly of soap. Somebody needed to tell the people who ran convenience stores that you don't use soap on coffee urns.

I dumped the coffee, threw the cup on the floor of the passenger side, and settled in to watch Reyland's, where an old man was raking pine straw out from around the azaleas. He was in no hurry.

It was ten to eleven before anyone arrived to mourn Alvin Hopkins. Two large old black women, wearing bright dresses and walking as though it were a struggle, their arms locked for support, went up the stairs, passed between the columns, and then on through the front door, which closed firmly behind them. A minute or two later, another old woman trudged up the steps and went through the door. Then, another woman, this one weeping and drying her face with a white handkerchief which she strangled in one hand. The other hand was on the shoulder of a young, awkward boy in a Sunday-school suit with pants that were almost two inches too short. The kid was growing too fast to keep in suits. He had a boy's face with adult torment fixed on it like a mask. He led the weeping woman up the walk, then took her arm as they went up the stairs. It was almost exactly eleven.

Nobody else came to Reyland's to pay last respects to Alvin Hopkins. The weeping woman had to be his mother. The boy with her would be another son.

I got out of the truck, locked it, crossed the street, and went up the walk and into Reyland's. A tall, slender man in an ash-gray suit stood inside the door with his hands folded in front of him and his head slightly bowed, as though in thought and regret.

"May I help you, sir?" he said in voice thick as crude oil.

"Hopkins?" I said. I wanted to sound like a not very close friend, come to pay my respects, but it wasn't working. He looked at me and thought *cop*.

"Please sign the book," he said.

He pointed to the proper page and I wrote my name. One of four.

"Second door, sir."

"Thank you."

I slipped into the little chapel and took a seat in the rear, nearest the door, and bowed my head. The room was full of the scent of flowers and the sound of recorded organ music. I listened to the music for a few seconds, then raised my head.

The casket rested on a raised surface in the front of the room and I wondered, for a moment, who would carry it. There were only the four women and the boy in the pews ahead of me. A man in a suit sat on a chair next to the casket, and another woman, this one in a white robe, sat on another chair a few feet to one side. I supposed that Reyland's would provide pallbearers for a slight additional charge.

The man in the suit cleared his throat, stood, and began speaking in a soft voice. He spoke effortlessly about leaving this vale of tears and crossing over Jordan. The four women in the pews in front of me moaned softly, and when the man in the suit said with conviction that Alvin had been "gathered into the Lord," one of them said "Amen," in a voice drenched with grief.

I felt like the worst kind of intruder.

"Alvin had a hard life," the man in the suit went on. "A life that was hard on him and hard on the ones who loved him. He wandered in a wilderness without God and he suffered. But we know that God pities those who suffer, and in time gathers them to Him and an eternity of peace."

More mutterings of *amen*.

The preacher went on a little longer but the words seemed to blur like images going slowly out of focus. My mind wandered and settled on the convicts who would come around preaching and citing Scripture to anyone who would listen. There was one in particular, an old bull with a long ugly scar across one side of his face and a patch of waxy skin where his eye had been. He'd killed the man who cut him, held him by the neck until he'd crushed his throat and the man stopped breathing. But that took a while and all that time, the knife was doing its work. There were other scars which you saw in the shower.

The man liked to call himself Jonah. He had another name but nobody ever used it. He was Jonah, swallowed up and trapped in the belly of a beast, where he preached the word to anyone who would listen. Some did. I wasn't one of the group but you couldn't help hearing them when they held their services. They would read Scripture and take turns talking about its meaning. Then, just before their meetings broke up, Jonah would preach. He was not ordained as far as anyone knew, not even by one of those mail-order outfits. But that didn't make any difference. He could preach and nobody was about to try to stop him. So you shut out the individual words, and the sound of Jonah's deep, sorrowful voice became just one more element in the mix of prison sounds that never seemed to change or stop. The noise was so constant, so reliable, that sometimes you began to think it was something that you carried around with you in your head, and that in your life, it would never be quiet again. That was one of the hardest things.

Listening to the preacher, I heard Jonah and all the rest of the background noises again. I wanted to get out of Reyland's.

Then the preaching stopped, replaced by a complete silence, a hush, and then the sound of a few notes played on a piano. The woman in the white robe stood and began to sing in a clear, sweet soprano.

What a friend we have in Jesus
All our sins and grief to bear

The women in the pews in front of me began to weep. They were still weeping when the song ended and the last notes faded from the room and six strong-looking black men in gray suits like the one worn by the man at the door stepped out from behind a red curtain. They lifted the casket and carried it down the aisle between the empty pews. The women wept as it went by.

When it was gone, the women started after it, still weeping. When the dead man's mother and the young boy were next to me, I spoke to her.

"Mrs. Hopkins?"

They stopped and looked at me. Her face was wet. The boy's was dry and very still.

"Yes," she said.

"May I talk to you?"

"You with the police?" she said. "The papers?"

"No ma'am. I'm an investigator. For a lawyer."

"Who?"

"I don't think I ought to say."

"You want to talk to me about Alvin?"

"Yes ma'am."

"Why? My boy is dead. Jackson Coleman shot him."

"There may be more to it."

She looked at me. Her face did not change.

"Would you know who your son was seeing and talking to in the last couple of weeks? Anybody he didn't usually spend time with?"

She shook her head but that was a refusal, not an answer.

"I know about that," the boy said.

"Hush," the woman said.

I looked at the boy. His expression was made up of fear, grief, and determination.

"He told me. Said he had to talk to this man and do what he said if he wanted to stay out of trouble."

The woman glared at him, but the boy's face did not change.

"Did he say who it was?"

"Name was Grant. That's all he said."

"I told you to hush."

"Thank you," I said to the boy.

"You gonna make it worse for us?" she said. "Worse than it already is."

"No ma'am," I said.

"You and your lawyer going to bring my boy back?"

I shook my head. "We won't make it worse for you. We're trying to find out why this happened."

"It happened because of guns and dope. That's why most bad things happen. Guns and dope." Her voice rose slightly. "You try hard as you can but that's what happens to so many of them. They get to taking cocaine and carrying pistols. He was a good boy before he found out about that stuff. Now we had to bring him here and look how many people came to see him off. You won't find out any more than I already know. And you won't make it any better. It won't never get any better."

"I'm sorry."

She looked at me and shook her head. Her wet cheeks glistened.

"Come on, boy," she said to the determined-looking kid at her side. "Let's go to the cemetery. That'll be the end of it."

She put her hand on the boy's shoulder and followed him out of the little chapel. I waited long enough that when I left Reyland's I was sure they would already be on their way, following the hearse down the street in a pitiful four-car cortege.

12

After barging in on a funeral and generally adding to other people's misery, I felt like driving around and listening to some
oldies until I got over feeling like something without legs. Since I
needed a photograph of Stitch Folsome, it seemed like a good time
to visit Carver High, which was out in what people call "the
county." This puts it beyond the expanding belt of little develop-
ments that are hacked out of pine plantations and farmland, built
around a shallow pond dug by a dragline and called something
like Lake Wisteria, with the whole project being named Wisteria
Estates. Nat Semmes says those places are covering up the South
worse than kudzu and that the day will come when you can walk a
straight line from the Gulf Coast to the Potomac River and never
be off somebody's patio.

Carver High is where the kids who still live on farms go to
school. It took me half an hour to get there. The oldies station
played Fats Domino, Chuck Berry, and Hank Ballard with no
commercials, and by the time I parked next to a big yellow school
bus I was no longer feeling like something with scales.

I spoke to a woman at the front desk and simply told her
that I was looking into something for Tom Pine of the Sheriff's
Department and wondered if she would help me. She recognized

the name and said, "What do you need?" without suspicion, a sure
sign that I was out in the country.

"I wonder if I could put my hands on some old yearbooks, one
from six years back, one from five, and another from four. I'd keep
them for a couple of days, long enough to copy some pictures. Then
I'd get them back to you."

I gave her a card with my name and phone number and the
word *investigator* on it.

She looked at the card and said, "I don't see why not."

I liked her attitude.

She left her place behind the desk and went down the hall.
After a couple of minutes, she was back with a load of books under
one arm.

"Here you go," she said. "I hope you'll find what you need."

"Thank you," I said. "I'll take good care of them."

It had been a rare thing for these days, a friendly transaction.

I went back to the truck and flipped through the pages of the
book from five years back, past the individual shots of smiling
seniors who'd been voted "best" and "most likely" and the teachers
of math, history, and industrial arts until I came to the section
devoted to athletics. Five pages to the football Wildcats. Another
five for what the yearbook editors called the "hoopsters."

Coach Folsome's photograph took up nearly half a page. He
looked young and intense, in the manner of coaches who believe
the games are not meant to be fun. He had thinning, curly hair.
Narrow eyes. Fat, petulant lips. He wore a sweatshirt and a lanyard
around his neck for the whistle he would blow when he was dis-
pleased in practice. Not the picture of a likable man and maybe
not a flattering angle. But perfect for my purposes, better than the
best mug shot.

I drove back into town to the mustard-colored building where
Tom Pine worked and parked in one of the visitor slots. I surrend-
ered my keys and pocket knife at the door, then walked through a
metal detector, signed in, and showed my identification. I told the
desk sergeant I could find my way and went down a long dim
corridor to Tom's office.

He was working a keyboard and studying a computer terminal.

"Morning," he said. "You want to wait one? There's coffee in
the pot."

I got myself a cup. It was very strong and did not taste like soap. I sipped it and listened to the soft tap of the keys.

After a minute or two, Tom said, "Thanks, babe," to the machine and swiveled his chair to face me.

"Damn thing will answer just about any question I can figure out how to ask it. I don't see how we got along all this time without them."

"What are you working on?"

"Hot cars. It's about as sexy as chopping cotton, but this machine here cuts down on the donkey work, anyway."

Pine stood and stretched. His big body seemed to uncoil and expand.

"I need some help with a name, Tom," I said. "I figure you'll know of somebody, a civilian, who has the city police wired. That's who I need to talk to."

He looked at the floor for a minute. He wanted to know why and a lot more besides but he knew he couldn't ask. "I got a guy who knows them like that computer there," he finally said. "Does some business with us, too. Man is a born shit-heel but he knows everything. Got a brain like a sponge. I'll give you his name and I'll call him and tell him to be nice to you."

"I'd appreciate it."

"Sit still while I call him."

Pine lowered himself back into his chair, picked up the receiver to his phone, and began pounding buttons so hard the phone rattled on the desk. I wondered how he could be so delicate with the computer and so hard on the phone. Probably because he still thought of the computer as something mysterious and therefore delicate. Phones had been around forever.

"Let me speak to Roulon. This is Tom Pine."

He waited for a minute, then said abruptly, "Yeah, Rou, I'm fine. Wife too. We're all fine as can be. Listen, you need to talk to a man. His name is Hunt. He'll be around and if you're good to him, I'll do you a favor and let you keep on living."

After another pause, Pine said, "Fine. Take care of yourself, Rou. Always a pleasure talking to you."

Pine put the phone back in the cradle and said, "Roulon Staggers is a bailbondsman. Did some lawyering once, but got himself disbarred. About half too smart for his own good. He knows everything there is to know about every arrest and every cop in this country. I suspect there are a lot of them driving cars that Roulon helps make the payments on. A model citizen."

"Thanks, Tom."

"Nothing to it." He looked at his watch and said, "Almost noon—you want to go put your teeth to some ribs?"

"Not this time."

"All right. Now listen, if Roulon doesn't deliver, let me know. I'll straighten him out."

Pine made it sound as though he'd like nothing better.

Staggers's bailbond office occupied a small cinder-block building painted a sour green color. There was a sign over the door advertising twenty-four-hour-a-day service and supplying a number to call. There were bars on the windows and the door was made of rolled steel heavy enough for tank armor. I pushed the bell and a buzzer sounded.

I walked into a small front room with benches on either wall and a waist-high counter near the back. A man stood behind the counter. He had a thick body and a round, doughy face with small, deeply set eyes and thin, wiry hair. His mouth formed a puffy smirk.

"Step right in," he said.

I already had.

"What can I do for you?"

"I'm looking for Mr. Staggers."

"You found him," he said. "First try. Now what can I do for you?"

"My name is Hunt."

His face did not move and his little black eyes did not change. They stayed locked on me.

"I need some information," I said.

"That's not my business usually. But as long as it's for Lieutenant Pine."

"It's confidential."

"Wouldn't have it any other way."

"The information is confidential," I said. "And the fact that I came here asking is also confidential. Pine told me I could count on you."

"Gave me a good recommendation, did he? That's nice of him."

"He told me to let him know if anything went wrong."

The man's face darkened just slightly and his mouth formed something between a grimace and a pout.

"What do you want to know?" he said. "I've got other things to do."

I had nothing to hold over the thick, motionless man behind the counter and he didn't do anything without security. That's what he understood. He'd help you make bail, but first he'd need the deed to your house.

"Listen, Mr. . . . hell, I've forgotten your name," he said. "But whatever it is, let me assure you that you don't have anything to worry about. You ask your question and I'll give you an answer if I can. If I can't, it will be because I think somebody might be able to make more trouble for me than your friend Pine could and I don't know who that could possibly be. People try to lean on me and get over on me all the time and I don't even notice. But Lieutenant Pine is somebody I notice. You can't miss him."

"You know the cops?"

"And the lawyers," he said. "They bring in referrals."

"Do you know a cop named Grant?"

He managed a minimal sort of smile.

"He's a nice boy."

"Where can you find him when he's not working?"

"At the Bayside, like most of the young ones."

"All right," I said. "That's all I need. Thanks very much."

I turned to leave and was still pushing on the ponderous steel door when he said, "I'll tell you one more thing. Gratis."

"What's that?"

"Whatever he did, somebody put him up to it."

"How do you know?"

"Like I said"—he shrugged—"he's a nice boy."

He smiled again. His best oily, professional smile. The one he would use later, after the sun went down and business picked up.

There was a pay phone not far from Staggers's office. I put a quarter in the slot and dialed information, thinking that one of these days I'd have to look into a cellular phone even though the primitive side of me hated the idea. New gizmos never seem to make life easier in any real way. Just busier.

I got the number of the Bayside from information and dialed it.

"Grant there?" I said to the voice that answered.

"Not yet," a surly, impatient voice answered.

"How about Stitch?"

"They usually get here about the same time."

"When's that?"

"Three o'clock. Now if you want to wait for the beep, you can leave a friggin' message."

He hung up the phone.

I looked at my watch. It was two thirty. I called Semmes's office and his secretary put him on.

"Sorry to bother you," I said.

"*Ce n'est pas un problème*. What's going on?"

"Dinah Coleman heard from our boy yet?" I said.

"No. She hasn't called here, anyway."

"All right," I said. "I believe I've got a make and model on the redhead who came to her with that proposition. I have a picture and I'd like to show it to her. What if I came by your place around four, four thirty and we rode out there together."

"All right. I'll call her and set it up. Good work, Morgan."

"We'll see about that," I said and told him I'd give him the whole story when I saw him.

The Bayside Lounge was close enough to the bay to deserve the name, but it wasn't exactly a desirable waterfront location. This was a commercial zone. The neighbors in one direction were several fish houses where the shrimpers and mullet netters sold their catch and took on ice and fuel. On the other side, there was a large tank farm where the barges that worked the intracoastal came in to unload. The view from the Bayside, then, was not restful and uncluttered, and the air carried the mingled odors of fish and diesel oil.

The lot was nearly empty, which was probably normal for early afternoon. Still, viewed in the clear light of day, you had to wonder why anyone would ever pick this place to drink.

It was a low, rectangular building that had once been painted some kind of hot, tropical pink. The color was bleached, faded, and mottled so the building made you think of unpeeled shrimp. The windows had been painted black, except for one that had been broken out and replaced with raw plywood. The front door appeared to be working and the sign next to it said OPEN. So I went in.

When I was inside and my pupils had dilated, I made my way

to the bar and ordered a beer. The bartender brought it and took my money without a word. I took a table along the wall near the door. I wanted to get a look at Grant and Stitch and then get out. I thought I might be able to do it before they even knew I was there.

It was ten minutes until three when I sat down. At three, a couple of men walked across the dark room to the bar, both fairly young and unmistakably cops. Their clothes looked trim and tailored and their mustaches were neatly clipped. They carried themselves with a kind of exaggerated confidence.

In the next ten minutes, five more out of the same mold came into the room and took up places against the bar. Somebody played the jukebox. Somebody else racked the balls and then he and another man lagged for break.

I remembered winding down that way in the afternoon after duty hours in the service. A shower, clean clothes, and some cold beer in a dark room with music on the jukebox. I don't especially miss those times but I can remember being a lot less happy than I was back then.

The pool shooters played hard but not very smart, concentrating more on a conversation about a high-speed chase than the lay of the table.

"Dudes were some kind of dumb, you know? They're in a rental car, dressed for Miami Beach right down to the shades. Wearing the Ray Bans at night just so everyone who looks at them will know that they are certified bad-asses. We saw 'em coming the other way off the bay bridge. Heading for the interstate, probably."

"Speeding?"

"No. Even those two weren't *that* dumb. But you know what?"

"What's that?"

"They didn't have to be speeding. We just had to *say* they were."

"You got that one."

"We spun around and hit the gumball. What they should have done, if they'd had any brains, is pull over and make us get a warrant or prove we had probable cause. But if brains was cotton, those two between them couldn't put enough together to make a Q-tip for a pissant. They see the gumball and they floor it. Man, what a ride."

It sounded like a good war story and that was probably a good part of the reason they came to this bar, to tell war stories. For a few hours in the afternoon, it was their clubhouse. No civilians allowed.

Another man, plainly a cop, eased into the room. One of the pool shooters recognized him and said, "Well, well, Officer Grant. What's shaking, my man?"

They gave each other a high five, like a couple of ballplayers after a score.

"How about a beer?" the pool shooter said. "I believe you've been known to drink beer."

"Only on odd- and even-numbered days," the newcomer said. He looked like the other young cops. Same trim body, clipped mustache, and vaguely hostile eyes. His long face and drooping eyes were distinctive enough that I would recognize him if I saw him again, and I suspected I would. He looked around the room as though he might be meeting someone. I was far enough away, deep enough in the gloom, that he could only tell that I was not someone he knew.

He took the beer the other man handed him and raised it for a long drink.

"Heard you had a little action," he said to the man who had given him the beer. "Something about a high-speed chase. Rental car, with certain illegal substances in the trunk."

"You got it," the other man said. "Illegal substances *and* weapons. Interesting stuff, too. Couple of AKs. You should have seen the eyes on those two when we opened that trunk. They knew they were in the deep brown."

The story went on and I listened the way you listen to music in an elevator. I didn't watch much of the pool game because my eyes were on the door. The next man through it was Stitch Folsome.

He and Grant nodded to each other, and when Stitch had gotten himself a beer from the bar, they broke off from the cluster of cops telling their war stories and took a table against the wall opposite mine. They bent themselves over the table so their faces were close and they wouldn't have to shout over the music. What they were talking about, they didn't want to share.

I took my eyes off them, and when I saw Stitch back at the bar for more beer, I stood up and slipped out. After breathing what passed for air inside the Bayside for an hour, the smell of diesel and ripe fish was a sweet relief.

13

Semmes was alone in his office. He had his feet up on the desk and was reading the papers. He looked content.

When I knocked, he folded the paper carefully, threw it in the trash, and stood up.

"We've got some time before we have to leave for Dinah Coleman's. You want something to drink while we talk?"

"Ice water?" I said.

"Sure."

Semmes crossed the room to a small bar with a refrigerator and a cold-water tap. He filled a glass for me and then poured an inch of bourbon in another glass and added a single ice cube.

He handed me my glass, went around the desk, sat, and put his feet up on the desk again. He took a very small, ceremonial sip of bourbon and exhaled with real satisfaction. Semmes drank bourbon with a respect that bordered on reverence.

"Might as well start at the beginning," I said.

"All right."

"I'm working on the theory that Jackson Coleman was set up."

"Just like he says."

I shrugged.

"If you could prove it, then that would be the best possible news for Jackson. Entrapment—the accused committed criminal acts because of police encouragement. He was *seduced*"—Semmes smiled—"or otherwise, his virtue would still be intact."

"Hard to think about Jackson Coleman in those terms."

"We're talking about the law here," Semmes said. "Abstraction is everything."

"If you say so. But I figured you needed more to work with than just Jackson Coleman *saying* the man he shot was trying to set him up. He's not exactly . . . what's the lawyer word?"

"*Credible*," Semmes said, rolling the word around happily in his mouth. He enjoyed this kind of thing, along with the bourbon, at the end of a day.

"Right," I said. "Jackson Coleman tests real low on *credible*."

"But he might have a measure of street smarts. Even if it isn't as much as he gives himself credit for."

"I wouldn't trust his street smarts to find me a parking place," I said. "But the way the bust went down . . . I discussed it with the cocktail crowd at the Midnight Rose yesterday afternoon and they agreed it was just too wonderful. The law got there right away with plenty of men and firepower, and they knew Jackson was their man."

"Police efficiency," Nat said. "A jury isn't going to see that as something sinister."

"But you know better."

He nodded.

"I knew you weren't going to make a circumstantial case that he was set up. Matter of satisfying myself first."

"Absolutely. Test the hypothesis."

"But," I said, "I figured the best way I could get inside some kind of setup was to ID the man who came to see Dinah Coleman with that proposition and then make him as a friend of the cops."

"That would damn sure tie things tighter."

I told Semmes about meeting with Grantham, getting the name and then the picture of Stitch Folsome. When he didn't interrupt, I told him about going to the funeral, coming up with the name Grant, and then watching Grant and Folsome drinking together at the Bayside.

"I've just come from there and that's what I've got so far."

Semmes took another small sip of bourbon and looked at me over the rim of his glass.

"You've got that photograph of Folsome?"

I held up an old canvas map case that I used when I needed a briefcase. "In here."

"Let's go show it to Dinah Coleman and make sure he's the man."

He left enough whiskey to cover the bottom of his glass and turned out the office lights behind him. He carried no work out with him. He never does. Just like he never finishes a drink.

We rode down in the elevator and then he followed me to Dinah Coleman's house, driving the pearl-gray Porsche that is one of the few extravagances in his life. "I got the old southern gene for fast cars," he'd told me once, "it just got mutated somewhere at one of those eastern schools I went to. I'd rather walk than drive a stock Dodge."

The Porsche was as out of place on the street in front of Dinah Coleman's little house as it would have been sitting on the pole at Talladega. Semmes locked it carefully and led the way to the front door.

He knocked, and after a few seconds the door came open deliberately, almost urgently.

The woman who'd opened it was not Dinah Coleman. She was much younger, in her twenties. Thin, like Dinah Coleman, but not with the same depleted leanness. Thin from healthy food and exercise, not a lifetime of wear and worry. She wore trim cotton slacks and one of those knit shirts with a polo player embroidered over one breast. The expression on her face was strong, almost defiant.

"Good afternoon," Semmes said. "I'm Nathaniel Semmes and this is my associate, Morgan Hunt. I called a little earlier. We're here to see Mrs. Coleman."

"I'm her daughter," the woman said. "Denise Coleman."

"Pleased to meet you," Semmes said.

She nodded and said, without warmth, "Please come in."

Semmes and I followed her into the tidy little living room where Dinah Coleman was sitting in her comfortable chair, dressed in a starched white uniform dress, the kind nurses and food service people wear. She stood up slowly.

"Mr. Semmes," she said wearily, "I appreciate you coming by. Can I get you something? A cup of coffee?"

."No thank you," Semmes said.

"How about you, Mr. Hunt?"

"No thanks," I said.

We all sat down. Denise Coleman sat on a hard kitchen chair, with her hands folded in her lap, and studied the rest of us with furious suspicion, as though we had come peddling cemetery plots.

"Are you going to be able to help my boy, Mr. Semmes?" Dinah Coleman said.

"We're working on it," Semmes said carefully.

"He was set up," Denise Coleman said. "That ought to make it easy."

Semmes looked at her. His face was calm.

"Now, Denise," Dinah Coleman said.

"He was *set up*, Mama. Jackson isn't any *murderer*. Somebody got him into that trouble so they could lean on you and William. It's about *basketball* . . . white men wanting William to come play ball and make money for their school."

"So far," Semmes said, "we don't have any substantial proof of that."

"*Substantial*," Denise Coleman mocked. "There was a white man here in this house before they even let Jackson make a call from jail, and he was offering Mama a deal. Send William to the university and he'd keep Jackson out of the electric chair. That's not *substantial* enough?"

Semmes raised a hand and turned the palm up in a small gesture of appeasement. "We know that, for sure. But we don't know if that man really had anything to offer. We don't even know who he is."

"Well, *we* could find out," Denise said, "if we really wanted to. And we could find out who else is in on it and we could make a lot of noise in the newspapers and on the television if we didn't have a white lawyer who lives in this town and has lived here all his life and wants to keep on living here."

"Denise," Mrs. Coleman said, trying to sound stern but realizing only the sort of pleading tone parents use when a child is grown and beyond them.

"Mama, it's true. I could get a lawyer from Atlanta who would come down here and make things *happen*. He would get Jackson out of jail and put the men behind this in there."

"Mr. Semmes is a good lawyer, you know that. One of the best there is. And he helped Jackson out before."

"Wasn't like this, Mama."

"Let's listen to him."

Semmes spoke to the angry young woman on the hard-backed chair. He spoke with soft, persuasive control and not a trace of hostility, which was a lot more than I could have managed.

"Before your lawyer from Atlanta or your reporters could do anything, they would have to know who the man who came here the other night *is*. And even if they knew that and could find him, what would they do?"

"They could pressure him to talk. Pressure him hard."

"And he could say, 'Yes, I went to talk to Mrs. Coleman. I told her I'd try to help her son if she would help me. But that's all I did.' You might be able to get somebody to see that as obstruction of justice, but I doubt it. So you wouldn't have anything to hold over him. You could embarrass him, maybe, in the news stories, if he is the kind who can be embarrassed. But you need more than that if you are going to get him to tell you who else is involved— what other white men." Semmes gave her the stern stare he uses on juries when he wants to impress them with the gravity of their work. "If you want that, then you are going to have to find this man and then be able to threaten him with more than a few embarrassing stories in the papers. Stories that the papers might not run, by the way, if they were afraid of libel suits. What you'd need—and what Mr. Hunt and I are looking for—is something a little heavier than that. What I want is a club that I can use to beat his goddamned brains out."

Semmes turned halfway in his chair and said, "I apologize for the language, Mrs. Coleman."

She nodded.

"How are you going to get that club?" Denise Coleman said. "And don't try your plantation manners on me. It won't work."

"I'm sure it won't," Semmes said, smiling. "So let's just say that the first thing we need to do is make sure we know who the man is and then we need to get him to make his offer again. We'll make sure he can't deny making it and then we'll squeeze him like a sponge."

"And when are you planning on getting started doing all this?"

"No time like the present," Semmes said and nodded in my direction. I took the yearbook out of the map case and turned to the page with Stitch Folsome's picture. I had used tape to cover the name. That was for me to know.

I handed the book over to Mrs. Coleman and said, "Is this the man?"

She took a pair of steel-rimmed glasses from the table next to her chair and put them on slowly, with great care. She was beyond haste.

She studied the picture, and for those few seconds there was no sound at all in the room.

"He was younger when they took this," Dinah Coleman said. "But it's him. Every bit."

Denise Coleman wanted the name and tried to insult Semmes into giving it to her. He said he would "abide by his client's wishes," which was a bluff since he knew he had Dinah Coleman's complete trust.

"Let the man do his job, Denise," she said. "He's trying to help us."

Denise shook her head. For a minute, I thought that Semmes might be about to launch a speech to win her over. But he knew better. Her anger was too big and too generalized to be soothed by anything less than the Sermon on the Mount: Part II.

"Well, then," Denise said, "what do you want us to do while you're doing your job?"

Semmes looked at me.

"Wait," I said. "I'll find out what I can about this man without getting too close. I doubt he's given up. If he was willing to come here once, right after the murder, I'd bet he'll be willing to come again. I think he's playing for high stakes."

"Why do you think that?" Denise said, just to be saying something. She wasn't going to take a passive role and I could understand that. Admire it, even.

"I'm just guessing, actually."

"He tests very high on intuition," Semmes said. "I don't think anyone else could have found that man this quickly."

Semmes loved to blow smoke about me.

"All right. But what about *us*?" Denise insisted. "What do we do?"

"When he gets in touch, tell him you'll meet with him right here in the evening, after William gets through with practice. I want him here with you. But nobody else."

I looked at Denise when I said that, expecting resistance. But for all her anger, she was smart.

"I can dig that," she said. "Don't want to spook him."

"Right. Now when he gets here, Mrs. Coleman and William need to make him talk. Get him to say exactly what he is promising and how he intends to deliver. Don't push too hard, but the more he says, the better for us and the worse for him."

"I understand," Dinah Coleman said.

"Once we've got him saying those things, we can put the pressure on."

"Who do I call once I've heard from him?"

"Call Semmes," I said. "He'll know where to find me."

14

Semmes and I walked out into the cool evening air. When we reached his Porsche, he said, "What are you going to do next?"

"Go look for Stitch Folsome," I said.

"Right now?"

"The night is young."

"When does Jessie get back?"

"She's here. Got in last night."

Semmes nodded and said, "Why don't you give it a rest? Go out to dinner with Jessie. None of my business, but I think you've done enough for now. Citizen Stitch will be there in the morning."

I nodded. Semmes believed in the slow stalk and I liked to push. But I'd learned to listen to him.

"There's more to this than Stitch, anyway. We're just getting started. We've got a lot to learn."

"Such as?"

"How about motive?" he said. "They say it almost always comes down to love or money, unless you're talking about an assassin. Somehow, I don't think this crime has anything to do with the liberation of Palestine."

"It would be a reach," I said.

"And I'm going to rule out love for the moment on the grounds of . . . where's the evidence?"

I nodded.

"Leaving money. I strongly suspect that our boys see a big pot of cash somewhere if they pull this thing off and can take credit for William Coleman leading the U to glory. The question, of course, is . . . whose money?"

"What about the prosecutor?" I said. "If Stitch is going to deliver, then he's going to have to reduce the charges."

Semmes shook his head. "Nobody at the courthouse makes the kind of money I suspect we're talking about. They're all driving leased Fords until they can get out into private practice and start making enough to afford something German."

"But Stitch did tell Dinah Coleman he could arrange it with the prosecutor," I said.

"He did. But that doesn't mean some prosecutor knows that Stitch was speaking for him."

I gave Semmes a dumb look that he has seen before on countless occasions. Usually, he'd set me up. He enjoys making explanations, weaving them like a mosaic. It is one of the tactics he uses on juries, and by the time he has finished they are like students in some celebrated professor's seminar. Even if they don't understand, they believe fiercely that they do.

"Prosecutors are not immune to influence, Morgan," Semmes said. "They'll push a case or back off of it depending on how it will play or, as often as not, according to who is pushing them . . . and which way. It could be that Stitch and Grant are dealing with someone who knows he can push a prosecutor whichever way he wants. Someone who knows the prosecutor will reduce the charges against Jackson when the time comes, even if the prosecutor doesn't know it yet."

"All right," I said. "I'll buy that—as theory, anyway—but does it make any difference as far as what I'm doing? Seems like we just need to prove entrapment to get Jackson off the hook. And that's what we're trying to do, isn't it?"

"You never struck me as someone who played for small stakes, Morgan."

I gave him the look again. The one that says I'm three steps in back of him and falling further behind.

"We'll get Jackson Coleman off. I know that as sure as I know the sun's going to rise tomorrow morning. We could nail Grant and Folsome but it would be like picking off cripples. I want the big boys. There is some high trash behind this, I know that in my bones. The kind of trash that plays around with lives because it gives them a pump. It would give me some real satisfaction to put their hides on the wall. I suspect you'd feel the same."

"Yes," I said.

"We're like astronomers here. Trying to locate some big, invisible mass that is influencing the orbit of everything around it. We're looking for a black hole and you won't find it by staking out Stitch Folsome's house all night. Take Jessie out to dinner. Forget about it for a while. Call me in the morning and let me know how to get in touch if Dinah Coleman calls."

"Talked me into it," I said.

"So where are you taking me tonight," Jessie said. I'd picked her up at the house she had built a couple of miles upriver from mine. We had just turned onto the blacktop.

"I thought we'd shoot a little pool first," I said.

"All *right*. Morgan, you know how to please a woman. Pick her up in your truck and take her out to the pool hall. You know what redneck foreplay is, don't you?"

"Haven't heard that one."

"That's when the man says, 'Git in the truck, bitch.' "

"Very funny. Anyway, I brought you flowers." I'd stopped for some roses on my way back from Dinah Coleman's.

"You did. And I love 'em. And I also love to shoot pool. You know that. I shoot better than you."

"More practice."

"Just proves you spent your life hanging out in the wrong places."

"I'll buy that."

She leaned across the front seat and kissed me. "That's okay," she said. "I love you even if you can't shoot pool."

"Whew."

"Stick with me and I'll teach you how."

All three tables at Jimmy's were open when we got there. It is an old pine-board place on the water next to a fish house where the mullet netters and the bay shrimpers come to sell their catch. When they have their money, they go to Jimmy's to drink a beer, eat some shrimp, and shoot a rack or two. It is a clean place, and safe, given the neighborhood.

"Hey, boy," Jimmy said from behind the bar. "An' you too, Miss Beaudreaux."

"How you doing, Jimmy?" Jessie said affectionately. She thought he was a sweetie, even though he was as big as Tom Pine and almost as tough. He had run shrimp boats until his wife got sick enough to need him on the beach. That's when he opened this place and the fish house next door. "That way," he said, "mos' of what I pay 'em for the fish and shrimp, I take back in my pool hall."

His wife had died a couple of years ago but he was doing too well on the beach to start shrimping again.

"I'm doing good," he said, "even if I ain't got no customers."

"You've got two."

"And two of the best." Jimmy smiled. He had come out from behind the bar. He was wearing an apron over a clean white T-shirt and faded old khakis. His face was lined and red. When you looked at it, the word that came to mind was *jolly*. Except for the eyes.

"I got some fresh shrimp," he said. "Like always. And I also got something special for you." He looked at Jessie when he said this. "I must of known, somehow, that the bayou lady was coming, cause I got some fresh crawfish."

"*Bugs*," Jessie said happily. "Jimmy, I love you. Run away with me."

"Nah. This big ugly sonofabitch would come looking to kick my old fat ass. But I'll bring you some crawfish."

"And a cold beer," Jessie said.

Jimmy looked at me.

"Crawfish," I said. "Three million coon-asses can't be wrong."

"Don't be calling us that," Jimmy said. "You outnumbered."

"Yeah," Jessie said.

She racked and broke while Jimmy served the plates.

"Straight pool to fifty?"

"Fine," I said.

"Five dollars?"

"You want me to give it to you now?"

"Come on, Morgan. You could beat me if you'd just concentrate."

She played safe on the break. Jimmy brought two plates piled with scalded red crawfish.

"Run a few," Jessie said. "I feel like eating."

I missed my shot.

"You did that on purpose," she said.

She wiped her fingers, then stood up and surveyed the table

like a general studying a map. She ran nine balls while I ate three crawfish. Then she missed an easy shot in the corner.

"You must be hungry."

"Go on and run 'em. I left you the table."

I missed.

"Morgan, you shoot too hard. Just like all the oil field boys. I'd tell 'em its not a game of strength but they'd just go ahead and bang away like they was trying to *hurt* those balls instead of just kiss them into the pocket and leave themselves in shape for the next shot. Why won't none of you men listen to me?"

"I dunno. Just dumb, I guess."

"Well, I'm going to sit and eat for a while, then I'm going to run the table."

Which she did. Easily.

We finished the crawfish and then the game. I gave her a five-dollar bill and she said she felt guilty, like she was stealing the money.

We talked about another game and she said, no, she felt like dancing. So we said goodnight to Jimmy, who told us to hurry on back, then we drove on down the beach to a club where the house band played old music like it had been played when it wasn't so old.

They were playing "Good-Hearted Woman" when we got there and we danced until they took a break. The floor wasn't too crowded and we had room to move. She looked good. Looked happy, I suppose, among the telephone linemen and construction workers dressed up like cowboys and the secretaries and real estate agents trying to look like Texas debutantes. None of them looked as good as she did. None of them came even close.

The music had a rank, heavy bottom sound and the piano man had nimble fingers and could do all the good honky-tonk licks cold. The music was all the old feeling-good stuff. Bobby Bare, Jerry Jeff Walker, Waylon, and Willie. It went right inside you and made you want to move and not think about anything, even thinking. The walls, the floor, and the ceiling seemed to throb with the energy of it and by the time the band took a break, I had worked up a decent sweat.

"Want to stay around for another set?" I said.

"No," she said, "I've had enough people. Let's you and me go home together."

We took a long way around to her house, listening to the radio and not talking much. When I parked the truck in her drive, she said, "You can come in for a drink if you want. But just because you took me pool shooting, fed me crawfish, and danced with me, don't be getting any wrong ideas."

We went inside and Jessie said, "I don't believe in cold showers like you. I like hot water. You want to take a hot shower with me?"

She had a big bathroom done in bright red tile and we stood in the middle of it and undressed each other, leaving the clothes on the floor. Then we stepped into a big glass stall where she turned the water up as hot as we could stand it. We soaped each other slowly, back and front, with the water running over us and carrying the suds away and steam rising all around us and clouding the glass. Her pale tight body turned a kind of livid pink color with her skin smooth, flawless, and slick under my fingers.

We stayed under the water for a long time and then dried each other off with big, soft towels that we left on the floor with our clothes. She lit candles in her bedroom and opened a bottle of cold wine. It tasted clean and dry as desert air. We drank and made love with the same kind of urgency and before she went to sleep, we had finished the bottle.

We hadn't talked about Semmes or the Coleman business all night. And we still hadn't when I left just before dawn the next morning and drove back down to the river house, taking it slow because of the fog and because I was in no hurry.

15

When I got back to the river house, I ran a few miles, as usual, and I lifted weights in the old mule stable I had converted into a gym. The smell of mule sweat and mule shit was better than the smell of any gym I'd ever known.

When I finished, I showered and ate a couple of eggs and a grapefruit. I was ready to fight a bear with a switch.

The morning, however, did not live up to its early promise.

First I looked in the Pensacola phone book under Folsome. There were about a dozen listed. I tossed out Louise and Josephine and a few others that were out of the question and still had seven names. I started calling numbers and asking for Stitch, then apologizing when people said "Who?" or "Wrong number."

Eventually, I hit pay dirt. The phone rang four times and on the fifth ring, the answering machine kicked in, the tape hissing softly until the message began.

"Stitch and Sandy are not here right now. Leave a number and we'll catch you on the rebound."

Followed by the beep. And nothing. No messages backed up on the tape, so Stitch and Sandy, whoever she was, had been getting their calls.

I looked back in the phone book. The listing had been for Henry

Folsome. I wondered why Stitch was better than Hank. The address was a number on Red Bluff Road. I wrote it down.

It was not quite nine o'clock when I left the river house and drove out to Carver High to return the yearbooks. The woman who had given them to me was behind the desk. I thanked her and she thanked me. By quarter after ten I was parked in the lot of a liquor store that had not yet opened, looking across Red Bluff Road at the Deluna Arms where Stitch Folsome, among others, rented an apartment.

The Deluna was one of those new brick and particle-board complexes that come complete with a pool, tennis courts, and exercise room. The occupants are mostly young and childless, and frequently single. Working transients drawn together, like herd animals, in places of this sort.

This particular model was a few miles out of town, nearly to the interstate, on a high bluff over the bay—accounting for the street name. There was no access to the water a hundred feet below, but the view was good and the air was saturated with the ripe scent of tidal marsh water. I'd smelled it as soon as I parked and rolled down the window on my side of the truck.

I had come prepared, with a thermos full of my own coffee so I didn't have to taste soap. And an apple in case I got the hungries. Watching a building wasn't my idea of a good time but I'd had plenty of practice watching trails, lying on my belly with the leeches and the mosquitoes sucking on me. Spending the morning in a parking lot wearing clean clothes and drinking hot coffee was light duty.

There wasn't much action at the building. These were working hours and most people were off at the office or down at the construction site or out on the road, earning their way. In the evening, they would start to trickle in to rest up and regroup. I hoped I didn't have to wait that long. I didn't have that much coffee.

After the first cup, I decided to ration myself. Half a cup an hour. So while I waited for my next coffee break, I got busy changing position so my legs wouldn't go to sleep. Then I got out my pocket knife and worked on my manicure. When that was done, I checked my watch.

I'd killed a whole half hour. In thirty minutes, I could drink some more coffee. I'd always wondered how prison guards kept from going mad with boredom. I wouldn't have lasted a week.

I watched a distant flock of pelicans doing a little formation flying out over the bay. Then I measured the progress of a tug pushing a coal barge down the channel. Standing watch on that boat, I thought, would be almost as bad as working the guard tower.

But then, I suppose, what is boredom to some is serenity to others. For a while, I followed that thought like a fresh track in the woods. For me, I decided, boredom was not necessarily inactivity but the lack of an objective. I wasn't bored, really, sitting in the truck and watching a shabby apartment building, because I had an objective. I was just restless.

So I shifted my weight again, threw my arm over the back of the seat, and checked my watch. Time for more coffee.

After four more hours of this, I was out of coffee, my bladder was full, and the distinction between boredom and restlessness had lost its meaning. I got out of the truck and stretched, then went to the pay phone next to the liquor store and called Semmes.

"Where are you?" he said.

"Watching the apartment where Stitch lives."

"Well, you can drop that. Stitch called Dinah Coleman an hour ago. He's coming by tonight."

All the stiffness left my body and I felt suddenly light enough to fly. "I'll be there," I said, "in fifteen minutes."

Bored no more.

It was twilight when I left Semmes's office and took my place in what passed for rush hour traffic on my way out of town, back to the high-school gym where I'd first seen William Coleman play basketball less than a week ago.

There were a dozen cars in the large lot, most of them new, mid-sized rentals. The scouts were here to watch William Coleman do his stuff at practice. I pushed open the big steel doors to the gym and was hit in the face by the sounds of basketball practice. The thump of the ball and the skid of sneakers on the floor, the pushing of bodies as they moved for position and went up for the ball when it rattled off the iron, the shrill notes of a cheap plastic whistle blown in exasperation.

"All right, all *right*," a deep voice said loudly and impatiently. "Do it again and do it right. When you cut, you got to *cut*. It's like a knife. If it ain't sharp, it ain't worth spit."

The gym was bathed in bright, electric light and smelled of work, sweat, and mildew. There were ten players on the floor wearing old shorts and ripped T-shirts, along with a lean man in faded sweats with a whistle in his teeth. Several men in street clothes lounged in the bleachers. One or two sat alone and took notes. The others were clustered together, talking softly and not following the action on the floor.

The man with the whistle in his teeth looked my way, nodded briefly, then turned his attention back to the ten sweating boys spread out at one end of the court. He blew his whistle, and they began to move.

The boy on the in-bounds line found an open man who took the pass and then began dribbling slowly, watching the other players weaving under the basket and drifting out to the corners. William Coleman came open at one corner and took the pass. Without hesitating, he made a move as though to drive the baseline and when two players bit and came out to take him, Coleman pulled up sharply and threw an effortless bounce pass to a man who had come back door, headed for the basket. The ball seemed drawn to his hands and he took it on the way up, without breaking stride or rhythm, and laid it softly against the backboard. The ball fell neatly through the net and the man with the whistle clapped his hands twice and shouted.

"All right. All *right* now. I'll buy that. I'll buy that every time. Mr. Robinson himself isn't going to stop that one. You can take it to the bank every day. Give me ten laps and then hit the showers."

The boys groaned and began to run around the court wearily in groups of two or three, smiling and talking as they ran. William Coleman, I noticed, ran alone, head down, as though he were contemplating the floor as it passed under his feet.

The man with the whistle let it fall from his mouth as he approached me.

"You the one Mrs. Coleman called about."

"Yes," I said. "Morgan Hunt."

I stuck out my hand and he took it.

"Louis Pete. I'm Coleman's coach. He'll be another fifteen or twenty minutes doing his laps and getting cleaned up. I can cut him some slack on the running if you're in a hurry."

"No," I said. "That's all right." We had a couple of hours, still, before the meeting with Stitch.

"Come on in my office, then," he said. "I don't like to talk with all these ears around." He nodded in the direction of the bleachers where the scouts were still sitting.

I followed him through a steel door, past the entrance to the locker room, and into a little institutional office with a metal desk and a single chair for visitors.

"Sorry about this," Pete said. "High-school coaches don't fly first-class."

"It's fine."

"Those scouts out there are probably going crazy trying to figure out who you're with and what kind of in you got, talking to me in private. They'll have you working for UNLV or Arizona in no time. I never seen a more paranoid bunch of grown men in my life."

"They're here every afternoon?" I asked.

"Oh yeah. And this ain't a particularly big crowd. I've seen it where there was twice as many as this. Almost as big a crowd as used to come to games, before we got Coleman."

"They're all over him, I guess?"

"Him and anybody who might get close to him. Several of those fellows out there in the gym have talked to me, real sincere, about what a fine coach I am and how with my talent, I ought to think about moving up in class. Consider being an assistant in the college game."

"Is that a bribe?"

"Not so's you could prove it," he smiled. "Maybe I *am* a good coach." Pete smiled, put his large feet up on the desk, and ran his hand over his head.

"Anyway, I'd rather coach high school anytime than be an assistant like them at some big Division One school."

"Too much pressure?"

He shook his head. "Coaches *like* pressure. If you didn't, you'd find yourself another line of work. But these fellows live with a different kind of pressure. They might as well be salesmen, humping a route with a satchel full of samples. It's sickening to watch. Grown men, hanging around some teenager, telling him how wonderful he is. Begging him to buy what they're selling. *Begging*.

"At least in high school, I don't have to beg no teenagers. County decides where they go to school. Not them and not me. I just coach 'em; I don't have to recruit 'em. Those scouts out there all have one-year contracts and they all want to be head coaches. The one who signs Coleman will be taking a long step in that direction and the others will all be wondering if their contracts are going to be renewed. So they beg and try to pretend they like doing it."

"How's Coleman holding up?"

"You wouldn't believe it. Most any kid his age, it would go right straight to his head. But Coleman just ain't made that way. He could run these guys around, make 'em do back flips through a flaming hoop, but he won't do it. He actually worries about them. He doesn't want to hurt their feelings. In a lot of ways, he's a real choirboy. But inside, the kid is tough. The best kind of tough."

Pete looked at his watch. "He ought to be dressed by now. I'll go get him for you. And I'll tell those scouts that you aren't competition. That they got to leave you and William alone on the way out. It'll break their hearts."

Pete left, and a couple of minutes later William Coleman knocked at the office door.

"Mr. Hunt?"

"Hello, William," I said. "I'm Morgan Hunt. Your mother told you about me."

"Yes, sir." He spoke softly but his eyes stayed on mine. He was still damp from his shower; dressed in jeans and a sweatshirt, and carrying a load of books under one long arm.

"All right, then," I said. "We ought to get going. We can talk while we drive."

"Yes, sir."

Several of the scouts watched us as we crossed the parking lot and got into the truck. I felt like I was back in high school myself, leaving a party with the head cheerleader.

When we were on the road, I said, "Why don't you tell me how much you know and then I'll fill in the blanks."

"I know Jackson is in jail," he said. "For murder." The words came out soft and slow but there was a hard, unmistakable crust of anger around them.

"Did your mother tell you about the man who came by to see her the night it happened?"

"Yes, sir. Said he could get Jackson down to manslaughter if I go to the U."

His eyes were fixed firmly on the road.

"All right," I said. "That's about where I came in. What I've learned since then is that the man who made the deal may have at least one partner, who is a cop, and they may have set your brother up. If we can prove that, we can get the charges against him thrown out."

"For sure?"

"The man I work for says so."

"Mr. Semmes?"

"Yes."

"He wouldn't lie," William said.

"No, he wouldn't," I said. "Now, the man who came by to see your mother is coming back tonight, to see if you're willing to deal. And I've got somebody out there right now who is setting up a system to tape everything that is said."

William nodded.

"We need for you to talk to the man, ask him questions and make him answer them. We need as much as we can get on the tape. But it has to sound natural. We don't want him to get suspicious. Do you think you can handle that?"

"Yes, sir. I think so."

"All right. I'd tell you what to ask, but maybe you know better than I do. Nobody ever tried to recruit me and from what I've heard, you've got plenty of experience."

He smiled mournfully. "Yes, sir."

"I saw you play the other night," I said. "You've got a real gift."

"Seems like it just causes trouble," he said. "Times like this, I could wish I'd never played."

He sat very still, almost unnaturally so, and his eyes stayed firmly on the road. We drove in silence for a mile.

"William, you get plenty of cheap advice," I said, "but would you mind just a little more?"

"No, sir."

"Don't think that way."

He waited for me to go on with my pitch, but I said nothing for another half mile. Finally he spoke, "You can't help what you think."

"You're wrong there," I said. "I can't tell you anything about basketball, but I can tell you something about thinking. You ever been in prison?"

"No, sir."

"Well, I have. I can't recommend the experience, either. But I did learn one thing there."

"What's that?" He was interested now. Somebody was telling him something new. Not just the same old stuff about how he had the best jump shot since Danny Manning.

"Well, I learned I couldn't change the fact I was in prison. If

I forgot it for a minute or two, all I had to do was open my eyes and look at the walls and the wire to remind myself. And I could feel sorry for myself, blame the world, hate everybody, make it just as hard on myself as I possibly could if I wanted to. That was easy. They call that 'prison thinking.' "

"Yes?"

"Or I could think like I was still a man, free in my own mind. My thinking was about the only thing that *was* mine. I didn't have any choice about the walls and the wire, but how I thought about it was my decision. You start thinking that you're nothing but a sorry, whipped, useless convict and, friend, that's what you are.

"In a way, it was easy for me. My choices were real clear. It's harder for you."

"How am I supposed to think?"

"You want my advice?"

"Yes, sir."

"Well, I'd start with the gift. I don't believe you could play ball the way you do without loving it. You do love playing basketball, don't you?"

"Yes, sir."

"Then start by thinking that you aren't going to let anyone poison it for you. It belongs to you, not some creep who wants you to go to his school so he can keep his coaching job, go to the big tournament, and get his face on television and make a lot of money for the school. That doesn't have anything to do with you and your gift."

He said nothing.

"Do you follow me?"

"Yes, sir."

"It wasn't you or your basketball that caused this. It was a couple of men—maybe more—who are your enemies. You can't let them beat you."

"No, sir."

"And as long as I've got your attention, do you mind one more piece of advice?"

"No, sir. You're making good sense."

"Well, thanks," I said. "That's the first time anyone has said *that* to me in a long time."

He smiled. Not so mournfully this time.

"Since we're talking about thinking here, let me ask you when you find yourself doing the least amount of thinking."

"When I'm playing basketball," he said.

"Okay," I said. "That ought to tell you, right there, just how important basketball is to you. It's the things that keep you from thinking that will get you through the times when you don't have any choice but to think. Not everybody has something like that. It's part of the gift. Maybe the most important part."

"Yes, sir," he said. "I understand what you're saying."

"All right. We're just about at your house now and I want you to do a little thinking. What I want you to think about is talking to this man just like he's another basketball recruiter. Ask him questions and make him explain his deal. Get him to spell it out so we'll have it all on tape. And then we'll nail his sorry ass. Can do?"

"Yes, sir," he said. "I can handle that. No sweat."

16

Duke Wagrum had the Coleman house fully wired. "Took ten minutes, Morgan," he said. "Piece of cake."

Duke was a retired navy chief who had spent thirty years in aviation electronics. He kept his hand in repairing televisions, VCRs, computers, toasters, and anything else people brought by his trailer at the end of a little dirt road a mile from the back gate of the naval air station. When we first met, over a telephone answering machine that had been fried in a lightning strike, I asked him if he ever did anything with surveillance equipment. "Hobby of mine," he'd said. "It's where a lot of the action is. I got some gear myself. Trouble is, I don't get much call."

Now I'd called.

"There is a little voice-activated mike in the living room that will pick up anything," he said. "And I mean *anything*. Mouse farts, and you'll hear it. That mike is wired to a line-of-sight transmitter out in the back yard. Thing goes about the size of a deck of cards. Range of maybe a mile on a clean frequency. I figure you can sit in your truck with the receiver and listen in. You want to tape it, I suppose?"

"I think we have to," I said.

"That's Jake. I've got a unit that is both a receiver and a

recorder. You can listen through the speaker or the headphones, don't make any difference."

"Okay," I said. "Why don't I take the receiver down the block, find a place to park, and we'll give it a test."

"Okay," Duke said and handed me the small black unit. "All you got is a power switch, volume control, and a squelch," he said. "No channel selector. It's a single crystal, and I selected that and checked it out myself. Here's the jack for your headset and this here is the recorder. All the usual stuff—forward, rewind, pause. Nothing to it."

"Okay," I said. "Give me five minutes, then run a test."

"Wilco."

I got in the truck and eased down to the end of the block. I parked around the corner from the Coleman house, killed the engine, turned on the power to the little unit, and rocked the squelch back until I heard a soft rush of static. I turned the volume up, then eased the squelch forward until the rushing sound was barely audible.

I waited for a minute or two and then heard Duke's voice very clearly and loud enough that I had to back off the volume. "Remote, this is base. My short count follows. Five . . . four . . . three . . . two . . . one. One . . . two . . . three . . . four . . . five. End of test."

I put the unit under the seat and locked the truck. As I walked back to the Coleman house, it occurred to me that I might look out of place, the only white man in a black neighborhood. But then I remembered the scouts who'd been coming and going for weeks now. To anyone who looked at me and wondered, I'd just be one more man come to talk to William about basketball.

"You read me?" Duke said when I was back at the house.

"Loud and clear."

"Then you're ready to ramble."

"I appreciate your help, Duke," I said. "How soon do you need this stuff back?"

"When you get through with it."

He left for his trailer and I checked my watch. Almost seven thirty. Stitch Folsome had told Dinah Coleman he would be there at eight.

"Just try to be natural," I said. "He'll expect you to be a little nervous, so don't worry about that. Ask him questions. Make him tell you as much as you can so we can get it on tape."

Dinah Coleman and her son both nodded.

"Feels wrong," she said, "to be doing something so *sneaky*."

"I understand. But he pulled you into it."

"Yes," she said softly. "I suppose he did."

"Do you think it will work?" William said.

"Yes," I said. "For some reason I do." I was feeling none of Dinah Coleman's qualms. I felt like a hunter setting up on an active trail. Action.

"Well, I hope so."

I squeezed his shoulder. Had to reach up to do it. "Don't worry," I said. "I'll be right around the corner. And, anyway, it's going to work."

I went back to the truck and fitted a little plastic earpiece that Duke had given me into my right ear, away from the window, and ran the lead down behind my shoulder, then plugged the jack into the unit. When I turned it on, I heard the soft rush of static in my ear, like I had gone to sleep with my pillow over a hive of bees. No voice for now. I checked my watch. Ten minutes.

I wished I'd thought to stop for coffee. Even soapy coffee.

Folsome was right on time. I recognized the voice from the tape on his answering machine. Nasal, country, and vaguely combative. Also, probably owing to the circumstances, just a little haughty. He probably still considered any black his inferior by some mystical, unchangeable measure.

"And how are you folks tonight?" he said.

"We're all right," Dinah Coleman said with cold dignity.

"How about you, Tiger?"

"Fine," I heard William answer firmly.

"Good," Stitch said. "Real good. But you *do* have a problem, don't you. A very *serious* problem."

"We know why you're here, mister," Dinah Coleman said.

"Okay. But just to make sure that we all understand each other, I'll tell William what I told you. Before I can help you people with your problem, you have to do something for me."

"What's that?" William said, not belligerent but still with enough reserve that I knew it had to bother Stitch. He didn't like being talked to that way by anyone and especially not by young black men. Someone he would always consider a boy.

"Well, Slick," he said, "what you have to do for me is sign a

letter of intent that says you'll go to the U and play basketball for
four years. You'll get the full boat and there will be plenty of ways
for you to pick up some extra spending money and somehow you'll
get lucky and wind up driving a nice car. But none of that gets put
in writing.

"You'll be an all-American, probably go the final four one or
two years, come out a lottery pick, and sign for a truckload of
money. So it ain't exactly a hardship tour you're signing up for. You
can even get a college education and a degree, if that's important to
you. Probably be the first person in your family to ever go to
college, right?"

"His sister went to West Florida," Dinah Coleman said.

"That a fact? Well, I admire initiative. Everyone does. And
what I'm offering is a chance for William here to better himself."

"He could go to lots of schools."

"Yes. He could. But for someone with his talent, it doesn't
make that much difference, the way I see it. He'll be playing in
the NBA four or five years from now, no matter where he goes to
school. Doesn't make any difference what kind of physics department they've got. Doesn't even make much difference what kind
of basketball program they've got, because wherever William goes
he'll be the program. But the U has a good program, especially
when you consider they've been on probation the last couple of
years. With William, they'll come back gangbusters."

I watched a little dial, illuminated in red light, while Stitch
made this speech. A tiny black needle danced to the tune of his
voice, indicating that everything he said was being preserved on
tape.

"If I sign, what will you do for us?" William said, in the same
soft but firm voice.

"If you sign that letter of intent," Stitch said, "then within two
weeks time, the prosecutor will reduce the charges against your
brother to manslaughter and recommend that the judge set bail at
something low enough that you could get him sprung on what
you've got in this house. Then your brother's lawyer can go to the
prosecutor and make a deal. Plead guilty and get a year. Do six
months. He'll be out in time to see you play your first college
game."

Nothing was said for what seemed like a full minute, then
William's level, unemotional voice came through the earpiece.

"How do I know you can deliver that? Are you with the prosecutor?"

God love that kid, I thought.

"No. I'm not. Be nice, though, if we could just trust each other."

"Phooey," Dinah Coleman said. I hadn't heard that word in a long time.

"All right, then," Stitch said, some exasperation creeping into his voice. "Then consider this. The signing period for letters of intent doesn't open for two weeks. I can't do anything with that paper until then. If the paper becomes public before then, the U is in trouble but so are you. It could cost you a year of eligibility, maybe more. Put the U back on probation. But if the prosecutor does what I say he'll do, then you don't have any reason to go public.

"But," Stitch said with an edge on his voice now, "if you try to get out of the deal after we've held up our end, then you can expect us to take it seriously. It might cost the U, but we'll make sure you pay in a lot bigger way."

"You're making threats," Dinah Coleman said.

"No. Just making a deal that is good for everyone and protecting our interests. We'll deliver, and when we do we expect you to deliver. That way, everyone wins. Your son got himself in this trouble and we're going to help him get out."

"You want me to thank you?"

"I want William to sign the paper and postdate it. I'll take care of getting it notarized." I could almost see Stitch smirk as he said this and I couldn't wait for it to end so I could get my hands on him.

"I can study what I want to?" William said.

"Sure. No problem. Home ec, philosophy, phys ed, or hotel management. Makes no difference."

After a long silence, Dinah Coleman said, "Seems like you don't have any choice."

"All right," William said.

"Good boy," Stitch said.

I turned off the tape, removed the earpiece, and started the truck. My impulse was to take him on the street, but if one of the neighbors looked out the window and saw two white men fighting, it would mean a call to the law. So without turning on the headlights, I eased up the block and waited for Stitch to come out of the Coleman house. I could feel my pulse in my neck and I was breathing a little hard, the way you do when the game you're laying for comes right down the trail where you've set up. Stitch wasn't even remotely aware of my presence. I had him dead in my sights and it felt great.

17

He walked down the sidewalk and turned up the street with a kind of confidence in his step, as though he had just scored twenty in the big game and helped his team to victory. He was wearing a tan sport jacket, and while he walked he put a sheet of folded paper in the inside pocket.

He stopped next to a dark black car, one of those indistinguishable little fastbacks that are supposed to take to the road like Cleopatra took to Mark Antony. He unlocked the door, got in, and started down the street. I waited until he turned at the first intersection, then I put on the lights and followed.

I hung back until he was in some traffic, then I got as close as I thought I could. He led me straight back to the apartments on Red Bluff Road.

I parked a few spaces away from him and caught up with him before he was out of the parking lot.

"Got a minute?" I said.

"Who are you," Stitch said with the contempt he was feeling for the whole world, which he had just beaten.

"I'm the man who is going to bring the walls crashing down on you," I said.

"Is that a fact?"

"Yes." I said. "It sure is."

"And just how are you going to do that, Slick?"

"That's what you called William Coleman just now, isn't it? Called him that when you offered him a 'full boat.' You also made some promises about his brother that sounded like the kind of thing that could be hard to explain to grand juries and judges. They're fans, too, but they play a slightly different game."

His small eyes widened, like the eyes of an animal that is suddenly aware of danger but doesn't yet know where the predator is. Only that it is close.

"Now, you should know," I said, "that everything you said in there is on a tape the grand jury can listen to. And I've got the tape. You're familiar with the legal phrases *obstruction of justice* and *conspiracy*?"

He nodded slightly, still testing the wind and trying to locate precisely the source of the sudden threat.

"Good. Then I don't have to explain to you that you have just stepped into a world of hurt. Now what I want you to do is hand me the paper that you just got William Coleman to sign by committing about a half a dozen felonies." I tried to sound procedural so he would take me for a cop. One who worked at a higher level than the cops he knew.

It must have worked. Stitch and his kind always believe that there is somebody around with more muscle than they have or can call on. His hand moved tentatively toward the inside pocket of his sport jacket. But when his fingers touched the paper, his hand stopped and stayed there.

"I could call for some backup," I said, "and we could take it from you. Or you could be cooperative and hand it over without a fuss. Makes no never mind to me."

He glared at me like a small, defiant animal in the grip of a steel trap.

"I want a lawyer," he said.

"I'd want one, too," I said, "if I was in your place."

"If you're going to take me in, then let's go. I want to make a call."

"Where would I take you?"

"Who are you?" he said. "Show me some identification."

"I'm nobody," I said. "Just a friend of the Colemans."

"Not a cop . . ."

"Nope. Lucky for you."

"Then I don't have to talk to you. Or give you anything."

"Maybe not. But I've got everything you said on tape. And in a minute or two, I'm going to have that paper."

He took a step forward so there was less than a yard of space between us and I could feel his breath on my face. He had a couple of inches on me and maybe thirty pounds. But they weren't very good pounds.

"If you've got help, *Slick*, you'd better start yelling for it."

While my hands were still down, he swung his right hand in a big, sloppy arc. He kept his head up and back, instead of tucked down into his shoulder and forward, and as I ducked under the big, lazy punch, I brought my right hand, fingers stiff, straight up and into his throat. As the fingers struck flesh, I used my right leg to get behind him and kick his feet out from under him. He went down in a heap, trying to scream but with only spit and air and a choking, guttural noise coming from his mouth, a sound of panic and pain.

But he wasn't through. He tried to kick me, aiming for the crotch but missing and catching me on the point of the hip. It stung but did not do any damage. He came off the ground with his fingers clawing for my eyes. He was tough, in desperation. Most men would have been too desperate for air to think about fighting. I grabbed his hand and twisted it away from me.

I should have stopped then and I might have. He was finished. I was on top of him now and could have pinned the arm behind him and applied enough pressure that he would have stopped fighting and done whatever I told him to do. He wasn't anything to me.

But he tried to bite me in the face, and when I moved out of the way he did the last thing left and spit. In an instant, everything went hot and his face, six inches from mine, became a red, watery blur.

I twisted his hand with all the force I could manage and felt the bone in his finger break. The sound of sheering bone was followed instantly by his broken scream. The tension went out of his body like air from a punctured balloon.

"My hand," he croaked. "You broke my fucking hand."

I let go of his hand, reached inside his jacket, and took the paper from the pocket. I stood up.

He stayed on the ground, moaning. He held his hand in front of his face and in the thin light from the windows of the apartment building and the traffic on the highway, I could see his middle finger bent back on itself with a small spur of jagged bone coming through the skin and blood running down his wrist from the puncture.

"Jesus Christ, look at my hand."

"You'd better get to a hospital," I said.

"My *hand*."

"They can fix it."

"The bone. You can see the fucking bone." His face was twisted in pain, disbelief, and fear. Even in the weak light, I could see he'd gone pale with shock. He was still having trouble getting air through his throat and was gasping like a beached fish. In a minute, he would hyperventilate and pass out.

"Get up," I said. "I'll take you to the hospital."

He looked at me without comprehending.

"Come on," I said. "Let's get you to the emergency room." I held my hand out and he took it with his good hand. I pulled him to his feet.

"Don't look at it," I said. "And try to breathe slow and deep."

"God, oh God."

"Come on, Stitch, it's just a broken finger. You won't die from it. Now suck it up. Breathe and walk. You can do it, big tough guy like you."

I pushed him to get him started.

"Oh, my hand."

"Shut up and walk."

He shuffled a few steps, breathing and spitting, trying to clear the airway. He was slow but getting steadier. Probably he wouldn't pass out from shock, I thought, especially if he didn't look at his hand. I did look at it. The stump of the bone was plain, jagged at the end, like the stump of a broken pencil.

The walking must have steadied him. He stopped walking and stopped moaning and looked at me. His eyes were full of dumb, primitive hate.

"I'll drive myself," he said.

"All right, Stitch. Suit yourself."

"This isn't the last you'll see of me."

"No. I'm sure it isn't. You're going to get burned by this thing." I held up the paper. "The only way to fireproof your sorry ass is to give me a name. I already know about Grant. So you'd better tell me a better name than that."

He didn't have to tell me. He could tell the prosecutor or a grand jury. But I thought I'd try.

"I don't know who you are, buddy," he said, forcing the words, "but you are in way over your head."

"Stitch," I said, "you don't seem to understand. Why don't you go get your hand fixed. They'll give you some codeine for the pain, and tomorrow, after you've slept that off, the hand will hurt like a bitch but you'll be able to think clearly. I'll be in touch and you can tell me who you've been carrying water for. That's your best shot at staying out of jail."

"Fuck you."

"Listen, Stitch, why don't you get yourself to the hospital while you've still got one good hand. Keep talking that way, and you'll never play the piano again."

He turned away and I watched him walk unsteadily to his car and reach across his body with his good hand to get his keys out of his pocket. It took him a while. When he was on his way, I got in my own truck and left the lot in a hurry in case somebody had seen our little dance and called the law.

It was getting colder outside so I stopped at the first convenience store I saw, bought a cup of scalding hot coffee, and sipped it on the highway home.

The radio was on and when I searched the dial for some old music—I don't get all weak and sentimental about the old days but I do miss the music—I heard the voice of Mike Grantham. He was arguing with somebody, insisting that sports were better back in the old days even if the athletes were not.

"Show me the Johnny Unitas of today," he was saying with something that sounded like real feeling. "Show me the Bill Russell of today. Show me the Ted Williams or the Willie Mays of today."

"You got plenty of ballplayers that's as good as they was," an earnest, country voice came back, hot and ready for argument.

But Grantham cut him off.

"These players today," he said, "they don't care about the team. The don't care about tradition. They don't care about sacrifice. All they care about is themselves and their money."

"Ah, come on—"

"No, *you* come on. Look at them. They sign a contract and hold out or take a scholarship and quit to go pro. If they get hurt the tiniest bit, they don't play. They complain about the press, they charge money to sign autographs, and when they get bored they go out and find some drugs to take. And when they get caught doing that, they check into a rehab clinic somewhere and say they've found Jesus. They're spoiled creeps and we're letting them get away with it."

"You're just living in the past—"

"You bet I am," Grantham said, sounding like a man at a wake who'd been grieving and drinking for two or three days and wanted now to tell everyone present how he felt about the departed, "this wunneful humin bein." I felt a twinge of embarrassment for him.

"Let me ask you something," he said and did not wait for his caller to answer. "Do you remember Billy Cannon?"

"Yeah, sure. LSU. Won the Heisman."

"Good. Very good. Most of the people who call can't remember any Heisman winner past Bo Jackson."

"Gimme a break—"

"No. I'm going to give you an *education*. Now listen. Do you remember when LSU played Mississippi in Baton Rouge Cannon's senior year?"

And with that, Grantham was off telling all his listeners out there in radioland the same story he'd told me.

I listened for a few moments, which was as long as I could stand it, then went back to the dial, scanning until I found Huey "Piano" Smith doing "Rocking Pneumonia and the Boogie Woogie Flu." Seems to me that if you are going to dwell on the past, you ought to take some pleasure from it, and the music just about always made me feel good right down to my bones.

18

I played the tape through once when I got back to the river house. Every word came through clear and precise enough to put Stitch in jail and get Jackson out. I put the tape in an envelope, along with the agreement that William Coleman had signed, and took the envelope out to the old mule barn that I had made over into a gym. I put the envelope in the bottom of a lead-lined icebox that had not been used since the advent of the electric refrigerator. I assumed the icebox was more or less fireproof, the lining anyway, and used it to store old papers and various documents such as my birth certificate, passport, and car registration.

It was ten o'clock but I was wide awake, full of the kind of agitation that had kept me lying on my bunk with my eyes wide open through a lot of long nights behind the wire. I hadn't gone out to the Colemans' with breaking Stitch Folsome's bones on my mind. He was nothing to me and probably not much more than that to anyone else. Useful, probably, to someone who was behind the scheme that had put Jackson Coleman in jail, but still just an errand boy. When I'd watched him climbing in his car like some kind of wounded animal going to ground, holding his maimed paw for some relief, it hadn't been with any sense of pleasure or triumph. I'd felt just as small as he looked. And dirty.

I only knew of two things that worked when I was like this. One was time—reliable but slow. The other was sweat. It was a little less reliable but much quicker. I took off my clothes, hung them on a nail, and put on a set of sweatpants and a T-shirt. Then I got down on the bench with two hundred and twenty-five pounds on the bar above me and began lifting. Ten repetitions. Then I added weight and did ten more. I worked hard, barely pausing between sets. In five minutes, I had broken a heavy sweat, even though the barn was not heated and I had no fire in the woodstove. The sweat carried a foul, oily odor, the kind you smell on yourself when you work out after a long spell of drinking.

I did curls and military presses. Flies and pullovers. Everything that felt right, in no particular order. I paced the stable between sets, breathing the dusty, moldy air deep into my lungs. I worked until my muscles burned and then worked them some more. I was quivering with the strain and my sweatpants were black. I was still working, doing heavy squats until I felt like the strain would pop something in my back, when a voice came through the door, soft and curious, startling me nevertheless.

"Morgan? Hey, Morgan, what on earth are you doing in there this time of night?"

It was Jessie.

She watched from the porch while I showered outside.

"Damn," she said, "isn't that *cold*?"

"Yes."

"How can you stand it?"

"Feels good."

"There's times," she said, "when I don't think men have good sense."

"You could say that about me," I said. Turned off the water, dried myself, and wrapped the towel around my waist. "Especially if you'd seen me earlier tonight."

"You sound like you had a bad one, Morgan."

"Pretty bad."

"Is that why you were out there in the stable punishing yourself?"

"I suppose."

"Well, listen, get yourself dressed. I'll build a fire and make you something to drink. See if I can't do something to get you feeling better."

I felt better already. It could have been the old sweat remedy

or it could have been Jessie's company, which was almost as reliable
as time.

When I came back to the living room, she had a couple of
sticks of fatwood going under some split red oak and was sitting on
the old sofa watching the rising yellow flame. I sat next to her.

"Here," she said, "take this. It's good medicine for the thing
that's ailing you."

I took the short heavy glass and tasted. Bourbon and something
else.

"I put a little bitters in it. Little sugar and a squeeze of orange.
Poor man's Sazerac. You like it?"

"Just fine."

"One of those New Orleans drinks," she said. "In the old days,
folks used to drink 'em at breakfast. Can you imagine that? Believe
it would put the day away before it even got started."

"It's a night drink," I said. "No doubt about it." The whiskey
seemed to spread through me like smoke, warming my insides the
way the fire warmed my skin.

"So what happened?" she said. "You get tied up in knots over
this basketball thing? You want to talk to me about it?"

I took another measured sip of whiskey and told her the story.
I watched her face while I talked. In the light of the fire, it showed
a kind of deeply attentive concern with no trace of judgment.

When I finished, she smiled a little mournfully. "Morgan, you
know what?"

"What's that?"

"You've got a bad way of being too hard on yourself."

"Oh?"

"Yeah," she said, firmly. "You sure do. You're feeling all low
because you broke that creep's hand for him. Right?"

"There's more to it than—"

"Naw there isn't. You don't want to be a bully and a hothead.
You want to be like Nat Semmes and handle things like a gentleman. But look what you did. You found this Stitch person and, in
the second place, you got him on tape. And *then* you got him to
hand over the paper he made that boy sign. You think Nat Semmes
could have done that, doing things like a gentleman?"

"Probably not."

"Not for sure, he couldn't. Won't ever happen. But you did
it. That's why he calls you up when he needs something done.
Because he knows that with you, it's going to get done."

"Kind of you to say."

"Now you keep on listening to me, Morgan Hunt, 'cause I'm not finished. You're feeling bad because of what you did to that Stitch person. Well, I think he got off light. Most people, if they knew what he did, would say, 'Go on and break his other hand, so he's got to get some help unzipping his pants when he wants to pee. Break his foot, too. The boy needs it.' "

"I *am* good at that," I said. "Everybody needs to be good at something, I suppose."

"Oh hush. Stop feeling sorry for yourself. You got no call to feel bad about anything. Thing about you, Morgan, is what you do, you do real good."

"Well, thank you."

She smiled, showing her bright, uneven teeth and the deep creases that bracketed her mouth.

Then, as though the image on a screen had suddenly been changed, her face turned solemn. "I'm not a silly little girl, Morgan. I don't go all to pieces because people get tough and hurt each other. I've seen plenty of that and I don't expect the world is going to change if we can just get everybody to smile and be nice and start growing flowers and caring about each other."

I nodded.

"I care about you and it scares me, sometimes, what you do. Things go wrong. Even to people who can handle themselves. I know that, too. It isn't like television. You could get chopped down real quick and I don't like to think about that happening." She gave me a melancholy sort of smile. "I'd miss you."

"I'm not—"

"Hush. Listen. I admire the way you get things done. I truly do. And I know you've got good reasons. I wouldn't spend five minutes in a room with you if you were just one of these old boys who needs to go around proving what a bad-ass he is.

"But I'm not going to just smile and say, 'Whatever you need to do, Cowboy.' I'm not that way either. I'm not going to *lie* to you. You're a big boy and I think you can probably live with that."

I nodded.

"And, anyway, maybe if you know I'm worried and I'm some-body good to come home to, then you might not do anything too stupid. You understand what I'm trying to say?"

"Perfectly."

"Okay. No more of this whipped dog stuff. It ain't like like you."

I started to say something but she told me to hush and put my arm around her and watch the fire and drink my drink and stop talking about it and thinking about it.

Just then, between the workout, the shower, the whiskey, and Jessie's little pep talk, I felt about as good as it is possible to feel. If I'd felt any better, it would have been a crime.

I was still feeling good in the morning after Jessie and I had coffee on the porch and she left for her place and the business of her day. I waited around for a while, drinking more coffee and listening to the farm report on the radio. I was thinking about feeder cattle. The price had been good for a long time now, long enough to have brought enough people into the game to saturate the market. I saw a lot of steers grazing between the rows of the local pecan orchards, put out there by farmers who figured to cash in, long as beef was high. Next fall, the feedlots would be crowded like a Tokyo rush hour, the way I figured, and the price would drop like a stone.

I listened through the reports on rice, wheat, and cotton. Feeder cattle were holding firm. I even liked that. For as long as there has been a cycle in the price of beef, people are always surprised when the price starts falling and act like they have been blindsided by some totally unexpected and unprecedented calamity.

By seven thirty, I'd had enough and left for town, first to talk with Semmes and then to brace Stitch Folsome for some names. That would be a lot easier now that I wasn't feeling so guilty about breaking his finger.

I tuned the radio in the truck to the same station I'd been listening to in the house. The farm report finished up with some tips on controlling broad-leaf weeds. Cut to commercial. Then back to the local news.

The body of a man who appeared to have been beaten to death was found early in the morning in the alley behind a local bar known to be a hangout for bikers. The body had been identified as that of local insurance salesman and former basketball coach Henry Folsome.

Goddamn.

I bit down hard enough on my back teeth to knot a muscle in my jaw and slammed my fist on the steering wheel, then on the dash. I felt like hitting myself.

I hadn't been too rough with Stitch; I'd been too easy. I should have kept on breaking fingers until he gave me the name I wanted. He still might be dead, or he might have had the sense to know that once he'd given me the name, he had to go to ground and ask someone, even me, for protection. But either way, whether he'd played it smart or stupid, I'd have a name . . . or names. Instead, I'd gone all to pieces over the kind of wound that would have gotten you out on the last chopper, with the body bags and the captured weapons, and now all I had was the tape and the signed letter, neither of them worth a bucket of warm piss without Stitch and the names.

Goddamn.

I stopped the truck and pulled as far off the shoulder as I could. Then I got out and leaned against the sheet steel of the bed and tried to breathe deeply, calm down, and think. No more blunders. And especially, no more sentimental blunders.

I decided to put off seeing Semmes until after I'd checked out the bar where Stitch had been greased. I didn't expect to find out much, but then I only wanted to know which side of the border the place was on. City or county. If it was county, and Tom Pine was handling the case, then I'd give him everything including the tape and hide in the grass and watch him work. But if it was city, then Officer Grant could be in a position to muddy the waters, or worse. So I wouldn't give them anything.

Then, later in the morning, I'd go see Semmes and bring him up to speed. Even this sort of feeble planning was better than thinking about how badly I'd blown it with Stitch. So badly that there would be no more chances, ever.

Goddamn.

19

The bar was called the Iron Horseman and it was well inside the city limits, about half a mile from the main gate to the navy yard on a rough strip it shared with pawn shops, used-car lots, tattoo parlors, and evil little girlie bars. The Iron Horseman was painted some kind of lurid purple with various Nazi insignia, skulls, and birds of prey stenciled over it in black. A sign above the door read CHAINS AND LEATHERS REQUIRED. The big, dirt parking lot was littered with empty beer cans and one discarded biker's helmet painted in bright yellow metafleck. You almost expected to see a head still inside it.

There was a city cruiser out back where some sawhorses had been set up. Yellow tape ran between the sawhorses. One cop in uniform sat on the front bumper of the cruiser, drinking coffee from a Styrofoam cup. The other cop was asleep in the front seat of the cruiser.

I gave the Iron Horseman a two-minute once-over. I wasn't going to learn anything poking around the scene of the crime, whether or not those cops were standing watch. But I did wonder what Stitch Folsome had been doing there. I'd have bet just about anything he was not a biker, not even in some kind of deeply secret life. And even if he had been, would he have come to this place after surgery to repair a compound fracture? He probably had a

steel rod in his finger, along with several stitches, and a head full
of codeine. Also problems of an unknown but serious nature with
both the law and whoever he'd been conspiring with. It didn't seem
likely he would have been in the mood for a night of hard honky-
tonking and whipping asses with the motorcycle crowd.

I left the parking lot of the Iron Horseman for Semmes's office.
I'd left the house planning to tell him of my great success. Now I
felt like a man coming home to tell his wife he'd just been fired.

"No way you could have known," Semmes said when I'd finished telling my story. "And even if you had, what could you do?"

"I could have gotten it out of him."

Semmes shook his head. "You're no torturer, Morgan. You
might pop your cork a little too quickly but that's the precise
antithesis of what it takes to sit there, smoking a cigarette and
twisting the thumbscrews or shooting the volts to a man's gonads.
So let's drop the *mea culpa* stuff, all right?"

"All right."

"Stitch is dead. May the Lawd have mercy on his sorry soul.
For the living, it's on with the hunt. So let's consider what we have
to go on."

"The tape," I said. "And the letter William Coleman signed."

"They're still in that icebox where you squirrel things away?"

"Yes."

"What else do you have in there?"

"Passport, insurance papers, my will, that kind of thing."

"Probably got a little gold buried in there, too. Right? You
ever heard of deposit boxes, Morgan? This is the twentieth century,
you know. Damn near the twenty-first."

"I'll put the tape and the letter in a bank box," I said. "Unless
you think I should give them to the law."

"Now *why* would I think that?"

"You're not worried about withholding evidence?"

"I've got better things to worry about."

"If you say so."

"I do. Indeed I do. And I'll take the heat. You were acting
under the advice of counsel. I've had a lot of interesting experiences
working in the law industry, but I've never been through a disbar-
ment proceeding. Might be fun. So you put those things in a bank
vault and bring me the key."

"Whatever you say."

Semmes had been looking out at the bay while we talked. Now he turned away from the window, rested his elbows on the clean, polished surface of his desk, and looked at me. He had his game face on.

"There are two problems with that material right now. First, by itself that stuff doesn't prove anything useful to us. It doesn't even prove that Jackson Coleman was set up and that's what we got into this thing to do. Just going by that stuff, you could make a reasonable case that Stitch Folsome was operating alone, taking advantage of an opportunity he saw after Jackson was arrested. It's plausible enough, according to courtroom thinking, that his plan was to get William Coleman's name on the dotted line and then shop it at the U in return for something. Maybe he wanted a job or just some money as payment for his initiative. I don't believe it for a minute; common sense tells you it didn't work that way. But then we are not working in the realm of common sense. This is the law and the law is what they call counterintuitive. That means it is about half full of shit."

"I see."

Semmes smiled. "True understanding of any system—law, politics, religion, or catfish farming—comes when you learn to appreciate its flaws and contradictions."

I nodded and wondered what the flaws and contradictions in catfish farming were. A man could make a lot of money, I thought, if he understood *them*.

"The second problem with that material," Semmes went on, "is that if it got into the wrong hands, it could hurt us a lot more than it could help us. And as long as Officer Grant is on the force, giving that stuff to the police would be putting it into exactly the wrong hands.

"That material would have been raw gold if Stitch hadn't gotten himself killed outside a motorcycle bistro. With that tape and the letter, a good prosecutor could have put him in front of a grand jury—if it came to that—and sweated the whole story out of him. But Stitch has gone to his reward and that makes that stuff worthless."

"What about Grant?"

"What about him?"

"Put him in front of the grand jury?"

"And ask him if he told an informer to get close to Jackson Coleman, maybe even purchase some drugs from him? He'd say, 'Yes, sir, I did. That's my job.'

"So then you ask him if it had anything to do with basketball and maybe pressuring William Coleman into signing on with the U and leading them to glory. And he'd say, 'No, sir. What it had to do with was drugs. Jackson Coleman had a long and distinguished record of selling drugs and I wanted to catch him doing it one more time.'

"And then if you ask him, under the pain of perjury, if he and Stitch put the thing together, Grant could say, 'No. I never spoke to Stitch about anything like that. This is the first I've heard of it.' And Stitch wouldn't be around to say he was lying."

"I see your point."

"The departure of Stitch is a real inconvenience."

"So what do we do?"

"Two possibilities. You should always have two different plans of attack because one of them surely will go bad on you. The first plan would be to do nothing; just watch and see who comes crawling out of the weeds. Whoever is behind this thing wants William Coleman bad enough to set up this whole scheme and he's got to know he's close. If he's one of those who think they're born bullet-proof, he might try to close the deal himself. William and Dinah Coleman may be hearing from him in a little while."

"And if they don't?"

"Plan two," Semmes said and smiled with the thin, anticipatory pleasure of a card shark sitting down to play a few hands with some fish.

"Which is?"

"We bait him?"

"What do we use for bait?"

"Well," Semmes said, smiling more broadly and with real delight now, "actually, I thought we'd use you, Morgan."

"Wouldn't be the first time."

"My thoughts exactly. Now, what we do if the man behind this thing doesn't show himself in a couple of days is this: I go to the papers, on background, and tell them that I am representing both Jackson Coleman and his brother, William, and that my investigator—which is you—has put his hands on hard evidence of illegal and felonious pressure being put on my client to attend the U. And I'll say I intend to make a case.

"The big boy behind all this knows that somebody has a tape and that signed letter because right after you got through breaking his hand for him, Stitch called this man and told him. Stitch also told the man that he hadn't given you any names or anything except the paper you took from him. But the man didn't know whether or not to believe that. Stitch could have been lying. So he arranged for his boy to get his brains beat to jelly at that motorcycle bar.

"Stitch couldn't tell him who you were because he didn't know. But once I talk to the newspapers, he'll know. Or know how to find out real damned quick. So he—or his helpers—will come around for the letter and that tape."

"And me."

"That, too."

"It might work."

"Are you willing?" Semmes said.

"Entirely." I wanted to make up for losing Stitch.

"I knew I could count on you." Semmes smiled again and this time, I smiled back. I like to see a man having a good time.

"But it seems like the bait ought to be allowed one or two questions," I said.

"Shoot."

"Just one, actually. Why?"

"What do you mean?"

"Why are you so keen to mount this operation? I understand about proving entrapment and getting the case against Jackson thrown out. But the truth is, you could pick up the phone, call the prosecutor and tell him you were defending Jackson and you wanted to talk deal. Show him the letter, play him the tape, and even though they wouldn't stand up in court, in two days time you could deal him down to low-grade manslaughter. Jackson would get three to five, maybe less, and be out in a year. Might even do him good. And William could go to school wherever he wants to. So why do you want to do it the hard way?"

Semmes nodded and put the tip of a long finger against his cheekbone.

"The obvious answer," he said, "is that it might be interesting. You aren't the only one who gets bored. Making deals and working juries gets old."

"All right," I said. "I'll buy that for your apparent motive. What about your concealed motive?"

Semmes sighed, and as he did his face took a darker, graver set, the way it does when he contemplates his enemies.

"Do you think for a minute that whoever is behind this would be doing things this way if William Coleman was a white kid whose daddy owned a bank?"

I shook my head.

"William Coleman is a good kid," Semmes said. "But whoever is behind this, William Coleman is nothing to him. Just property. I despise that kind of thinking."

I nodded.

"Whoever he is, he needs to be punished," Semmes said. "If I made a deal for Jackson, if you gave that material to the police, it wouldn't happen."

"No."

"Maybe we can make sure it happens."

20

Semmes had told me once, when we were talking about something he'd read in the papers, that you cannot libel a dead man. "The thinking," he said, "is that once you've rolled back your eyes, you can't be harmed. If somebody writes a story that says you slept with goats, you won't be embarrassed. The goats, however, are another matter. They can sue."

"Makes sense," I said.

"Every now and then, there is wisdom in the law."

I didn't plan on printing any libels about Stitch Folsome. If it were up to me, I might not even print the truth. He probably had family somewhere and they could believe the best or the worst about him.

But I did think I would invade Folsome's privacy a little and I wondered if that would be illegal. Not that I cared.

I used a pay phone in the lobby of Nat's building to call a man named Hawkins who did things with a computer. Most of what he did was legitimate but he liked a challenge. For a fee, he would open up a stranger's life like a heart surgeon opening up his chest.

"Morgan," he said. "What can I do for you?"

"Some telephone records," I said.

"Is that *all*?" He sounded disappointed.

"Sorry."

"Hardly worth the effort," Hawkins sighed. "But for you . . . what's the name?"

I told him.

"Didn't I hear that name on the news this morning?"

"Yes."

"Sad. All this senseless violence. Must be drugs. How soon do you need it?"

"How soon can you have it?"

"No time at all."

I gave him Stitch's phone number and we agreed to meet at a place on the water not far from his house. Hawkins lived on the beach in a big house where he used his computer to play the stock market when he wasn't putting together dossiers for people like me.

I drove out over the bay bridge. A cold front was coming in from the east with a lot of wind ahead of it, kicking up a ragged chop on the bay and skimming the foam from the tops of the whitecaps. The gulls that tried to make it head up into the wind looked to be standing still. The storm made me think about being back at the river house in front of a fire.

Hawkins had picked a little doughnut and coffee place with a long counter and a couple of tables. The air smelled like cake frosting—sweet enough to gag you. I got there before he did and had a cup of black coffee.

I was thinking about a refill when Hawkins pulled up in his Range Rover. I wondered why he had decided on that car. It is supposed to be a great off-road machine, but Hawkins hardly ever left his house, much less the road. What he liked to do was play with his computer and spend his money, which explained the British wagon, I suppose.

He is a short, thin, intense man whose pleasures are almost certainly all cerebral. If he has any vices, they are probably mental. He ordered tea with cream and sugar. We aren't very much alike, Hawkins and I, but I like him. And I think he finds me amusing.

"Morning, Morgan," he said briskly. "Good to see you."

"You too, Frank."

"Looks like you've got your hooks into something pretty interesting."

I shrugged.

"I did what you asked. I've got it right here." He tapped an envelope that he'd put on the table between us. "Going after the phone records was like asking me to eat one peanut. I just couldn't stop myself."

He smiled.

"What else did you get?"

"Not that much, really. Credit report. Bank statements. Police record. Car registration."

"Did you find out if he's ever had his appendix taken out, Frank?"

"No," he said happily, "but I could have. Matter of fact, that kind of medical stuff is very big these days. You own a business and you want to hire somebody, but you want to make sure they're not carrying any *diseases*, you know. There are some things you can't test for and there are people who lie. So you'll pay to get a look at their medical records."

"Sounds like the coming thing."

"Oh, it is. It *definitely* is." Hawkins sipped some tea, so delicately that it seemed like it should have been served in fine china instead of cheap plastic.

"I didn't think bookies killed people anymore," he said. "I'd heard that the new thinking was, if you killed them, they could never pay up."

"I missed something," I said.

"Look at the printouts, Morgan. They'll tell you why your man was killed."

"Gambling?"

"I'd bet on it," Hawkins snickered.

I picked up the envelope. "I'll be able to understand everything that's in here?"

"Oh, sure."

"What do I owe you?"

"I'll send you a bill. You don't have a computer, do you?"

"Afraid not."

"Too bad. I could have gotten it to you by modem. Instead, I'll have to use the mail. Primitive. Very primitive."

I drove back across the bay. It was raining now and the wind had fallen off some. But whitecaps still covered the bay. The gulls were all roosted on the barge fenders, waiting out the storm.

I pulled off the road into a little park at the end of the bridge, opened the envelope Hawkins had given me, and studied the papers inside.

Stitch's bank statement was a mess. A couple of overdrafts and several charges for returned checks. He'd also had one car repossessed. A bank card had been canceled. And he was in the deadbeat file of a couple of clothing and sporting goods stores.

The phone bill showed some fairly heavy long-distance charges. About a third of the calls were to the same number. It had a 900 prefix, so it was one of those numbers you could call to listen to a woman talk dirty or a man telling you how to buy properties that had been seized by the government. You were billed by the minute and every call was padded with a long pitch at the beginning.

None of the other numbers meant anything to me. No reason they would, but I could go to a number directory and check them out if it came to that.

There was a phone stand in the little turnoff so I got out of the truck and used it to call the 900 number, using my phone credit card to pay for the call. I stood in the rain getting wet while a recorded voice thanked me for using AT&T.

The call went through and a voice at the other end, very male and very hearty, welcomed me to Scorespot, the nation's most comprehensive, reliable, up-to-the-minute sports information service with all the latest scores and lines from all the action across the country, guaranteed accurate and blah, blah, blah. My shirt was soaked and I was in for two minutes of charges by the time the pitch was over.

Stitch had pretty plainly been gambling or making book. Going by the bank statement and credit report, it seemed like a dead solid lock that he was betting, not booking. Bookies always paid on time. In cash.

I got out of the rain, dried off with a towel I keep under the seat, and thought about what I'd learned. Nothing much, I decided, except that Stitch had a pretty clear motive for monkeying around with William Coleman's life not to mention Jackson's. If somebody was willing to pay him for the service, he could use the money to get well and stay in action. Which is the only thing in this world that a gambler cares about.

Knowing that didn't get me any closer to who Stitch had been working for, the same one, most likely, who had killed him. Or had him killed. I considered my next step and, lacking anything better, decided to drive out and take a look at Stitch's apartment building again. I was just killing time. Waiting for someone to take the bait.

I could see before I even reached the parking lot of the Deluna, where Stitch had shared an apartment with someone named Sandy, that the law was ahead of me. An unmarked cruiser with a small gumball on the dash was parked in the lot, as conspicuous among all the bright-colored fastbacks as a vintage Bentley.

No surprise there, I thought, and parked in the lot next to the liquor store across the highway. Maybe the detectives were just finishing up and I could talk to Sandy when they had left, if she still felt like talking, which was not real likely.

But I stuck around for another half hour until a news crew from the local television station arrived and started taking equipment out of the sliding side door of their van. The talent wore a suit and the technicians wore jeans, windbreakers, and watchcaps. They seemed to be doing a lot of yelling at each other but I couldn't hear what they were saying. After a few minutes, they headed off toward one of the apartment stairwells, carrying their gear and still arguing.

I turned the key in the truck and pulled into traffic on Red Bluff. I might take leavings from the law. And I might take seconds from television. But I wasn't going to come in behind both the law *and* television. There is such a thing as pride.

And compassion. Sandy, whoever she was, would have been through enough for a whole lifetime, much less one morning, by the time the cops and the newsies were through with her. I couldn't see myself hitting her for another interview. And, after all that, she would probably be talking gibberish anyway.

What I would do instead . . . well, maybe I would eat lunch. No, better than that, maybe I would call Jessie and see if I could take her to lunch. Bait needs nourishment and companionship, too.

"Lunch?" Jessie said. "With you?"

"Well . . . yes."

"I'd love it."

She had to drop some proofs off at a print shop back toward town and I said I'd meet her there. Then she could follow me to the place I had in mind. As soon as I hung up the phone, the impatience and agitation I'd been feeling since I heard about Stitch Folsome on the radio lifted like a morning fog. It was a stormy afternoon and a good time for a long lunch. Later, we could go back to the river house, where I could build a fire and maybe thaw out a venison backstrap and cook it over coals for supper.

Being bait doesn't necessarily mean being miserable.

I beat Jessie to the print shop. I went inside with her and while we waited for the man behind the counter to finish a copying job, I told her about my morning. I finished at the point where I'd left the Deluna just about the same time the man behind the counter said, "I'm sorry to keep you waiting, Mizz Beaudreaux. I'm here by myself today."

"That's all right," she said. "I understand."

When she finished telling him what she wanted, I started for the door. It was still raining outside.

"Wait a second, Morgan," she said. "Let's talk about something."

"Okay."

"You want to talk to this Sandy person, don't you?"

"Not anymore. I want to eat lunch."

"But you *did*."

"Yes. But it's not important."

"How do you know?"

She had me there.

"Truth is, you were probably glad when those TV people showed up so you didn't have to go in there and talk to some woman who was crying and going to pieces because of what happened to her man."

She had me there, too.

"You want me to come with you and do the talking?"

I may not test very high on sensitivity but I knew what she was doing. It was her way of letting me know that, in spite of her feelings about the work I did for Semmes, she didn't disapprove of me. She was on my side even if she didn't like the game. You can't turn down that kind of offer.

"Well, sure."

"Okay then, I'll follow you there. Let me do the talking and don't interrupt unless I miss something important."

"Yes ma'am," I said and smiled.

"And when we're finished, you can take me to lunch."

21

There were no police cruisers or TV vans in the Deluna parking lot this time. Jessie and I went to the front hall and found the apartment number on the directory.

She followed me to the apartment. I knocked softly on the door.

I could hear movement behind the door. It sounded furtive.

I waited, then knocked again. Heard movement again, a little louder and closer this time, as though whoever was behind the door could not decide whether it was safe to answer.

I knocked once more.

"Who is it?" The voice was weak and frightened.

"Miss Gilbert?" I said. Her full name had been on the building directory. Henry Folsome and Sandra Gilbert.

"What is it?"

"Mizz Gilbert?" Jessie said, stepping in front me, just slightly.

"That's me. Who are you?"

"I know this is a hard time for you, Mizz Gilbert," Jessie said. "I hate to bother you now and I wouldn't do it except for something important."

"Are you police?" the voice said, making it sound like an accusation. "Or reporters?"

"Neither one," Jessie said. "But I know how hard they can be to deal with, believe me."

159

"What, then?"

"We're working for a lawyer, trying to help somebody who has got trouble almost as bad as your trouble. We can't talk to Mr. Folsome about it like we wanted to, and we were hoping you could take a minute to help us. I know it's a bad, bad time and we wouldn't be asking except we really do need some help. We won't stay long." Jessie sounded just right, like the kind of person you would trust and not feel right about turning down. Better than I could have been in a hundred years of trying.

The door came open reluctantly.

"All right. Come in."

She was a tall, heavy-boned woman with a wide and undistinguished face that would look better with makeup. She had artificially blonde hair and wore jeans and a sweatshirt. Big gold loops in her ears.

We followed her into a room that was cheaply and sparsely furnished. Deck chairs, mostly, and the kind of pine stuff that is unfinished when you buy it and still looks that way even after a couple of coats of paint or stain. Throw rugs on the floor and framed prints on the wall. It was the kind of place inhabited by people who could break camp quickly. There were half-filled cardboard boxes scattered around the room.

"I'm getting out of here," she said offhandedly, sat on a futon, and motioned toward the deck chairs. Jessie and I each took one.

"Do you have some place to go?" Jessie said, sounding like she would be willing to take the woman in if she said no.

"Friends, for now. I'll find something."

"You got somebody to help you move all these things?"

The woman nodded. "We'll come by this weekend with a U-Haul. I don't know what I'll do with his stuff. He didn't have much, really. Mostly clothes. And some old basketball trophies."

"You could give those to his parents, maybe," Jessie said.

"I don't know them. Don't even know where they live or even if they are still living. That's how much I knew about him after living with him for three months. You believe that? I've been thinking, ever since the police came by here this morning and told me that Stitch was . . . had been killed, about what I really knew about him. I knew what kind of beer he liked. I knew he played basketball when he was in school. I knew he liked to watch *L.A. Law* and *Gunsmoke* reruns on the television. And eat Mexican food." She shook her head and her teased blonde hair caught the light. "That's about all I knew," she said helplessly.

"You can take the clothes to the Goodwill," Jessie said. "They can put them to use. Hold on to the trophies, maybe, in case he does have some family somewhere and they want them."

"Yes," the woman sighed. "I suppose."

"You'll remember a lot more later," Jessie said. "It'll come back to you when this part passes. The good parts come back to you."

"It's like a big, empty hole," the woman said. "It was so, I don't know, so *sudden*." She looked away from us, made her hands into fists, and softly pounded her knees.

"Miss Gilbert," Jessie said.

"Sandy," she said, "call me Sandy."

"All right, Sandy. Did you see Stitch last night? Before he went to that bar?"

She shook her head and the light gleamed in her hair again. Then she began talking in a flat, abstracted voice, almost as though she were reciting lines she had memorized and had no feeling for one way or the other.

"There were a lot of nights when I didn't see him. He sold insurance and said he made calls at night, when people were home. Sometimes he called and sometimes he didn't. We had fights about that. He said he didn't have to account to anyone for his time. I quit pushing it."

"Did he have any other jobs besides selling insurance?"

"He wanted to be a basketball coach. I guess he'd done that once. He hated selling insurance. He told me, a couple of nights ago, that he was close to something that was going to set him up so he could quit."

"Did he say what it was?"

"No. He just said it was a coup. A 'monster coup.' "

"That's all?"

"Yes," she said. "I could ask but he wouldn't tell me. We almost broke up over it. Then, later on, he was nicer. He took me out to eat and told me that we'd be going on a vacation soon. He wanted to take me to Las Vegas." That thought must have been especially keen, because she stopped talking as though something were suddenly caught in her throat and went for her eye with the back of one hand.

"I just feel so *stunned.*"

"I'll get you some water," Jessie said and stood up. She left the room and the woman put her face in her hands. Jessie was back in a few seconds with a kitchen glass full of water. She handed it to the woman, who took it gratefully.

When she sat back down, Jessie looked at me and nodded in the direction of the door. I didn't want to leave. There were some questions I wanted to ask and I wasn't sure that Jessie would ask them. But she had connected with the woman in a way I never could. So I got up and eased out of the room, shutting the door softly behind me.

I waited outside for ten or fifteen minutes, watching the bay and some ducks that were rafted up a couple of hundred yards offshore. They'd be heading out in a couple of months, I thought, migrating back up the coast to their breeding grounds in Nova Scotia. Something about that instinct, the deep urgency of it, always got to me. In a world defined by hard labor and short, brutal lives, the human species craves the shortcut to comfort.

I was deep into that thought when Jessie came out of the passageway and across the lot to where I was leaning against the side panel of my truck. She looked uneasy and a little grim.

"That poor thing," she said, shaking her head. "She's frightened about half to death."

"She thinks they'll come after her, right?" I said. "For the money Stitch lost gambling."

Jessie gave me a look. "You weren't listening at the door, now, were you?"

"No," I said. "It was a guess."

"Well," she said, "it was a good one."

"He was in pretty deep, then?"

Her mouth took an angry curl. "So deep he had to ask her for money. Took all she had in her savings. Two thousand whole dollars, to pay off *his* bookie."

"You have to wonder why she ever teamed up with him," I said. "Or stayed with him once she had."

"That's an old, old story, Morgan."

"I suppose."

"Anyway, you want to hear what she told me?"

"Absolutely," I said. "Do you still want to have lunch?"

"I sure do," she said, brightening a little.

"Good. We can talk while we eat."

22

Jessie followed me out the highway as it contoured the shoreline of the bay and left the town behind. In fifteen minutes, we were back among the patch farms, pine plantations, and occasional small churches with graveyards out back. I turned off on a county road that wound down toward the bay through the cypress and gum swamps and ended, after a mile or so, in a red clay lot in front of a small frame building next to a blackwater river. The sign in front of the building said MIKE'S FRIED CATFISH. There were half a dozen cars and pickups in the lot.

"Now this here looks uptown, Morgan," Jessie said. "You bring all your girlfriends to this place?"

It was cool inside, even though the air was thick with the smell of fried food. There were picnic tables in three ranks along the rectangular floor. We took one near a window that looked out over the slow-moving river.

A young woman, thin and sinewy, wearing blue jeans and a cotton work shirt, came over to the table with two menus.

"Special today is kicking chicken—" she said, "frog legs and fries. Three ninety-five."

I nodded.

"You want something to drink while you're deciding?"

"Pitcher of beer?" I said to Jessie.

"For sure. I'm parched."

The woman left to get our beer and returned in a minute or two. The pitcher was beaded with moisture. She put it on the table with two heavy jars, the kind you use for preserves.

"Is the catfish farmed?" Jessie said.

The woman shook her head and said, "Not ever. Comes from the river or we don't cook it."

"I'll have a plate of catfish, then. Slaw."

"Same," I said.

The woman left us and I filled the jars with beer and handed one across the table to Jessie, who raised it, nodded, and took a long drink.

"Oh sweetness," she said.

The beer did seem to taste unusually good. Cold and just bitter enough.

"You know," Jessie said, "that poor woman really was afraid. After you left, I asked her if she knew anybody who might have wanted to hurt Stitch, and she went real still. I think she wanted to tell somebody, but figured she couldn't."

"Why's that?"

"Maybe nobody would believe her or do anything. And if she was out there telling, then the people who killed Stitch would come after her. She'd need protection but nobody would be there to protect her."

"What did you say to her?"

"I just told her I understood how it was. Being all alone and not sure there was anyone you could trust enough to talk to. I just sort of eased her along that way until she felt like even if there wasn't anything I could do to help her, at least I wasn't going to do anything that would make it worse and wind up hurting her. She just wanted to *tell* somebody so she wouldn't feel like she was all by her scared little self. The police had asked her but she felt like she couldn't tell them because they'd use the information but they wouldn't protect her."

I nodded. "Did she tell you that somebody had threatened Stitch?"

"After a while."

"She know who it was?" I felt my pulse rising. Maybe Jessie had gotten the answer in her private interview. I suppose my vanity should have been wounded and maybe it would be later on. But right now, I felt like I'd take help where I could find it and taking it from Jessie seemed like a bonus.

She nodded and took a swallow from her glass. "A man who called all the time. She said he was friendly most of the time. Just asked to talk to Stitch and when he was expected back if he wasn't there.

"But then, once or twice, he'd turn mean and say something like, 'Well, you tell him Danny called and that he *needs* to talk to me.' She'd be scared and tell Stitch about the call and he'd just tell her not to worry about it. But he'd duck calls for a few days. She knew what it was about, but Stitch wouldn't talk about it. Except for the time he asked her for money. That was right after one of those calls from Danny. She said she'd never seen Stitch that way, all pale and trembling,"

"Had Stitch been getting those calls lately?" My pulse eased. Jessie had done good work but the Gilbert woman hadn't told her who'd killed Stitch. Just the name of his bookie.

Jessie shook her head. "She said she hadn't taken any calls like that. But Stitch had been on the phone a lot, all agitated when he was talking. She figured he was in trouble, digging himself a deep hole with the gambling."

"You learned a lot," I said. "Damn sight more than I would have found out."

"Did I miss anything? Is there something you would have asked if you'd been there?"

"Nope."

"You think it was the gambling that got him killed?"

I shook my head.

"How come?" She sounded disappointed, as though her work had been for nothing.

"They don't get the money if he's dead. If you've got a gambler on the hook, there are ways to get the money."

"Such as?"

"The first thing you do is the thing he fears the most. Cut off his action. Tell him if he can't pay, then he can't play. He needs the action more than anything. It's what he lives for. There were a couple of convicts in prison for things they'd done to support the gambling. Embezzled money, defrauded banks. Fountain-pen stuff. They'd been lying to their families—stealing from the wife and kids the way that Stitch was stealing from Sandy—and from anybody else they could con or cheat out of a few dollars. And finally it got to the point where they did something stupid *and* illegal, just so they could stay in action. That was more important than anything. It was life to those boys and they'd risk anything for it. When you're dealing with somebody like that, you threaten to cut off his action and he'll do anything to find the money."

I finished my jar of beer and poured another. "Those were actually some of the sweetest men in the joint. Wouldn't harm a soul. They just had this need and couldn't get control of it."

"And the bastard gamblers just help them dig themselves deeper into the hole," Jessie said. She had a hair-trigger sense of injustice, a feel for the innocents. But it wasn't soft. She had a reciprocal hatred for those who preyed on them. That's one of the things I like most about her.

"Well, nobody goes out and breaks someone's legs to make them lay bets," I said. "The State of Florida, you'll notice, runs a lot of slick advertising encouraging people to get down on a fifteen-million-to-one shot. The state wins every time, just like the house in Atlantic City or the track in Saratoga or the local bookie when he does a good job of balancing up the action and skims off the vigorish. The State of Florida spends the take on schools, I believe."

"Doesn't make it right."

"No. But if you want to launch a genuinely futile crusade, try to get the lottery outlawed."

She nodded and stared out the window at the river, its oily surface randomly dimpled by a million raindrops.

"Some people get hurt by gamblers," she said. "You hear about people getting their legs broken and stuff like that."

"Sometimes," I said. "There were guys in prison who'd done a little of that. It was actually a good place to learn about the gambling culture. And other interesting things, too, I suppose."

"I'll bet."

"But the leg-breakers were usually a last resort and even then, you didn't kill the man. You didn't even necessarily hurt him too bad. Not bad enough to cripple him so he couldn't work, because then how was he going to get the money to pay you? Gambling is a business," I said. "It's about money. Blood and honor and all that happy stuff doesn't really come into it. You can't garnishee wages, so you put a scare into someone occasionally to make him pay and to give the others something to think about. But you don't go as far as they did with Stitch. Not good business."

The waitress brought the food in straw baskets lined with butcher's paper that was darkened in spots from the frying oil. The fish fillets were crisp and yellow from the corn meal they'd been rolled in before they went into the grease.

"Another pitcher?"

"Please."

She left and we tried the fish, which was still hot to the touch and broke cleanly in our fingers. It had been fried just right, so that it hadn't soaked up any grease but was still cooked through and flaky, the way it is supposed to be. The taste was very clean and sweet, not at all what you'd expect the flesh of a scavenger to taste like.

"Ummm," Jessie said. "They know how to do it here, don't they?"

Sure did, I said.

"What's the best bait for catfish, Morgan?"

"You sure that's something to talk about while we're eating?"

"Come on," she said. "I'm not some squeamish little old *girl*. I've caught lots of catfish. I'll bet I can skin one quicker than you."

"I'm sure of it."

"All right, then. What's the best bait?"

"Chicken guts?"

"Nah. Farm boys say that just because they like things messy."

"Blood-soaked doughballs?"

"Better. I knew an old black man who swore by them and he could surely catch catfish. But there's still something better."

"I give up."

"A soft crawfish. I believe a catfish would swim a mile upstream past all the doughballs and chicken guts in the world, just to eat one soft craw. With soft crawfish and a fairly clean river, I could always catch a mess."

She smiled at the memory.

"Almost makes them taste better to think they fed on crawfish, doesn't it?" she said.

"Absolutely."

We finished the fish. She ate my slaw and hers and we lingered over the second pitcher of beer, with the room and the view of the river to ourselves.

"So you don't think Stitch getting killed has something to do with gambling?"

"I didn't say that. I just don't think he got killed because he

stiffed a bookie. I wouldn't be surprised if the whole thing didn't
come down to gambling and that Stitch is just playing a bit part.
He probably doesn't even know the whole script."

She looked at me like a curious child.

"Every now and then, some gambler comes up with a big idea.
Almost like he's been divinely inspired or something. He's going
to pull off the *Paradise Lost* of fixes. Somebody fixed the world
series a million years ago. Bought off a bunch of players—including
Shoeless Joe Jackson—for chicken feed. I imagine there are still
gamblers who dream big."

"That could be a reach, Morgan. Maybe it was just a bar fight
and it wasn't Stitch Folsome's day."

"Maybe. But that is a lot of coincidence. Somehow, I just can't
believe that Stitch died because he insulted some old boy's tattoos."

"What I still can't get a grip on," she said pensively, "is that
this whole thing is about basketball."

"I don't think it is. That's what I'm saying. I think it comes
down to money and somebody wanting to pull off the epic inside
job."

"Well, if that's so, then they might be a lot badder than Stitch
was."

"Are you going to start worrying about me again?"

She smiled, touched my hand. The rain had slacked off so that
now there were only a few scattered drops hitting the river, sending
precise, expanding circles out across its surface. It felt good to be
inside, talking and watching the weather change.

"This does beat working, Morgan," she said. "But don't you
have someplace to be?"

"You know what they say. Everybody has to be somewhere,
and I'm here." It was an old Vietnam line.

"You and Semmes don't have anything working to find out
who killed Stitch and is trying to pressure the boy?"

"Nat thinks the best thing is to wait for a few days. See if
somebody makes a move."

She thought about that for a moment. "And what if nobody
does?"

"Well, then, Nat is going to put a hook through my tail and
fling me out into the river like a soft crawfish. Then we'll see what
bites."

23

By the time we paid up, the rain had stopped, leaving a thick, cold mist that had turned everything a kind of dispirited gray, the color of primer paint.

"Let's go to my house," Jessie said. "Build a fire, drink something warm, and see if we can't do something to build an appetite. Then I'll fix you some supper."

I said that sounded fine. Actually, it sounded better than that.

"But first follow me to the garage. It's on the way. I've got to get somebody to look at the front end of this car. If it shimmies any worse, it's going to fly apart."

So I followed her for five miles back into town to a little two-bay garage where she left her car with a short, bald man who wore Carheart coveralls with grease stains that looked a hundred years old. Jessie talked to him seriously for ten minutes. He nodded as he listened and then wrote up an estimate which she went over carefully, then signed. She knew cars, maybe not quite as well as she knew catfish, but well enough.

"Bad?" I said when she was inside the truck.

"Bearings," she said. "I probably ought to get a new car, but I purely hate how much they cost."

We drove out of town, back toward the river. It was last light but there was no sunset. The horizon was a thick, continuous gray, impenetrable as stone.

Five miles from the river house on a long straight stretch of two-lane, with fog beginning to settle in the low places, I looked in the rearview mirror and saw two headlights. The distance was closing fast and something wasn't right about the headlights. After a second or two, I realized that they were not from a single car but two different motorcycles. I'd seen plenty of motorcycles on this highway. But this was the day that Stitch Folsome had been killed at a motorcycle bar . . . and these two bikers were coming up very fast.

"Look behind the seat," I said. "There's a shotgun wrapped in an old towel."

Jessie looked out at the side mirror, saw the motorcycles, and without a word reached behind the seat for the shotgun. She unwrapped it quickly, ignoring the oil that stained her skirt.

"Shells?"

"In the tool kit."

She reached around the seat and brought out the small canvas bag, unzipped it and searched through the box wrenches and screwdrivers until she had found some fat, blunt shotgun shells. Without asking, she began feeding them into the magazine of the shotgun, an old model-12 pump with the blueing mostly gone and the stock nicked and dented in a dozen different places.

The motorcycles were four car lengths back, side by side, and still coming up fast. I could see the riders. They were large and wore leathers. No helmets.

"Buckshot?" she said.

"Copper twos. They'll do fine. Why don't you slump down in that seat in case they've got pistols." I rolled down the window. "If I tell you to shoot, just stick the barrel out the window and cut loose. Three rounds. That ought to scatter them."

I cut my eyes in her direction. She was pale and her lips were pressed tightly together. She was scared but not immobilized by it. She eased down in the seat as far as she could go, with one hand on the pistol grip of the shotgun, finger outside the trigger guard. The muzzle was against the floorboard.

"You can't outrun them?" she said.

"No chance. If it comes to it, don't aim. Just shoot."

"It's going to be loud."

"I know."

"Don't wait too long, Morgan, on account of me."

"I won't."

The lead motorcycle pulled up even with me. My face was not more than six feet from the rider's. He was looking at me with a kind of dumb, satisfied leer on his round, fat, stupid face. His forehead was receding but the rest of his head was covered with long, tangled, greasy black hair, kept out of his eyes by a bandanna. He took one hand off the handlebars and pointed to the shoulder of the road. I shook my head and cut the wheel quickly in his direction. He backed off the throttle and drifted back so the front fender of the truck passed harmlessly into his lane. When I straightened it out, he gave his machine some throttle and pulled back even with me. He smiled and shook his finger at me, like a teacher scolding a kid for misbehaving in class.

When he pointed at the shoulder and I shook my head again, his expression changed and his hand moved down toward his waist. I could see the grip of a big pistol. When his hand touched it, I said, "Okay. Blast him."

I leaned back as far as I could and Jessie came up from her crouch, maneuvering the barrel of the shotgun awkwardly across my body. I heard the slide work as she chambered a round. Then the inside of the cab seemed to explode around me and I strained to keep my concentration and not jerk the wheel and send us into the ditch. On the edge of my vision, I could make out the face of the man on the cycle as his expression changed from the dumb, cruel satisfaction a kid feels when he is torturing a cat to something full of desperation. Then his front tire turned into shredded rubber and the bike went over onto the road, sliding along the surface of the blacktop, throwing sparks and leaving a trail of ripped steel.

I seemed to feel it when Jessie worked the slide and ejected the empty shell. It landed on the dash, over the wheel.

"That's enough," I shouted, unable to hear myself over the ringing in my ears.

I checked the mirror and saw the other motorcycle braking, then turning as though on a pivot and accelerating off in the other direction. The one that had gone down was off the road in the weeds and litter along the shoulder, twisted and deformed. The rider was crawling into the ditch.

I stood on the brake. The deep tread on the all-terrain tires did not let me down. The truck came to a smooth stop about a quarter of a mile from the spot where the motorcycle lay on the side of the road.

"Give me the shotgun," I said to Jessie. "You take the truck and get to a phone. Don't go to my house or yours. Call the sheriff's department and get Tom Pine. Nobody else. Tell him where I am and to get here, by himself, as soon as he can."

"Just keep going, Morgan," she said. She was pale and her voice was fluttering.

"I can't let that one get away," I said.

"Let Tom Pine find him," she said.

I put my hands on her shoulders. My ears were ringing and my own words sounded like somebody else was speaking them. I could have been shouting. I don't know.

"Listen," I said. "If the first person that creep talks to is Tom Pine, then he won't say anything except 'Get me a lawyer.' And Tom won't have any reason to hold him or charge him. He might have to arrest *us*. There's no law against dumping a motorcycle but you can get in trouble for shotgunning one."

"What are you going to do."

"I'm going to find him," I said. "And then I'm going to talk to him and find out who put him up to it. If I don't, whoever it is can just wait until the time is right and come try it again."

"What if the other one comes back?"

"He won't." I wasn't sure of this, just guessing that for all the brave talk about the colors and being brothers, the cycle boys were the kind who abandoned their wounded and left their dead behind.

"He might," Jessie said. She was still trembling a little but not as much.

"If he does, I can lose him in the woods. His kind needs pavement under their feet."

"Morgan, are you sure?"

"Close enough. I'll be all right. Just get Tom."

She nodded and I got out of the truck. I took the shotgun and a couple of spare shells with me.

I kicked the door shut behind me and said "Go." Then I sprinted across the pavement into the ditch and heard the truck behind me as she put it in gear and started down the highway. In a few seconds, the sound had faded and it was very quiet on the side of the road. I was kneeling on the hard clay, facing toward the spot where the ruined motorcycle lay, listening.

I watched the road. There was just enough light left that it looked like some kind of dim passageway, maybe on a ship, where you could see somebody coming or going in dim silhouette. I watched for a couple of minutes to see if he would try to make it to the road to get away. I didn't think he was the kind to stick in the swamp. Not his sort of terrain.

He didn't appear on the road, so I crawled a little farther off the road, where the ground rose slightly and firmed up. The gum trees were old enough and tall enough to have shut out the light and cut down on the understory so you could move without having to fight the bamboo briers and gallberry bushes. And the ground was spongy enough to soak up the sound of your step. I held the shotgun waist high, with the muzzle in front of me and my left hand on the slide. I had one in the chamber and four in the tube. Enough to tear up the woods and make anyone in front of me try to crawl down into the ground like a mole once I started shooting.

I used the trees. Took a couple of steps and listened. Then another couple of steps and listened some more. If he moved, he'd do it the way he did everything. No finesse. He'd be like a big tractor, and I'd hear him before he made three feet; if I could hear anything, that is, through the ringing in my ears.

The air was cold and it felt clean and sharp passing down my throat. The light had died, leaving the woods opaque and indistinct. It was like walking through smoke.

When I had gone a hundred yards and maybe a little more, I stopped and went to one knee. The ringing in my ears had diminished to a faint, steady whine and I guessed I could hear through it. It occurred to me, in one of those completely random and unsolicited thoughts that come at the goddamnedest times, that it must have been hell on the Indian hunters to grow old and lose their hearing. Worse, in a way, than when the vision began to dim.

A barred owl got off a "Who cooks for you?" from across the road and I heard that clearly enough. And then, fifteen seconds later, a soft involuntary moan about thirty steps straight ahead.

I had my man.

I marked the spot by a lightning-scarred pine tree and spent what felt like half an hour creeping up on it, testing each step with the toe of the foot I was about to plant, then easing the weight down on it so slowly that I could have been trying to walk across a field of light bulbs without breaking a single one. Ten steps from the tree, I could hear his steady, strangled breathing. And two steps after that I could see him, lying on the ground behind a large, rotting stump. He held one of those new thirteen-shot automatics in both hands and looked down its barrel toward the road, twitching every few seconds with pain or fear. Or both.

I pointed the muzzle at his hams.

"If you don't do anything dumb," I said, "then I won't blow your ass off."

He didn't say anything.

"Just lay the piece on the ground and then roll away from it. Two or three times. I want you on your fat belly when you stop."

He lowered the pistol and released it.

"My ankle's broke. Hurts to move."

"Well," I said, "I'm feeling for you, but I can't quite reach you. Roll away to your left."

When he did it, he gasped and let out a strangled sound of pain. "Agggggh, god*damn*."

Maybe his ankle was broken.

I switched on the little flash, focused the beam down, and put it on his face.

He was nobody I recognized. Just another porky motorcycle bad-ass.

"Well, now," I said, "what have we got here?"

"All right, man," he said through his teeth, "you win. Do what you're going to do."

"Who sent you?" I said.

"Nobody sent us, cowboy. We were after the babe."

"Nope," I said. "Try again."

"We watched you out of the garage back in town. She looked like choice meat. We didn't count on any shotguns."

"It's a break for you that I think you're lying," I said.

"I'm telling you the truth."

"In a minute you will be," I said. "That's a promise."

I'd let Stitch off light but it wasn't going to happen again. Not with this one. I put my foot on his ankle and applied a little pressure.

"Arrrgh, *Jesus*, man."

"Who sent you?"

"Nobody sent us."

More pressure.

He screamed again.

"Who sent you?"

"I told you . . ."

More pressure. He screamed and clawed at the dirt and I thought I could hear bone grinding but it was probably just my imagination. My ears were still ringing softly. It was cold but I was sweating.

"You'll tell me," I said. "Now or later. So make it easy on yourself."

I put all my weight on his ankle and he passed out.

When he came to a minute later, I said, "These are just the preliminaries. The easy part. I've got all night. And there are places that hurt a lot more than a little broken ankle."

"I don't know who it was," he said, sobbing for air. "Honest."

"How could you *not* know?" I said and applied just enough pressure that he would know I was still there, still interested.

"We got a call. From one of the guys. In Tampa."

"Tampa?"

"Yeah. The club runs big out of there."

"What were you supposed to do?"

"Get a tape and some kind of paper from you. The guy who called said you'd know what we were talking about."

"How were you supposed to know who I was."

"We had a description. And we were supposed to watch the apartment where that guy who was killed lived."

"You kill him?"

He didn't answer until I stood on his ankle. Not too hard.

"Oh *Jesus*. Yeah, we killed him. The guy in Tampa set up the meeting."

"How did you follow us."

"We had a third guy watching the apartment from a car. He had one of those car phones. Called from there and that place you and the babe ate lunch. Followed you to the garage and then called us when you got out on the road. We figured it was a good place, back in the woods and everything."

An excellent place.

"You know what this is about?"

"No. And I didn't ask. This brother in Tampa calls, and I do what he says. That's the way it works."

"All right," I said. "I want you to get up on your hands and knees and start crawling. Don't stop until we get to the road."

I followed him out of the woods, and when we got to the road there was still no sign of Tom Pine. I struck a match and tossed it on the gasoline puddling around the wrecked motorcyle so he'd have some light to steer by. The fire was almost out by the time he got there.

24

"One of them hogs from hell," Tom Pine said, shining the beam of his flashlight on the motorcycle bum's face. He was sitting down with his back against the trunk of a tall longleaf, shivering and glaring back at Pine through small, dull eyes.

"You're about as bad a piece of pork as ever rode a machine, I imagine."

The motorcycle man said, "Call me an ambulance," and it was plain that he wanted to add *nigger* to that. But he had looked into Pine's face and knew that out here, on this empty highway, he couldn't count on anything in the way of professional restraint.

So he merely said, "Goddamnit," to let the world know he was still plenty tough.

"You want me to call you an ambulance?" Tom said. "All right, shit-head, you're an ambulance."

"Very funny."

"He is hurt, officer," I said. I didn't want the creep to see that Tom and I knew each other. So far, Tom hadn't let on.

"You shut up," he said, looking at me like he might be ready to bounce me. It was a good act.

"Whatever you say, officer."

"All right," Pine said, turning back to the man on the ground. "You'll get a wagon. But *I'll* get some answers. What in hell happened here?" He looked down at the man on the ground, who looked back up at him and said, "I got too close to this man. I wasn't going to hurt him. I was just screwing around." It was what I had told him to say and he was saying it just right. I was relieved and also struck by all the lying and play-acting that was going on around me in this one little scene on a nowhere highway. So far, I was the only one who knew everything there was to know. Knowledge, they say, is power, but just then I felt about as powerful as a blind kitten.

"Is that what happened?" Pine said turning on me.

"Yes, officer."

"And what about the fire?"

"That's my fault," I said. "I was pretty upset. There was a woman with me, the one who made the call. She was nearly hysterical. I wanted to get even so I set fire to his motorcycle."

Pine fought to keep from laughing.

"You want to press charges?"

"No, sir."

"How about you, Hopalong?" he said to the man on the ground. "Man here set fire to your horse. *You* wanna press charges?"

"No."

"You sure, now?"

"Jesus Christ. Just get me an ambulance."

"All right. I suppose I'll call one now."

Tom walked over to the cruiser, which was pulled off on the shoulder of the road. The flashers were on, giving the night a hard, blue pulse.

In a few seconds he was back, carrying a blanket that he threw carelessly over the body of the man on the ground, who tried for a defiant, you-can-kill-me-but-you-can't-eat-me sneer. But he was in too much pain and could only manage a pout.

"Don't suppose you'd want to give me your name, rank, service number, and date of birth, would you? Maybe tell me why you were out here on this lonesome highway, harassing civilians, when you could have been back in the Iron Horseman, keeping dry and drinking beer."

"I want a lawyer," the man said through his teeth.

"I haven't even arrested you," Pine said.

"Either way, I ain't talking."

"Suit yourself," Pine said. "And next time, find a nice safe old
lady to pick on."

The wagon arrived ten minutes after Pine's call. The paramed-
ics looked at the injured man's ankle, put it in an air cast, and
loaded him on a stretcher. One of them asked Tom how he'd been
and Tom said, "Fine. How's business?"

"Pretty slow," the man said. "This here is the first call tonight.
But it'll pick up."

"I suppose so," Tom said.

We watched until the wagon had turned around in the highway
and was headed back toward town with the flashers growing dim-
mer in the distance.

"You don't expect me to buy all that horseshit, do you, Morgan?" Tom said finally, looking at me like it was time to get serious.

"No."

"All right. What do you say we sit in the cruiser and talk?"

"Fine."

The night turned dark and restful again when Pine shut off the
flashers. He sighed and leaned back against the seat.

"This has got to have something to do with the Coleman business, doesn't it?" he said.

"Yes, Tom, it does. And I'll tell you as much or as little as you
want to know."

"I'd like to hear it all," Pine said.

So I told him the whole story, and when I'd finished he shook
his head and said, "Thurston."

"Huh?"

"Danny Thurston. That's the man who would have been calling
Stitch and getting him all upset. He makes book. He's a small-town
lowlife who likes to pretend it's just an accident that he ain't doing
business in Miami or New York."

"Do you think he's running this thing?"

"Nah. He doesn't have the stones. Not likely he'll be calling
Tampa motorcycle creeps when he needs help."

"Can you do anything with that?"

"Maybe. I'll call somebody I know over there and talk to him.
See if he's heard anything about a job over here. But I wouldn't
count on anything. Fact is, even with everything you've told me,
I don't know what I *can* do. Fellow whose cycle you burned up

isn't good for anything and, anyway, I don't have anything to charge him with. Stitch is dead and his killing is the business of the city. I suppose I could ask you to give me the tape and the letter you took off Stitch before he so unfortunately passed. They might be proof that a crime was committed, but so far as I can tell, Stitch was the only one doing anything wrong. On the evidence, anyway."

"Right," I said. "But there is one thing you could do."

"What's that?"

"They saw Jessie's car and they know who she is. Can you provide some protection."

Pine shook his head. "Come on, Morgan," he said, "you know better than that. We get women, got an old boyfriend or ex-husband who has beaten on them and is under a court order to stay away, and we can't baby-sit them because we don't have enough manpower. Sooner or later, the guy comes around and does what he wants to do. You know what I tell those women?"

"What's that?"

"Get a shotgun, and if he comes close, don't hesitate. Paint the walls with him. Because all we can do is arrest him after the crime has been committed. And that ain't going to help you."

"Then she needs to get away for a while," I said.

"What about you?"

"I'm bait. The bait stays."

Jessie had called from a gas station a couple of miles down the road and was still there when Tom and I pulled up. She looked tired.

Tom waited in the cruiser while I talked to her.

"Are you all right?" she said.

"I'm fine. How about you."

"A little scared," she said. "No . . . a lot scared. I didn't like that business with the shotgun one bit."

"I didn't either. And I'm sorry it had to happen."

"You saying it was your fault, Morgan? That you could have done something to keep it from happening?"

I could see where this could go, the way that she was feeling.

"No. I'm not saying that. I'm just sorry it happened. But I'm glad you were along. It would have been a lot different if I'd been by myself."

She nodded without much conviction and said, "What happens now?"

"Let's go to your house," I said. "Tom's going to follow us. We can talk on the way."

"All right," she said.

The truck still smelled faintly of burned powder. I put the shotgun back behind the seat and pulled out onto the highway. Pine followed in the cruiser. Jessie sat with her hands in her lap and looked out at the dark wall of passing trees.

"I asked Tom if he could provide you with some protection," I said.

She shook her head slightly and said, "I know, without you telling me, what he said. They're not in the bodyguarding business."

"I could stay close," I said.

"That's no good, either—just waiting for somebody to come after you. It's not my business but I know that much. You do, too."

She sighed and went on, without looking at me, "I thought about it back at the gas station, and it seems to me that the best thing for me to do is get out of the way for a while. Let you and Semmes and Tom Pine try to take care of it without me getting in the way."

"I agree."

"I need to be in Naples in a couple of days, anyway. I'll just go early. There's a flight leaves early in the morning. If you'll take me in, I'll spend the night at one of those motels by the airport."

"All right."

We didn't say anything more until we reached her house.

"You and Tom come in," she said. "Have some coffee. It'll take me a while to pack."

25

The motel room was small, plastic, and sterile but it could have been a suite with walnut paneling and Persian rugs and Jessie and I would still have spent a bad night. But we did our best. She took a long hot bath and got into bed with a book. I watched a college basketball game on the television, with the sound turned down so I didn't have to listen to the announcers.

The players did remarkable things, all of which I could see for myself. There was nothing wrong with the way they played the game. But the game that you couldn't see on television was something else and it was rotten.

I was still watching, without much interest, when Jessie turned out her light and said, "Forget about it for tonight, Morgan. Come on to bed."

I turned off the television and slipped under the covers. I was wearing some shorts I had picked up when I stopped by the river house on the way in to get the paper and the tape. They were in an envelope on the little table next to the bed. Jessie was wearing a large T-shirt. She eased over to my side of the bed.

"Do me a favor, will you?" she said.

"Sure."

"Don't lose your head, start acting stupid because somebody

sent those motorcycle guys out while you were with me. Keep cool and keep being careful."

"I'll try."

"I'm getting away because its the smart thing to do. Not because I'm a woman and going all to pieces. You're better than I am at this kind of thing. It's what you do and you've had lots of practice. It's the smart thing to do. But if you start acting dumb just to prove you're a man . . ."

"Give me some slack," I said.

"You know what I mean."

"I know what you mean." I also knew what she was feeling just then about what I did. And it is hard to separate someone from what he does. She was trying. So was I.

"I'm on your side," she said quietly. "I just want you to be smart, Morgan. You and I will work things out about what you do. Or maybe we won't. But we won't, for sure, if you do something stupid and get yourself hurt."

"All right," I said.

"Promise?"

"Promise."

I put my arm around her and my hand fell on the hard flesh just above her stomach. I could feel her ribs, and though it was hard bone my fingers touched, it felt somehow tender and frail.

She moved my hand up a few inches until it covered her breast and I felt something urgent pass from my fingers deep into my body. I moved closer to her.

"Just hold on to me till I go to sleep, will you, Morgan? Please. I don't want to make love tonight. I just want you to hold on to me."

"All right," I said.

"Be thinking about me and what I said."

"I will."

"Good. That's good. You feel strong, Morgan. You're plenty strong and I know you're mad. Just be smart, too. Remember that while I'm gone."

In a few minutes, she was asleep. I stayed awake for a long time.

In the morning, we checked out of the motel and had a dismal breakfast of coffee and stale muffins at the airport. I saw her as far as the security checkpoint, where she gave me a commuter's loveless kiss, a weak smile, and told me one last time to be smart. I waited until her plane was in the air, then left the airport for the day's chores. It was still drizzling and cold, with the sky low and sullen and no sign of the sun. But my problem was not with the weather.

First, I went to a bank and rented a safe-deposit box. I put the letter and the tape in the box, slipped one key into my wallet and the other into a little magnetic box under the bumper of the truck where I keep an extra set of keys for when I lock myself out.

Then I drove downtown, which looked even more hopeless than usual in the rain, and went up to see Semmes.

I knocked at his private door and heard him shout that it was open.

He was bent over his desk, writing something in longhand on a legal pad.

"Sorry to barge in."

He shook his head, looked back at what he was writing, and said, "One minute."

I studied the lifeless, lead-colored surface of the bay while he worked. The sky was low and tarnished out over the Gulf, which looked unusually barren and hostile.

"Nice day, huh?" Semmes said when he'd finished. "Sort of makes you think life was filmed in black and white."

"I put that stuff in a strongbox, like you told me," I said. I gave him the key and the name of the bank.

"I wrote down that you were my executor in the event of my buying the farm."

"Excellent," he smiled. "A wise precaution."

"And almost a little too late," I said.

"Sit and tell me about it."

I took the chair in front of his desk and told him about the motorcycles and everything that had led up to it.

He listened, keeping whatever he was thinking to himself. When I finished, he said, "Well, I'll tell you this. Jessie Beaudreaux must be one hell of a shot. I'm not sure I'd know how much to lead a motorcycle myself."

"You'd be impressed," I said, "at what a load of twos will do to a tire."

He smiled. "I can imagine."

"It was good shooting," I said, "but it didn't do me a lot of good. Even with that motorcycle boy in my hands, I couldn't get anything useful."

"Yes," he said. "I can see that."

"I hate to think that whoever it is—now that he has gotten two people killed, another one thrown in jail, and put Jessie through the scare of her life out on that highway—after all that, the rotten bastard is not just going to get away with it, but we'll never even know who he is."

"Take it easy," Semmes said.

"Well *goddamn*, Nat," I said. I'd promised Jessie I would keep my head, but it wasn't easy. I wanted to get my hands on somebody. But I didn't know who it was or how to find out. My jaw was locked down tight and my hands were trembling. If I had been this way when I was stepping on the motorcycle rider's ankle, I might have killed him. It had happened before. I sucked air deep into my lungs, trying to settle down.

"Take it easy, Morgan. I know how it is," Semmes said soothingly. "Believe me. I've lost cases where the heavens themselves cried out for justice, but the jury or the judge had ears full of crud and couldn't hear. My getting all emotional was sort of like pissing in my pants. Felt nice and warm for a minute or two but after that wore off it was cold and smelly.

"Anyway, it hasn't happened yet. We've still got the letter and the tape and you're still hanging out there for bait. So patience, my friend, is what you need to work on."

I nodded my head. He was right, as usual, but that didn't make it easy.

"Another day," he said, "maybe two, and I'll plant my story with the papers. Have you got anything you could work on in the meantime?"

"A couple of things," I said. "Be convenient if I could stay here for a couple of hours and use the phone in your library."

"Help yourself," he said.

I stood up and took a couple of steps toward the door into the room he used as a library and conference room. Before I reached the door, Semmes said, "Hang in there, Morgan, and remember what Stonewall Jackson said once when things looked black for the cause."

"What's that?"

"Do not take counsel of your fears."

"I like that," I said.

"Yes," Semmes said. "It's real damned good."

I sat at a polished mahogany table in Semmes's quiet, dusty

little law library and studied the list of numbers on Stitch Folsome's phone bill. I drew brackets around the numbers he had called in the last ten days he was alive. Then crossed out the calls to the 900 number he used to check on the line and the results of games he had bet. Then I made a list of the other calls by area code and began using the reverse directories in Semmes's library to match the numbers with names. A couple belonged to collection agencies that had been after Stitch for overdue bills. And there was a woman in Perry, Florida. I called her, and when I said I was looking for Stitch, she didn't say anything right away, then spoke very slowly with a voice full of venom. "I haven't seen him and I want to keep it that way. And if you see him, tell him that for me." Then she hung up.

The next number I tried was unlisted. I checked my list. The last call Stitch had made to that number had been on the night I'd recorded him talking to William Coleman and broken his hand. The call had been made at ten o'clock that night and had lasted for almost fifteen minutes.

I went up the list, looking for other calls to that number. There were half a dozen of them. The shortest had been for five minutes. Two calls on the day before Jackson Coleman was arrested for murder. One the day after.

I called Hawkins.

"That stuff do you any good?" he said.

"Yes," I said. "It did. But I'm running up against an unlisted number."

"Piece of cake. What area code?"

I told him.

"Where can I call you?"

"I'll get back to you," I said, "in an hour or two."

Before I could start checking the numbers that remained on my list, Semmes buzzed me on the intercom.

"Yes?"

"Morgan, you'd better get in here," Semmes said.

"Right."

He was standing at the window, looking out at the sullen surface of the bay. "Denise Coleman," he said, "has lost patience and called in the cavalry. I just got a call from a reporter with the *Atlanta Constitution*. He's working on a story and he wants to talk to me."

"Did he say what his story is about?"

Semmes turned away from the window. He was grinning.

" 'The blackmailing of William Coleman's family.' That's the way he put it. Sounded very excited, he did. Like a dog that has just made game."

"What did you tell him?"

"I told him I don't talk to reporters." He smiled thinly. "I think *you* ought to see him."

"And?"

"Lie to him."

"I see."

"He has his needs," Semmes said. "We have ours. There is no law I know of that says you can't lie to reporters or mislead them, or manipulate them to further your own agenda. Anyway, *they* do it to us, so it seems like simple fair play."

"You want me to call him?"

"I don't think that will be necessary. I'm sure he'll find you. Denise Coleman gave him my name so I'm sure she gave him yours, too."

"You have any particular lie in mind?"

Semmes shook his head slightly. "We can't script this thing, Morgan. You'll be talking to him. Feel him out. You want him calling people, checking out what you tell him, and making them nervous."

"Right," I said. "And it seems like I need to make this reporter believe that he has a potential Pulitzer in his hands. We need him talking to a lot of people."

"Exactly," Semmes said. "You'll know how to handle it. This is just what we needed and it fell right in our hands."

"Aren't we lucky."

"*Fortunate*," Semmes said, as though he were correcting my grammar. "Wit, as well as valor, must be content to share its honors with fortune."

"Who said that?"

"Dr. Johnson," he said. "He could have said, 'Being lucky can beat being good.' "

"Okay," I said. "I'll buy that."

26

I left Semmes in his office and went back to the library to finish researching Stitch Folsome's paper trail. After the unlisted phone number, it was pretty meager. When I'd crossed off the last number, which turned out to belong to an outfit selling some kind of treatment that was supposed to help you hang on to your hair, I called Hawkins to see how he'd done on the number I gave him.

"Big medicine, Morgan," he said.

"How's that?"

"That number . . ."

"Yes."

"Well, I ran it down for you. It belongs to a Mr. Stallworth. Charles K. Stallworth."

That stirred up something but I couldn't quite get my hands around it.

"Help me out," I said.

"Come on, Morgan. He's one of the biggest men in the state."

"I give up."

"Charlie Stallworth is athletic director over at the U."

I remembered vaguely. I'd heard the name on the radio. Seen it in the papers. But it was no more than a name. I couldn't get interested in stories about coaches and athletic directors and agents. Watching a player with William Coleman's gifts might help you forget about the real world for a while. Reading about a man who runs a team just reminds you.

"That's right," I said to Hawkins. "Now I remember."

"You mixed up with Stallworth, Morgan?"

"Send me another bill," I said to Hawkins. "And thanks for the prompt work."

"Tell me about it some day," he said, "when it's all over. Okay, Morgan?"

"Absolutely," I said.

I hung up and called Mike Grantham at the radio station. He told me to come on over. On my way out I nodded to Semmes, who was on the phone. He gave me a thumbs up.

Grantham was in his office, reading and ripping the sports section of *USA Today* to get ready for his show that evening. He'd used a lot of aftershave that morning, probably to cover the sour smell of last night's drinking, still plain in the filmy red surface of his eyes.

"Have a seat," he said, his voice rough as pine bark. "You want coffee? Seems like that's your drink."

"No, thanks. Just a couple of questions, if you've got the time."

"Time? Sure. I got plenty of time. We could go out to Pepper's, get some lunch, if you want."

"I'm a little pressed," I said.

He looked disappointed.

"Some other time."

"Okay. You promised me an exclusive if I'd help you out," he said. "And I'm going to hold you to it."

"It's yours," I said and his face changed a little. He was not past hoping. Not yet.

"Then ask your questions and I'll see if I can answer them."

"What can you tell me about Charlie Stallworth?" I said.

Grantham blinked and looked at me.

"*Stallworth*? You after *him*?"

"I'm not after anyone, necessarily," I said. "I'm just interested in Stallworth."

"Well," he said, "Stallworth is somebody to get interested in. He might be one of the most interesting men in sports these days."

"You know him?"

"Nah. Shook his hand once or twice at banquets. Charlie Stallworth doesn't know people like me. He aims a lot higher than that."

"How long has he been AD?" I said.

"This is his fifth year, I guess. He played at the U. Made second-team all-American. Scuffed around the NBA for a year or three, but he had a bad case of white man's disease. In college, you can cover up the holes in your game. Not up there.

"When he saw he was never going to make it in the pros, he got a job coaching at some little school. But he always saw himself as somebody with bigger fish to fry. *Players* didn't interest him, you know. Not if they were athletes. He wanted to get out of short pants and into a thousand-dollar suit.

"He was always a favorite with the boosters. They remembered him for playing one game when he broke his nose in the first couple of minutes but wouldn't come out. His face kept swelling up like a boxer's, and you'd of thought, to look at him, that he would hardly be able to see out of his eyes. They were like slits. But he stayed in. Brought the ball downcourt, set up the plays, got back on defense. Kept the U in the game so they were tied in regulation. Went two overtimes, and just like one of the Greeks had written it, Stallworth sank a layup on a break to tie it up with one second left in the second overtime. Got fouled on the shot and went to line. If he sinks it, they win. But if you looked at his face, you'd think, 'No way. He probably can't even *see* the basket, much less concentrate enough to put the ball through it.'

"He made the shot, then passed out before he could get to the bench. Nobody who saw it has ever forgotten. If you took everybody who says he was there that day and tried to put 'em in a gym, there wouldn't be enough room in the Superdome."

"That's a good story," I said.

"Yeah, boy, and people down here remember that kind of thing. So five or six years ago, people started talking about Stallworth coming *back*, like General MacArthur returning, you know. He was doing good things as AD at a little school up in Tennessee and the U couldn't stop stepping on itself. The teams were mediocre and that was bad enough, but what was worse was that they were getting caught for cheating. Couple of NCAA investigations turned up some free plane tickets and extra cash for players. The U got warned and then put on mild probation. But instead of cleaning up, they decided to cheat a little harder. This time, when they got caught, the NCAA almost shut them down.

"That happened over in Texas, at SMU. The governor of the state was in on paying football players. The whole program got shut down for one year. They call it the death penalty, but of course it's the players who get hurt. The governor and the high rollers kept their jobs and their money. The kids on the team—the honest ones and the cheaters—for one whole year, they weren't allowed to do the thing they loved . . . play football.

"Well, like I say, it wasn't that bad at the U. But it was bad. Probation. No television games. No postseason games. Loss of scholarships. So they cleaned house. Fired the football coach, the basketball coach, and the AD. Then they brought Stallworth in to clean out the stables."

"How'd he do?" I said.

Grantham shrugged.

"He came on strong as onions. Cleaned out all the old dead-wood in the athletic department. Launched fund-raisers to expand the stadium and the gym, build a new athletic dormitory. Conducted a big search for new coaches and got a couple of bright young guys—rising stars, you know, not the kind of big, established names who'd be his natural rivals. He also made all the right noises about playing within the rules.

"And?" I said.

"Well, like I say, he made all the right noises . . . in public."

"But not in private?"

Grantham shrugged. "You hear a lot of rumors. Around here, rumors are cheaper than chinaberries. The thing is, if you know anything about Stallworth, you know that nothing means as much to him as beating you. He played that way when he played. Coached that way when he coached. And I expect he's administering that way now that he is an administrator. It's in his bones. He *might* play by the rules if he was absolutely sure everyone else would, too. But if he thought the other fellow was cheating, then Stallworth would make up his mind to *outcheat* everybody."

"And the other people are still cheating?"

"Depend on it."

"So you hear rumors about him cheating?"

He rubbed his head again, as though from grave indecision. It was plainly a topic he would as soon not talk about.

"Listen, you can't imagine how popular Stallworth is right now," he said. "Being popular makes him powerful. When people write stories or broadcast things he doesn't like . . . he makes phone calls. Got a guy in Jacksonville bounced right off the air."

"I understand," I said. "But anything you tell me . . . it stays here."

Grantham took a breath, as though his next words would be somehow decisive.

"I heard that Stallworth told one of the big boosters that he was going to do whatever it took to get players. And if that meant cheating, then they were going to cheat. He's supposed to have said that he was going to show the U how to 'cheat neat,' so nobody would get caught."

"I see," I said. I tried to make it sound like this was pretty heavy stuff. Hard to believe that Grantham was either afraid enough of Stallworth or fond enough of his job to worry about repeating something like that.

He read my mind. "Listen, this is a very small, inbred world. People in these little pointless towns and out on their stove-up farms . . . they love the U. It gives them something to pull for, something that has a chance at glory. Damn sure isn't much chance of it in their own lives.

"Now a man like Stallworth, he makes it better for those people. Makes it better for the hogs, too.

"He's more powerful than the president of the U. A *lot* more powerful. People who own things—things like radio stations, you know—they like to get next to powerful people like Stallworth.

"So," Grantham said, rubbing his hand over his head like a worried old man and blinking rapidly to clear his filmy eyes, "if some washed-up old sports hack was to start spreading rumors about Stallworth, in the papers or over the air or even in private . . . well, Stallworth could make one or two phone calls and get the trouble-making sumbitch fired.

"I talk a lot about how we've lost our sense of tradition and how the games have been tarnished by proximity to too much money and how we need to get back to the sources of purity in sports. But I don't fuck with Charlie Stallworth. Mama didn't raise no dumb-asses."

"I see," I said and smiled.

He wiped his eyes and rubbed his head again, then said, "You *sure* you don't want to fall by Pepper's for a bottle of lunch?"

"Can't do it. But thanks."

"All right, then, I guess I'll just have to go by myself."

"One last thing," I said.

"Yeah."

"Has anything come up, since Stallworth's been at the U, about gambling?"

"Gambling?"

"Yes."

"You're covering it all, aren't you, from Alpha to Omega?"

I nodded.

"Gambling is not the same thing as recruiting. Most recruiting sins are what your Catholics would call the 'venial' variety. Gambling is something else. Mortal sin from the get-go."

"I'm not suggesting Stallworth is a gambler," I said, wanting Grantham to think I was fishing, which I was. But I had a feeling about the water I was fishing in. Even when you can't see below the surface of the stream, you sometimes know, from studying the way the currents move, where to put your fly.

"Well, matter of fact, he is. On the golf course, anyway. I've talked to some people who've played with him and it seems Stallworth can't get interested unless there's money riding on the game. He plays a lot, like most of them in the business. I heard that he was in one of those charity tournaments once with some of these businessmen, and on the first tee he turns to one of them and says, 'How about a thousand-dollar nassau, just to keep it interesting?' Fellow almost choked. But they played it and when Stallworth got down, he pressed. And pressed again. Lost five thousand. And he's a *good* golfer. He doesn't usually lose. But that doesn't make him a *gambler*, if you know what I mean."

"Sure," I said. "I just wondered."

"Tell you one more thing," Grantham said. "It just occurred to me. I've been ranting away about Stallworth all this time when I could have been telling you how to get a look at him up close."

"How's that?"

"He'll be at the Holiday Inn out on the interstate tonight. Speaking."

"Open to the public?"

Grantham smiled wearily and shook his head. "No. *Hell* no. Stallworth works for the state university, friend. He can't be doing his business out in the open."

I waited for him to explain.

"He'll be speaking to a little group of the hogs. Boys who give ten thousand dollars and up to the athletic department scholarship fund. They call themselves Bull Gators. Besides the money they give outright, they also loan Stallworth and the coaches private jets when they need to go see a recruit somewhere. They find jobs for kids in the summertime. Line of credit down at the bank. Little things like that. And they don't ask much in return. They want good seats. They want to be able to wander around in the locker room after a game, slapping people on the ass. They want to call Charlie and the coaches on their private lines and go see a practice even when its closed to the press. And they want Stallworth and the coaches to come out and eat beef and drink whiskey with them every now and again and then, after supper, answer a few questions. They figure ten thousand ought to buy that."

"Tonight, huh?"

"At the Holiday Inn."

"Are you going?"

"Friend," Grantham said, helplessly, "I couldn't break into that thing with a gun."

I thanked him and left, thinking that a gun might not work but Tom Pine would surely know how to get me into that room.

27

I called Tom Pine and offered to buy him lunch.

"Out of the goodness of your Christian heart, I suppose," he said. "Not because you might be wanting something from me."

"Tom," I said, "how can you say that about me?"

"Easy. And anyway, Phyllis is on the warpath about my eating. Fed me greens and nothing else last night. I felt like I was grazing instead of eating."

"Plate of ribs sound good?" I said.

"You'd have to answer to Phyllis," he said. "Whatever you want, it ain't worth that."

"Quick sandwich," I said. "Nice crispy end pieces and we'll skip the dessert. Just black coffee."

"All right, Morgan. But I got to be the first police officer in history to go into the tank for a barbecue sandwich."

The sandwich looked almost dainty in Tom's hands, like it should have been cut square and filled with thin slices of cucumber.

"Oh, man," he said, "I was starving. Normal day, I'd do three of these."

"See, you're cutting way back. In a month, you'll be a perfect size eight."

"Okay," Pine said, "I took the bribe. Now what do you want?"

I told him about the function at the Holiday Inn.

"And you want to get in?"

"Just for a look."

"At Stallworth?"

"And the Bull Gators. Could be one of them behind this."

Tom thought for a moment, then said, "You know, it could be Stallworth. Seems crazy when you first think about it but I've known some like him. The way they see themselves, they aren't running sports programs for kids. More like they're the head of Ford or something, trying to cut the competition's throat and any old knife will do."

"Got any ideas?"

"For getting you in there? Sure, make a ten grand donation."

"You want to loan me the money?"

Tom smiled and shook his head. "I could probably get you on as a bartender for the party," he said. "The manager out there thinks he owes me one. Busted a couple of Cubans who used one of his rooms to pass out coke. He probably knew about it, might have even been paid a little, but I didn't bust him. He thought I was being Christian. Truth was, it would have been too hard to prove."

"Would you do it?"

"Sure. What the hell, I'm like an addict. Anything for a sandwich."

"Thanks, Tom."

He shook his head. "You wouldn't believe," he said, "what I'd do for some pie."

It had been a while since I'd done any bartending. Longer since I'd worn a white shirt. I shopped for one at a mall and found the price almost as frightening as the squads of teenagers walking around with their headphones on, soaking up the sounds and the spirit of recreational shopping. I paid cash for the shirt and got out of the mall in five minutes flat.

From there I drove to the Holiday Inn, a couple of miles north of town on the interstate, and introduced myself to the manager, a tense little man who rubbed his hands constantly and couldn't bring himself to look me in the eye.

"Oh, yes," he said. "You're the one Lieutenant Pine recommended."

"Yes," I said, wondering what Pine had told him about me.

"You've tended bar before?"

"Yes." It had been years. Bartending had been a backup job once. I might have worked at it a total of three nights, more than long enough to learn that I would never make a career out of being cordial to drunks.

The man didn't ask me about that, though. He merely hustled me out of his tight, airless office and into the banquet room where the help was setting up tables.

"There you are," he said, pointing to the bar, and left like he couldn't wait to get out of my sight.

I set up the bar and waited. While I was waiting, I counted the place settings at the banquet tables arranged in neat files across the room. Forty places. So this room would represent almost half a million dollars raised and donated for the purpose of winning football and basketball games. It seems like the big money is in the nonessential things these days.

I took my time skinning a lemon, turning it carefully on the blade of my pocketknife so that the peel came off in a neat little coil. Then I stacked some napkins, iced down a couple of cases of beer, lined up three or four dozen glasses, and checked to make sure I had enough scotch, bourbon, vodka, and such to keep a room full of Bull Gators wet and happy.

I didn't even notice when my first customer stepped up to the bar.

"Jack Daniel's, if you please, sir. Little ice. No water."

He was smiling, plump, and wore a good suit for these parts. Also a large gold wristwatch with diamonds the size of BBs embedded in the bezel.

I poured his drink.

"Thank you, sir," he said and stuffed a bill in an empty glass. My first tip.

Five more were right behind him. And then another five. Then a dozen. The room seemed suddenly full of middle-aged men in suits, talking loudly, laughing heartily, and waiting impatiently for me to pour some whiskey.

So I poured and they stuffed bills in the glass. A lot of bourbon. Some scotch and vodka. A beer every now and then. If temperance and sobriety were now in fashion, you wouldn't have been able to tell it by this crowd. These boys were *thirsty*.

"Mr. Bartender, I'll have a little helping of the sour mash."

"Same here, only not so little."

"One see-through with a twist."

"Johnny Red and soda."

I poured and they drank. For the first half hour, it felt like a race. One I could not win.

But after the initial burst out of the blocks, they settled into a groove and it was easy to keep pace so I could watch and listen while I poured.

"It's that four-game stretch in the middle of the season that worries me. Auburn, LSU, Tennessee, and Miami."

"It's a mankiller . . ."

"Yeah, but if we get through that minefield . . ."

"Lose one and we've lost the conference."

"Last two ain't no easy thing. Georgia and Half-Assed U."

"Them Dawgs ain't so tough anymore without Dooley."

"What about the 'Noles? Bobby's boys are still plenty tough."

"Yeah. But I got a feeling about this year. They're the kind of team, you got to show 'em some Dee. You shut 'em down and they got rattled. And this year, we got some hosses on Dee."

"You got that right."

And so on.

I surveyed the room in the lulls between filling glasses. I didn't expect to see anyone I recognized and wasn't disappointed. They were all strangers to me. This was fine, since it meant that none of them would be likely to recognize me either.

When they talked, they used more volume than they had to, so the room seemed to vibrate with noise. They also put their hands on each other a lot. One man would stand next to another with his hand on the other man's shoulder, rubbing it. Another man would move around from one group of men to another, slapping everyone on the back and shaking every hand.

Not one of them stood out in any conspicuous way from the crowd. They were all white; all wore suits or blazers; all looked to be between forty and sixty. They had lost some hair and put on some weight since the days when they would have played the games they were talking about. But only a few of them looked like they ever had. For the games they played now, they were in their prime.

In one lap of this room, I thought, you could find lawyers to take care of your estate, your divorce, your taxes, or your kid's drug bust. You could get a mortgage or a business line of credit at the bank. Open an account in tax-free bonds. Get a bypass done.

Get into oil and gas fractions. Insure your life. Or buy a nice forty-eight-foot sport fisherman. You would be one phone call from the sheriff. No more than two from a U.S. senator and probably not more than half a dozen from the president. They might not look like much, but the boys in this room, drinking their whiskey and talking high jockstrap, could get things *done*.

You could not find one man in this room, I thought, who would go off by himself and put the heavy arm on William Coleman and his mother. Certainly none who would be willing to kill two men to get to Coleman.

They'd resent the suggestion if you made it. Resent it or consider it ludicrous.

But as a group—a mob, almost—they were all in on it. Half a million dollars worth.

Near the end of the drinking hour, there was another rush as they crowded my bar for refills to last through dinner and the speeches. Most of the orders were for doubles and a few of my glassier-eyed clients wanted a pair of doubles. I filled their orders and they took their glasses with them to the tables. When everyone was seated, the help begin weaving through the room serving up plates of chicken and peas.

Nobody lingered over the food. By the time the last plate had been served, the first was being cleared. Dessert—some kind of limp pudding—went even faster. Coffee was poured. A few of the men slipped back up to the bar to ask me for refills. One of them had a lump of pudding on his tie.

Twenty minutes after the first plate of chicken hit the table, a man stood at the head table and banged his water glass with the handle of his fork.

"All right," he said. "All *right*. Now gentlemen, if I may have your attention."

The room quieted.

"Thank you. First, let me say what a pleasure it is to see all of you here tonight. I think you all know me. My name is Ted Griggs, and when you cut me I bleed orange and blue."

Lots of cheers and laughs. I took a closer look at the man. Grantham had told me about him. He was the one who had hired a boy's father and mother as a way to get the son to play football for the U. Then, when the son had been injured and couldn't play, Griggs got rid of both parents. Just like a racehorse.

He was tall and thick from a life of too many breadsticks with too much butter and a lot of mindless drinks. His hair was silver and combed down across his forehead and his mouth was thin and crooked. He had jowls, and when he smiled it took a while for his eyes to catch up with his mouth. He had the face of someone who is perpetually selling.

"Now, as you know," he said, "I usually have a bunch of boring announcements—"

A few groans and boos from the audience.

"But tonight," the man went on, "we don't have time for that. We have a speaker, same as always, but our speaker tonight is a busy man. If he had fleas, he'd be too busy to scratch. He came up here this afternoon on a Gulfstream from Gainesville. And right after we get through here, he'll be going back the same way. We got less than two weeks before signings of letters of intent, and our speaker tonight is busy recruiting and kicking some serious ass."

Loud whoops from all over the room. Griggs smiled broadly and waited for quiet.

"Now we all know that this year, the U has been tough on the hardwood and done all right. Better than a lot of the wise men who write for the newspapers thought we would."

Cheers.

"A lot better, when you come down to it, than any other school that's been persecuted by the En Cee Double Ay has ever done under the circumstances."

Loud cheers and whoops.

"And we're going to do better next year," Griggs said, almost snarling into the mike. "Count on that."

He smiled while he waited for the cheering to die. Then he said, "But when we are really going to get some people's attention is when the boys who'll be signing in a few days take the court. Fellow Bull Gators, I want to tell you, when that day comes, the U is going to take no prisoners. And you can take that to the bank."

The cheering was louder than ever, and across the room men in suits got to their feet and began barking like bull gators marking territory in a cypress swamp. Their faces were flushed and gleaming with sweat and alcohol and they kept up their barking for two or three full minutes.

Finally, Griggs held up his hands and the noise died and the men sat back down.

"Now," he said, "with no further ado or bullshit, I give you the Boss Gator, Mr. Charles Stallworth."

Everyone in the room stood and applauded.

The man who stepped to the mike to take the cheers was tall and erect, with a frame that he'd kept lean, plainly by the kind of hard exercise the rest of the men in this room just couldn't find the time for. He had a long, angular face, and when he smiled it was strictly with his mouth. His eyes held a level, combative stare that refused to take in any one man in the audience while he waited for the cheering to stop.

"I appreciate that introduction, Ted," he began, "and I want to tell you right off that I'm sorry I have to eat and run, because there is nothing better than being with a group like this. The way I see it, the men in this room are the A-Team."

He had a distinctive, hard-edged, country voice. He might be raising money but he didn't sound like a beggar.

"Now what I came up here to do," he said, "is answer your questions. You men are the soul of our program and, as you know, I believe in keeping you informed. About everything. I tell the men in this room more than I tell the newspapers."

Cheers.

"More than I tell the university president."

Louder cheers.

"More than I tell my wife."

Laughter and cheers.

"And a hell of a lot more than I tell the NCAA."

Whistles, cheers, foot-stomping, and more loud gator barks.

When the noise died, the smile left Stallworth's lean, carnivorous face, and he spoke firmly into the mike.

"Before I take those questions, though, I want to give you a quick progress report. A rundown of just what we've done since I was last in this part of the state talking to you men."

The next five minutes could have been the chairman's report to a meeting of the stockholders. Stallworth ran down the various accounts. Money raised. Money spent. Balance on hand. Capital improvements. Long-range goals. An appraisal of the competition. Crisp, precise, and all business. When he finished, you'd want to invest.

"Now," he said, looking out at the room, pushing his jacket back away from his chest and hooking his thumbs into his belt, "fire away with your questions."

A man at a back table stood and cleared his throat. "Charlie,"
he said, "I know I speak for everyone in this room when I say that
you have done a hell of a job in a very tough situation. And we all
appreciate it."

Stallworth flashed a ritualistic smile at the remarks and the
loud applause.

"Now," the man went on, "in this part of the state, there is
one name that everyone is talking about. One player we all know
and who we want to see sign a letter of intent with the U."

"We know the same name in our part of the state," Stallworth
interrupted. "Everyone in the country knows that name. They
know it in Indiana. They know it at UCLA. North Carolina. Duke.
Syracuse. LSU. They even know it down in Miami."

Laughter.

"Well, then," the man said, "you won't be surprised by my
question—How are we doing with William Coleman?"

Stallworth's face changed. Became even more grim and determined.

"William Coleman, as you know," he said, "is the finest prep
prospect to come out of this state—or any state—in maybe the last
five years. Coleman is a blue chipper. Maybe the ultimate blue
chipper, in my experience. I can't think of anyone close, except
the Anderson kid who went to Tech a few years back."

Mumbles of agreement filled the room.

"Do we have a chance?" the man at the back of the room said.

Stallworth paused and seemed to give the question very deep
thought.

"In the dark ages," Stallworth said, "back when I was playing,
I don't think there would have been any question. We'd have
gotten him. Except . . ." he smiled faintly, "in those days, there
were no blacks at the U.

"Now that's changed, along with a lot of other things. In my
time, I *wanted* to go to the U because it was my state's school. My
friends and my neighbors had gone there. Everybody I knew
wanted me to go there. I knew that if I went to the U, then I'd
make contacts that would help me in this state for the rest of my
life. There were people like you men who were willing and eager
to help me and my family out—and we didn't have much—if I'd
go to the U and give it my best.

"Well," Stallworth said, "I don't have to tell you it doesn't
necessarily work that way anymore. Most of these kids today, they

aren't interested in the future. What they care about is right now. A kid like William Coleman doesn't care about the things you men can do for him and his family down the road. Not the way he would have a few years ago."

"Has somebody bought him, Charlie?"

"Not yet. Not as far as we know, anyway."

"So we've still got a chance."

"Yes. We've still got a chance. And as long as we've still got a chance, we're going to be in there fighting. Just because things have changed the way I said, that doesn't mean you men shouldn't keep the pressure on that kid and his family."

"What's he want, Charlie?"

"Hard to know, actually," Stallworth said. "He's a quiet kid. Real serious. But he's been making noises about wanting to make sure he gets a good education."

Scattered groans from across the room.

"We've heard Duke is playing the academic angle very hard. Somebody said Princeton had been around."

"Is there anything we can do?"

"Well, I can't make the U into Duke or Princeton. That's the president's job."

More groans.

"Look," Stallworth said testily, "the kid still hasn't signed with anyone or made any kind of commitment that we know about. And we damn sure haven't given up on him. So don't you men be giving up on him either. We're working very hard. You work hard, too. And maybe we'll get him."

Tepid applause. And then another question, this time about a new defensive coordinator for the football team.

Stallworth answered that question and several others, then said he was sorry but it was getting late and he had an airplane waiting. The men in the room stood and cheered as he left the room. It was nine o'clock.

28

The airport was quiet, almost deserted except for a single Federal Express jet that taxied out to the end of the runway and took off into the empty night sky while I found a parking place and locked up.

I walked around the terminal until I saw a sign that read GENERAL AVIATION over a closed door. I tried the door and it was unlocked. One man sat at a desk in a small office, reading a magazine.

"Help you?" he said.

"I'm hoping. You had a Gulfstream come in earlier from Gainseville. Supposed to leave tonight."

He turned to a computer monitor and studied it.

"Yeah. Landed at seventeen hundred."

"What time did it leave?"

"Hasn't yet. Pilot hasn't filed."

I thanked him and backed out of the room before he had a chance to get a good look at me.

I went back to the truck and moved it around to the area where the private planes were parked in orderly rows. Everything from little Cessnas to old twin-engine Beechcrafts. There was even a DC-3 that looked old enough to have flown the Hump. The Gulfstream was easily the throughbred in that stable.

I parked close enough to watch it, far enough away that I wouldn't be noticed. Checked my watch. Almost eleven.

It was chilly and I smelled like smoke from several hundred cigarettes. A lot of the Bull Gators hadn't yet managed to quit, so the cigarette smell seemed to cling to my clothes like old oil. Given the choice of a shower, coffee, or a bed, I would probably have gone with the shower.

I got out of the truck and took off the white shirt. The cold felt sharp and clean on my bare skin. I let it wash over me until I was shivering. Then I pulled on an old military sweater, the kind with the patches on the elbows and shoulders. It felt rough against my skin but it smelled like wool, which was a big improvement over cigarette smoke. I balled the white shirt up and threw it behind the seat, with the shotgun Jessie had used on that motorcycle.

I sat and watched the plane, wondering why Stallworth had felt obliged to lie to the Bull Gators. He'd left that dinner more than two hours ago saying he was in a hurry to catch his plane. Maybe he'd gone to see a woman. Or maybe he'd been trying to clean up the mess Stitch had made.

I could only guess, though, and there wasn't much profit in that. So I closed my eyes and let my mind wander to the wreck of a navy training plane I knew about in sixty feet of water, about fifty miles straight-line distance from where I sat. Coral was slowly covering the sheet steel in a crust of red, yellow, and purple so the hard symmetry of the plane was changing to something wild and irregular. An octopus lived under one of the wings and I would tease him out with cut fish. After he'd eaten, he would sit in my hand and squeeze my wrist with pressure that came and went, rhythmic as your pulse. A gesture of gratitude, I suppose. People who have studied them say that the octopus is one of the smartest, most easily domesticated creatures in the sea. I caught a couple of lobster every time I dove that wreck, but I went there to see the octopus.

In my weary dream, I was swimming down the anchor line to that plane. I was just deep enough to make out its shape and the school of bait that moved around it, breaking up and reforming like a flock of birds, when I heard a car coming up the road behind me.

My eyes stung when I opened them and the image of the coral-covered plane vanished.

* * *

The car was a big Lincoln, black with lots of chrome.

I put my head down and watched.

The car stopped in front of the one gate in a cyclone fence around the apron where the private planes were parked. Five men got out of the car and waited while a guard walked over from the main terminal to open the gate. He was taking his time, as though there was no need to hurry at this hour of the night.

I recognized Stallworth. Also Grant, the cop who'd met Stitch at the dingy bar. He wore civilian clothes and paced. And I recognized Ted Griggs from the dinner I'd just left.

The last two men wore dark suits, white shirts, and fifty-mission hats. They would be the crew. They stood off to one side by themselves, talking and looking at their watches. Grant stood alone with his hands on his hips and his eyes on the ground. Griggs and Stallworth stood off by themselves, their faces very close as they talked. I figured I knew what they were talking about. While I didn't have the whole script, I felt like I knew the players. Stitch and Grant were the errand boys. Griggs was the banker. And Stallworth—he was the head hog. He gave the orders.

The security man arrived, unlocked the gate, and let the pilots and Stallworth through. Griggs and Grant got back in the Lincoln. Griggs was driving and he was plainly in a hurry. The car was gone before Stallworth and the pilots reached the plane.

I waited until both the car and the plane were out of sight, then I drove home on empty highways, alternately satisfied because now I *knew* and frustrated because I couldn't think of a way to prove it. A few miles from the river house, I stopped thinking about it and merely looked up at the stars in a dark and clearing sky and punished myself with thoughts of Jessie. I had a hard time sleeping.

The phone rang a little before eight. I had run a few miles, showered, and was drinking coffee while I listened to the farm report on the radio and watched a pair of mergansers swimming upcurrent in the river, diving every now and then for a fish.

"Mr. Hunt?"

"Yes."

"My name is Albertson. I'm with the *Atlanta Constitution*."

"What can I do for you?"

"I'd like to talk to you."

"What about?"

"I think you know."

I had been thinking about how this conversation might go. I wasn't going to tell this reporter any wild, entirely made-up stories. And I wasn't going to tell him the whole truth either. I was going to tell him what I thought might provoke him to do what I wanted him to do. I was going to deceive and manipulate him, in other words.

But he wasn't going to be dumb, so I couldn't be obvious about it. I had to come on the way he would expect me to come on. I had to smell right to him, which meant I had to play the part of someone who didn't necessarily want to cooperate and was probably hostile to media people in general.

I just had to play myself, in other words. And he was making it easy.

"Listen," he was saying, "I don't like talking on the tele-phone—"

"Why did you call me on the phone, then?"

"Ah . . . all right, what I mean is, I'd like to talk to you, probably at some length."

"Oh," I said, "in that case, I suppose I ought to just drop everything and come meet you somewhere."

"Listen—"

"No. You listen. If you'd like to talk to me, then say so. Tell me what you want to talk about and ask me when and where is convenient for me, since you are the one who is all eaten up to talk. I'll let you know if I want to talk to you and if I have the time."

He sucked in some air and said, "I'm doing a story on the recruiting of high-school athletes. One of the young men I'm writ-ing about is someone you know. William Coleman."

"He's a good kid," I said amiably.

"Yes," Albertson said, "he is. And since you feel that way about him, maybe you'd be willing to talk to me."

"This story of yours is going to help him out?"

"Yes," he said. "I think it is. It could be a *very* important story. And I need your help . . . if it's convenient."

"Have you eaten breakfast?" I said.

"No."

"How about we meet for breakfast, then?" I said. "In an hour."

"That would be fine."

*   *   *

Albertson had curly hair and a serious face. He was slightly stoop-shouldered and he wore a corduroy jacket and a plaid shirt. His eyes were alert and active. He reminded me of some of the better lawyers in the public defender's office.

"I'm glad you could make it," he said.

I nodded and said, "Let's get a table." I had to stay in character. I was a reluctant source.

We were in a short-order place a block or two from the water. The floor was rough concrete and the tables were bare wood, but the food was good and they served large portions. Except for a pair of men in jeans and gimme caps drinking coffee, we had it to ourselves.

We took a booth in a corner. The waitress arrived with a coffeepot and menus.

"No coffee," he said.

"You?"

"Yes, please."

He wanted oatmeal. I ordered eggs over easy with sausage and grits and understood, for the first time, how Tom Pine must have felt when the two of us went out to eat.

He told me what he knew, or thought he knew. It was what he had been told by Denise. He didn't know the identity of the man who had come to the Coleman house with the deal, didn't know he was dead. Didn't know about Stallworth or Griggs.

When he finished, I said, "So what do you want from me?"

"Can you confirm that story?"

I looked at him.

"And," he said hastily, "correct any details that are not accurate. Or add anything to it."

While he was waiting for his answer, the waitress brought our food. I put salt and pepper on the eggs, speared the yolks, and started eating. It gave me time to think.

Albertson picked at his oatmeal and looked across the table at me.

"I've got a problem," I said.

"What is it?"

"My professional responsibility. I work for someone. And he expects me to keep confidential matters confidential. He wouldn't be happy to learn I'd been talking to you about his case."

"I don't reveal sources," Albertson said stiffly, as though I'd called him a name. It has always baffled me how people in his line of work take pride in never betraying a source but don't mind asking other people to betray a trust in order to become a source. Why is it okay for me to betray Semmes, which is what he was asking me to do, and not okay for him to betray me? It's one of those mysteries that I'll never fathom.

"I don't know," I said.

"Listen, we're talking about someone's *life* here."

And a very good story, I thought, but didn't say so. Instead, I began to fiddle with my food and look around the room as though I was on the verge of talking but wanted to be certain that no one would ever know. Sourcing felt like pretty dirty work.

"Somebody needs to tell the truth about these people and what they're doing. This whole thing with college sports is out of control. A story like this could change that."

I wondered if even he believed that.

"I'm going to write something. I'll go with what I've got but if you could make it stronger . . ."

He stared at me while I drank some coffee, drummed my fingers on the table, and otherwise looked like a man under considerable agitation. Finally, I said, "Okay. You got a notebook and a pencil? You're going to want to get all this down. There is a lot more to it than what your source told you."

29

I gave him Griggs, Stitch, and Grant and kept Stallworth for myself. The way I told it, Griggs had paid Grant to bust Jackson
and Stitch to approach Dinah Coleman with the deal. They hadn't
counted on Jackson killing Grant's informer.

"Stitch and Grant considered that a minor screwup in an otherwise sound plan," I said. "They didn't see any reason to call it off."

"Did they actually have a prosecutor lined up?" Albertson
said.

"I don't know. Maybe Griggs thought he could handle that
part when the time came."

"Have you talked to Griggs?"

"No."

"Why not?"

"I don't have anything to ask him."

"What about the tape and the paper?"

"They make Stitch look pretty bad," I said. "But he's dead.
Grant and Griggs can say they didn't have anything to do with it.
I need to put them together with Stitch." I hadn't told him about
the scene at the airport.

"Can you do it?"

"I'm working on it."

He gave me a skeptical eye as though to say maybe I wasn't trying hard enough or wasn't resourceful enough.

"Without a witness," I said, "or somebody to lean on until he testifies, I'm stuck."

Albertson nodded but not in agreement. "Well, you've been a help. If anything else comes up, you can call me at the Ramada out by the airport."

"You actually believe you can open this thing up?" I said.

He made a grim face and nodded again. "Count on it," he said.

What a hero.

I didn't know what to do next. The plan according to Semmes was . . . wait. I didn't have much natural ability for it. Plenty of practice, though.

So I drove back to the river house, changed clothes, and spent the day working on my hearth. When all the brick was in place and the mortar was setting, I went out to the shed I use as a workshop and began to shape my mantel. I was hewing it from a single slab of magnolia off a tree that had been dropped by lightning. It had a four-foot girth and I'd used a chain saw to rip a slab six feet long and half a foot thick from the trunk. I had the piece on sawhorses and for some reason, when I walked into the shed and saw it, I was reminded of a body stretched out for viewing.

I spent the afternoon with that piece of wood, planing, sanding, and then oiling it. The room smelled of shavings, sawdust, and ripe, sweet linseed oil. I rubbed the oil in with a soft cloth and then with my hands and, when it had set up, I rubbed the wood down with very fine steel wool to bring up the grain. Then I rubbed in more oil until the colors of the wood—deep reds, oxbloods, and very rich browns—began to separate out and glow, and the weave of the growth rings seemed almost to come alive.

I took one break for a beer and went back to work. I was still working when the sun began to settle behind the tree line. I almost hated to quit.

The house felt lonely when I went back inside. Too big for one man, even one who wanted room to bounce around. I needed another dog. I'd had a good one, a pointer I called Jubal Early, who had been with me for almost a year when a man cut his throat to demonstrate just how bad he was. I kept thinking about looking for a replacement. Even had a name picked out. I was going to call him Bedford. But I couldn't seem to make myself take the first step. Maybe when this thing was over.

I showered. Put on some clean clothes. Poured myself two fingers of bourbon in a coffee mug. I needed some music, so I put on a Merle Haggard album called *Same Train, Different Time*. It was all the old Jimmy Rodgers stuff, the train songs and the hobo songs, done faithfully and straight by Haggard. His voice had just the right note of lonesome, hopeless longing.

I sipped while Haggard sang. Just a quiet night at home.

Ben Dewberry was a brave engineer.
He told his fireman, "Don't you ever fear.
All I want is the water and coal
Put your head out the window, watch the drivers roll.
Watch the drivers roll
Watch the drivers roll
Put your head out the window, watch the drivers roll."

I was getting into the whiskey and Merle was getting into the sorrowful Rodgers ballads when the phone rang.

It was Jessie.

"How you doing, Morgan?" she said. "I been missing you. Not still mad at me, are you?"

"Never was," I said. "I've been missing you, too."

"Well, I don't think it would have been too good for me to stay around. If I had hit something besides tire with that shotgun . . . would have been hard for me to live with, Morgan."

"Sure," I said.

"So this is better."

"Much better."

"I'm worrying about you, though. You need to be careful with yourself."

"I am."

"What's been going on with that business?"

I told her what had happened since she left. The part about Stallworth set off her alarms.

"Sounds to me like he's your man, Morgan. I'd put some strong dogs on him and run him hard. Wear him out."

"Intuition?" I said.

"There's worse ways of knowing something. At least it ain't voodoo. You got plenty of that, too, where I come from."

"I know," I said, happy to listen to her talk even at six hundred miles road distance.

"What about you?" she said. "You think it's Stallworth?"

"That would be my guess," I said, "but I've got to prove it. I need to smoke him out."

"You working on that?"

"Yes."

"Well, good luck. Even if I'm not there, I'm pulling for you."

We talked a little longer about this and that. For the moment, I forgot about the music and the whiskey . . . everything except the sound of her voice.

After she hung up, I felt better. I made myself something to eat. Had another drink and listened to a few more train songs, then I went to bed, read for a while, and went to sleep early.

In the morning, I did the weights and went back to work on the mantel. Just as I was quitting for lunch, with another two coats of oil rubbed into the magnolia plank, the phone rang.

"Would this be the investigator?" a throaty voice said. I thought I recognized the voice but couldn't place it.

"This is Morgan Hunt," I said. "Who are you?"

"This is Hercules Johnson," the voice said. "We met at the Midnight Rose a few days back. Had us a little discussion."

I remembered now. The bartender.

"How are you?" I said.

"Oh, I'm fine. Just fine. How are *you*? Getting anywhere with the business we was discussing?"

"Some."

"You know you got some company. We had a newspaper dude all the way from Atlanta in here asking questions."

"What did you tell him?"

"Nothing much. Didn't like his manners. But he told me something that got me thinking. He was talking like Brother Coleman's problem might have something to do with *basketball* and his brother going to the U. Imagine my surprise."

"Must have taken your breath right away," I said.

He laughed and it sounded something like a growl. "You wouldn't be interested in the same thing, would you?"

"Basketball?"

"Un-huh."

"I might be."

"Good. 'Cause I've got a man who can tell you some things about basketball and the U that will curl your hair. Man's name is Ricky Randolph. Mean anything to you?"

"Afraid not."

"Well, he knows the basketball scene over at the U on account of he played there for a couple of years. I think you'd be interested in his story."

"When can I meet him?"

"Oh, anytime. Drop in for a cold one and I'll set it up."

"Tomorrow?"

"That would be fine."

"All right," I said. "You mind if I ask why you bothered?"

He laughed again. "Because I'm a good citizen," he said. "And I get tired of seeing them mothers get over on kids like Randolph and Coleman. I'd like to see them get a little back. Figured maybe you could give it to them, you understand."

"Tomorrow afternoon, then," I said.

"I'll be the black one behind the bar," he said and hung up.

I put the phone down, thought a minute or two, then picked it up again and dialed Mike Grantham's office.

"You still dogging this thing?" he said.

"Yes," I said. "I may not be too smart but I *am* slow."

He laughed. Grantham liked those locker room locutions.

"Well, what can I do for you?"

"What do you know about Ricky Randolph?"

"Big old kid," Grantham said. "Must have been six ten when he was in high school. Comes from here, actually. Tall and strong and could move, but he never learned how to *play*, you know what I mean?"

"Not exactly."

"Well, there is such a thing in basketball—or any game—as technique. Fundamentals. The finesse stuff that you need to learn. It isn't enough to just have the physical tools. You have to *think* and that comes hard for some of these kids. A lot of them are just too lazy to ever learn. That was Randolph. He had plenty of good games. But he had some that were just plain awful. Laughable. He'd get called for three seconds, and next time back up court, he'd get called for it again. Or he'd throw a big moonbeam pass into a double for an easy steal. Never even see the open man. He got one coach fired—by Stallworth, who figured that you can coach smarts. Maybe you can, but not with Randolph.

"Anyway, Randolph had been kind of a tough kid in high school. Worked a little for some bookie. Big as he is, the fellow probably used him to lean on folks who had gotten behind on their payments. But that never came out. What did come out was that Randolph liked to make a bet himself now and then. Somebody got arrested and told the prosecutors about it. There was a small scandal."

"What happened?"

"Nothing much. Randolph was a sophomore at the time. It was fairly late in the season and the U wasn't going anywhere. So Stallworth kicked him off the team for the rest of the season—or had the coach do it. Then, when he hired a new coach, he said that Randolph wasn't totally to blame, he hadn't been properly supervised and counseled by the old coach, and he let him come back and play on some kind of probation."

"How did he do?"

Grantham sighed. He was getting tired of the conversation. Probably his mind was on a beer. "Same as always. He'd dominate one game, then throw the next one away. Kid was no more consistent than a Georgia politician."

"Where is he now?"

"Ah," Grantham said, wearily, "that's always the question about yesterday's glory boys, isn't it? Nineteen or twenty years old and in the spotlight, hero to millions, and then a few years later, people are trying to remember the name and saying, 'Where is he now?' The answer, in Randolph's case, is pretty much the usual—he's around."

"I see."

"First he'll get out of shape. Next he'll get into trouble. Then he'll die of complications following a gunshot wound. That's the pattern. If he's lucky, he'll go to prison real soon. At least he can play ball there."

I thanked Grantham and told him I hadn't forgotten his exclusive. I'd get to him just as soon as I had something.

"Okay, brother," he said. "I got to run now."

I hung up and thought for a while. Then I made one more call, this time to Frank Hawkins. I had a theory and he was the only person I knew who could test it.

Hawkins and I talked for ten or fifteen minutes and he seemed to grow more excited with every question I answered.

"My friend," he said, just before he hung up, "this is going to be fun. I just hope it plays out the way you see it."

"Me, too."

"Call me this evening. I'll know something then."

I hung up feeling like a man who has gone out to the track and picked the first five races in the pick six. If one more horse comes home, he can pack the job and fly to Paris.

One more horse.

30

I went back to work on the mantel, but without much conviction. I can usually lose myself in a project but not this time. I imagined Stallworth, Griggs, Albertson, and now Ricky Randolph all out there *doing* something while I stayed at home, screwing around in my shop. I got so distracted and careless that I missed taking off the top of my thumb with a wood chisel by about one thirty-second of an inch.

I quit and sat on the porch and watched the water. A single mullet jumped and seemed to hang for a moment at the top of his arc, turning a silver side so that it caught the sun. The move reminded me of a basketball player going up for a jam. I couldn't leave it alone.

It was a mercy when the telephone rang.

"Morgan," Semmes said, without preamble, "you need to get in here, son. Time to start reeling them in."

"Griggs?"

"He wants to see me this afternoon. He sounded like a man who has just heard from his wife's lawyer."

"I'll be right there."

Griggs came into Semmes's office strong, with an old-buddy handshake and a lot of stuff about how he hated to be seeing him

221

under these circumstances instead of out on a dove field somewhere. Or playing golf.

Semmes did not play golf. But he didn't bring that up. Merely
said, "Do you know my associate, Morgan Hunt?"

Griggs gave me the look he used on the help. No handshake.
His face was pale and his long forehead was creased with worry.
He did not look especially tough but he plainly expected things to
go his way.

"I know all about Mr. Hunt," he said. "Going back several
years. I'd say you backed a wrong horse this time, Nat."

"Morgan has a past, Ted. It's no secret." Then Semmes shot
him a stern look. "Some people have secrets."

Griggs looked like he'd been slapped.

"Nat, you know me. We've both lived here all our lives."

"Just like Dinah Coleman."

"Nat," Griggs said soothingly, with just the faintest trace of
desperation, "you want to hear me out?"

"Sure, Ted. Have a seat. How about a drink?"

"Bourbon would be good."

"Fine. I'll make it."

Semmes poured a generous drink for Griggs. Water for me
and for himself. Semmes did his drinking when the mood—and
the company—was right.

Griggs didn't seem to mind drinking alone. But when he took
the glass, his hand quivered slightly.

"Nat," he said, "there is a newspaper man from Atlanta who
is going around talking to people about me."

Semmes nodded. "You're an important man, Ted. That comes
with the terrain."

"He's not writing about the insurance business. Or the oil
business. Or the car business. Or any of the other things I do for
a living. And he's not writing about the Rotary Club or the Mardi
Gras Society or the Republican party, either."

Semmes nodded.

"Your boy here"—Griggs bent his head in my direction without looking my way—"got that newspaper man interested in me,
telling him a lot of bullshit stories."

"Why do you say that? Did the reporter tell you that?"

"No."

"Then how do you know, Ted?" Semmes bored in. "That's a
pretty serious accusation. Can you back it up?"

"I *know*," Griggs said. "Put it that way. Because of Hunt here, that reporter is looking into what I do for the U."

"Endowments, Ted?"

"Sports. You know that. Everybody knows that."

Semmes nodded again.

"I'm a booster. No secret about that. I fly a Gator flag on the office flagpole. Haven't missed a home football game since I graduated."

"Why would a newspaper man be interested in that?" Semmes said. "Some kind of human interest story?"

"Don't bullshit me, Nat," Griggs said, a little tint of red showing in his otherwise gray face. "That newspaper man is trying to prove I had something to do with blackmailing William Coleman into going to the U. And your boy there put him up to it."

"Wasn't there something about a killing, too?" Semmes said, mildly. If you knew him the way I did, you could see how much he was enjoying himself.

"Goddamned right there was," Griggs said. "One of those project monkeys gutshot another one in some drug deal and this newspaper man is trying to make me a *conspirator*."

"Is it true?"

"Christalmighty! No, it's not true. Come on, Nat, you know me. You've been knowing me for years."

"Well, if it isn't true and he prints a story, hire a lawyer and sue the paper. You can buy a whole backfield off the judgment. And if Morgan Hunt here is spreading slander about you, hire a lawyer and sue his ass, too. He doesn't have much more than an ass and a face, but you'd get it in a judgment."

"I don't want to sue anybody, Nat. I just want it to stop. I have a business and a reputation."

"You know somebody named Stitch Folsome?" Semmes said.

"*Snitch?*" Griggs said. I was watching him close. He was a pretty good liar.

"Stitch," Semmes said. "Stitch Folsome."

"Never heard of him."

"What about a cop named Grant?"

Griggs hesitated. "What's this about?"

"What did you and Grant and Charlie Stallworth talk about the other night after the banquet?"

"Nat, I don't know what the hell you are driving at, but you've got it wrong."

"I don't think so, Ted. I believe you and Grant and Stitch are guilty of conspiracy and maybe are accessories to a couple of murders. I've got tapes and I've got documents. I'm going to give 'em to the appropriate prosecutor and then we'll see what *he* thinks.

"You need to get yourself a good lawyer—not a libel lawyer but a good criminal lawyer, and you need to think about trying to win the race to the courthouse. You testify against somebody bigger—if there *is* somebody bigger—and you might be able to plead down to some kind of suspended sentence or community service so you'll never see the inside of Raiford.

"But . . . when the criminal trial is over," Semmes said, "I'll be seeing you in civil court."

"What . . . ?"

"My client will be William Coleman—and his family—and we'll be asking for damages for all the distress you and your conspirators inflicted on them."

Griggs shook his head helplessly.

"Nat, I've never tried to *hurt* anyone."

"Just trying to help the U, right, Ted?"

Griggs nodded.

"I'll have the jury dancing to my music, Ted. I saw in the paper a few months back that you are now one of the fifty richest men in the state. Pictures of you with your Brangus herd and your airplane and your boat. You won't make the list next year, I can flatly promise that."

Griggs put the glass down. There was still some bourbon in it, but in his state he probably wouldn't have been able to taste it. He stood up by degrees, like a man who had suddenly turned old.

"I'm wasting my time," he said.

"You've been getting an education," Semmes said. "That's worth all the time it takes."

Semmes stood up and went to the window. He looked out at the bay, which was turning a hard slate color in the dying light. He stayed at the window for a minute. When he turned back to face me, he was grinning.

"Got 'em, Morgan. By God, we *got* 'em."

I smiled back.

"Griggs isn't going to wait on the prosecutor's pleasure. He'll be talking to a lawyer and cutting a deal before morning. And he won't want to expose his fortune to a jury of his peers, either. He'll come to me asking for a settlement. I won't skin him too bad. We'll take enough so William has some money to spend, clothes to wear, and a car to drive when he goes to school. And it might be nice if Dinah Coleman could stop scrubbing floors. We'll get her a comfortable annuity and a small house in a better neighborhood."

"What about Stallworth?"

"If Griggs is going to make a deal, he's going to have to give them someone. And it can't be small fry."

"What about Grant? He's small fry but he *is* a cop."

Semmes thought for a moment.

"Possible," he said.

"So Stallworth might skate on out of it."

"Maybe," Semmes said. "And he might even be clean."

"I don't believe that for a minute."

"If Griggs doesn't tell it, Morgan, there's nothing we can do. Even without Stallworth, we'll have done more than it looked like we'd do back when we started."

I didn't like that.

"I don't think Griggs sent those motorcycle boys after me and Jessie."

"No," Semmes said, "I don't either. But you're going to have to find a way to prove it was Stallworth if Griggs doesn't put the finger on him. And I doubt if Griggs knew about it. There is a lot he'd do, but he's not up to a killing."

"No," I said.

"It's a victory, Morgan. And you did it. You did damned fine work. Don't get greedy. If Stallworth was in on it, he'll try something else, and sooner or later he'll trip."

"All right," I said.

"I'm going to be talking to the prosecutors first thing in the morning. After that, you can take Jessie to New Orleans and celebrate. Stay at the Royal Orleans and eat like a French king. You owe it to yourself."

31

I stood outside a convenience store in the glare of the lights de-
signed to keep the parking lot safe. They didn't do much good.
To the punks, those places are cash machines. Instead of a plastic
card and a secret code, you use a pistol and the magic words, "Give
me the money or I'll blow your fucking brains out." Twenty percent
of the talent on death row got there for killing convenience store
clerks. They ought to give them combat pay.

But it was early for that. Six thirty in the evening and most of
the customers were stopping in for a six-pack or a microwave pizza
instead of some quick spending money. I was using the pay phone
to call Frank Hawkins. We talked for ten minutes, and when I
hung up I knew my horse had come in. Now I just had to cash in
my slip.

I got back in the truck, feeling light and nimble and invulnerable enough to work the graveyard shift at the Stop and Shop. I
drove to the Midnight Rose to collect my winnings.

"Hey, look at here," a voice said from somewhere in the gloom,
"it's the in-*ves*-ti-ga-tor."

"Well, shit, I reckon."

The bartender looked at me with the same impassive menace.

"Another beer?" he said, as though I'd just come back from the men's room.

"That would be fine."

He put the bottle in front of me and I paid him. I left the change on the bar.

"You getting to be a regular," the bartender said.

"It's the friendly clientele."

"You come to talk to my man?"

"Can you find him?"

"Drink up," he said. "I'll get you another beer."

He put it on the bar and then went to a phone on the back bar, dialed a number, and spoke a few essential words into the mouthpiece. I could feel the other men looking at me.

The bartender hung up the phone and came back to his old spot. "He'll be right along," he said.

Ricky Randolph seemed big as a tree. Bigger than Tom Pine, but without Pine's hard core. Randolph had already reached the first stage in Grantham's odyssey of decline. He was fat and out of shape.

We sat at a table in a far corner of the Midnight Rose. He drank vodka and ginger ale. His face was big, puffy, and vacant. He looked like a man who was too big and too lazy to think hard about much of anything.

"What'd you want to see me about?"

"Basketball."

"That's history. I haven't played in two years. Haven't even touched a ball."

"Why?"

He shrugged. "Lost my enthusiasm. I got drafted. Real low. But I got cut. Couldn't learn the plays. It's not the same now."

"You had some great games at the U, though."

"Yeah," he said and, for a moment, his face seemed almost animated. "Scored forty once against Georgia and got twenty rebounds. SEC player of the week."

"That your best?"

"Yeah, easy. I was smoking. Like if I touched the net, the strings would catch fire. I had some other games where I was good, but nothing like that."

"You had some bad games, though."

"Just like everyone else," he said, looking sullen.

"What happened?"

He shook his head. "You never had you a bad day?"

"Sure," I said, thinking about that time when all my days had been bad days.

"Same for a ballplayer."

"Fair enough. But I've been wondering about your bad days. Seems like there was a pattern to them."

"Pattern?" he said nervously.

"That's right."

"How do you mean?"

"Well, it seems like on most of your bad days, the U was a two-digit favorite in the spread. You know about the spread, don't you?"

He lowered his eyes and said, "Yeah."

"And," I went on, "the U still managed to win those games. But it didn't cover."

"Uh-huh."

"You tanked those games, didn't you?"

I watched his face closely when I said it. Nothing changed much, but there was something. An expression, almost, of relief. As though he'd been expecting this, fearing it, and now that it was here, the worst had finally happened and he did not, at least, have to fear it any longer.

He took a long drink from his glass and looked at the floor. Finally, he said very softly, "How did you know?"

"Computer," I said.

"Huh?"

I explained it to him without using any names. Not Grantham's or Frank Hawkins's.

"I had a friend of mine go back over all the games you played your last two years. He used your stats. Points, assists, rebounds, fouls, and turnovers. He also used the spread. What he looked for was games where the U won, but didn't cover. It almost jumped out and bit you," I said.

He shook his head from side to side, in disbelief rather than denial.

"Six games?"

"Five," he said. "Three my junior year and two when I was a senior."

"Bad."

"The worst, man. The worst. I always tried to make good

passes, even when they went wrong. But *trying* to make a bad pass so it looked like I was trying to make a good one . . . that's the hardest thing I ever did. I'd be shaking for an hour after the game."

"But nobody said anything about the way you played, right, because the U won the game?"

"Yeah. In a way, it made everybody feel better because it showed they could win when the big man was playing ugly."

"Who'd you do it for?"

He shook his head. Forcefully, this time.

"I know," I said gently.

"How?" He sneered. "That computer tell you?"

"No."

"Why didn't I do it for myself, then?" he said, sounding like a child caught in a lie and still trying to lie his way out. Strange in such a big man. "Everybody knew I made bets. Got me kicked off the team sophomore year."

"You didn't even bet on those games, Ricky. Who'd take your bet? Everybody in the state knew who you were. Especially the books."

"Get a friend to do it."

I shook my head. "It would get out."

"So why'd I do it, then?"

"Because somebody had something to hold over you like a club."

"What's that?"

"Basketball. You wanted to keep playing."

A fleeting, fearful look on his face made me certain.

"If you didn't go along, then you couldn't play at all, right? And it didn't make any difference, really, because you weren't going to cause the U to lose any games. They'd just win them by a little less than people expected."

He looked around the room and sighed, as though his surroundings had confirmed for him that he'd made a mess of his life and there was no point in keeping any secrets now.

"He made it sound like he was doing *me* a favor," Randolph said, with bitterness in his voice now instead of defeat. "Said, 'Ricky, boy'—he liked to call me boy, something you shouldn't do to a black man. Anyway, he'd say, 'Ricky, I've hung my pale ass out bare for you. Most programs, you'd be history. But I saved you. Now I want you to do a little something for me. . . .'

"He told me that if he let me stay at the U, he'd hire a coach who would build a team around me and work with me so I'd get up to where I could play the NBA game. Said he knew coaches in the NBA—knew 'em *personally*, he said—and that if I did what he wanted me to, then he'd make sure they knew about me and gave me a look. He could do a lot for me—or he could put my ass out on the street. Depended on me."

He picked up his glass, which looked frail in his massive hand, drained it, stood up, and went to the bar for another drink. He didn't bother to ask if I wanted one. I sipped some beer while I waited.

"You know what, though?" he said, when he was back sitting at the table.

"What's that?"

"He might have been telling the truth about the NBA. He was telling the truth about the new coach. Man really did work with me and I should have gotten better. But it didn't make no difference once I started tanking games."

"I know," I said.

"No," he said, "I ain't real sure you do."

The apathy had gone out of his face. Where it was slack before, there was a kind of tension. He'd been waiting passively four years to be caught. Now that it had happened, he'd experienced a kind of release, a freedom to talk and to justify himself.

"You're a white man and I can tell by looking at you that you got brains. Probably some money. You might have played basketball—football would be more like it—but it wasn't nothing more than a *game* to you."

I nodded.

"Different for me," he said. "Like everything else."

Tom Pine would have said, "Son, you are breaking my heart." He had no tolerance for self-pity. None. But then, Tom could have said anything he wanted under these circumstances. He was black and big enough to handle Randolph and everyone else in the Midnight Rose—except possibly the bartender. I was not black and I might need help. Or a weapon anyway. And I could afford to indulge Randolph. I saw him as a witness, not a brother.

"Meant a lot?" I said.

"Oh, man," he said. "No way you could know."

I nodded. All sorts of people think they have the franchise on suffering, which is their problem. Would have driven Tom Pine to righteous fury, though.

"That's when things was right for me . . . when I was on a basketball court. The only time. High school might have been the best. I thought it was going to be even better at the U, but it was mostly white kids who called me Ape when they thought I couldn't hear. At games, kids from the other school would wave bananas when I went to the line."

I nodded.

"And the school part was hard. I never was any good at school. But I was still good at basketball. And I liked it even more because the school stuff was so bad. I could forget about it when I played. I *liked* going to practice. That was probably the best time. No fans waving bananas and doing monkey sounds. Just players and coaches. Working for the shot, trying to block out, going for the rebound. People said I was lazy, but they didn't know. I worked harder than anyone at practice."

"Tanking games killed all that, though?" I said.

"Yeah. Deader than a stone."

"You get any money?"

"Hah. I didn't get nothing. Free shoes. A few hundred-dollar handshakes, just like everybody else. But for tanking those games—I got to keep playing basketball and that wasn't worth nothing anymore. Nothing. What I did, just so I could keep playing basketball—it ruined playing basketball for me. Ain't that a bitch?"

"You never told anyone?"

"You're the first . . . well, first *white* man, anyway."

"Somebody come around to see you? After you didn't make it in the pros?"

He gave me a stare. "Man, that computer knows everything, don't it?"

"He didn't come himself, did he?"

He laughed bitterly. "No way. He didn't like to get his hair mussed. Sent a couple of motorcycle dudes, wearing leather and chains. All covered up with beards and tattoos. One of them carrying a gun. They had a contest between 'em to see which one could call me *nigger* the most times."

"What did they tell you?"

"Said they were friends of a man and that I could die if I forgot how to keep a secret. They didn't mention the man's name or say what the secret was. Didn't have to. I *am* smart about some things."

He swallowed about half of his drink and then looked at me

across the table without much hope. Without very much interest, even.

"So what happens now?"

"Depends."

"Probably I'll go to jail, right? Or get killed. Both, maybe."

"Or neither."

"I'd like that."

"Will you tell the whole story under oath?"

"I got to have protection."

"Telling it is your best protection," I said. "You lay low for a while. Tell the bartender where I can find you when I need you."

He nodded. "This going to cost the man his job?"

"Worse."

"Good. 'Cause that job is his life. I'll be doing the same thing to him that he done to me. I like that. First thing I've felt good about since I went in the tank."

I got up, nodded to the bartender, and left the Midnight Rose—for the last time, I hoped.

On the drive back to the river house, I hardly noticed the road. Ballplayers would say I was in another zone, feeling something very close to pure joy. Now I had them.

32

When I got back to the river house, I made myself a drink and took it out on the porch, where I sat and watched the dark river. I could hear the movement of the water and smell the salt of the marsh at low tide. The sky was clear and cluttered with stars. It was cold and getting colder. The whiskey tasted good and I felt myself settling down now, not so excited anymore but still feeling a kind of glow that the bourbon only helped.

I thought I might build a fire and cook myself a steak later on. It was about the best I could come up with in the way of a celebration as long as Jessie was away.

I considered calling Semmes at home to tell him about Ricky Randolph but decided to let it rest until morning, when Semmes could hear the story from Randolph himself and then get it in the form of a sworn statement and take it, along with the tape and the letter, to the prosecutor's office. For now, there just wasn't anything left to do.

So I went inside for more bourbon. I'd just made it to the kitchen when the phone rang.

"Morgan, this is Jessie."

"How are you?"

"I'm fine," she said. "Listen, I decided to come home early. Can you pick me up at the airport?"

Must be my night, I thought. Maybe I should run out and pick up a couple of lottery tickets.

"What time?"

"How about right now? I just got in."

"I'll see you in an hour. Little less."

"Okay. Bye."

It took me a little more than an hour because I stopped on the way in and picked up a bottle of champagne, which was on ice in a cooler in the bed of my truck. I thought we might drive out to some empty stretch of beach on the Gulf and drink it while we looked at the stars and talked. I wanted to tell her about Stallworth. Brag a little, I suppose.

I parked in the short-term lot and started for the terminal. It looked quiet, almost deserted, this time of night. It was a small town and most of the flights came and went between sunrise and sunset.

I was about halfway across the lot when a bearded man with a large, blubbery gut stepped out from behind a parked car. He was holding one of those ugly little machine guns they all like to carry these days for lots of firepower at close range. An Ingram or a MAC-10. One of those.

The man pointed the muzzle at me and said, "Evening, Slick."

Another man, smaller but stamped from a similar mold, stepped out from behind another car and smiled. "You'd better do exactly what we tell you. You hear?"

I didn't say anything.

"The deal is . . . we've got the babe. The cop, Grant, went by the garage where she left her car. He got her name and then, when she wasn't at home, he figured she might have left town. He started checking flight manifests. It's easy when you can say you're a cop."

"Where is she?"

"In the car. We drove her up today."

She hadn't sounded right when she called. I hadn't been paying attention. Too full of myself. When you think you've got it won, but it still isn't finished . . . my stomach heaved at the idea of Jessie in a car all day with these two.

"Come on. We'll show her to you. We've been nice . . . so far. But she is kind of a sweet piece if you like them clean and prissy. I'm keeping my dance card open."

They led me across the lot to a large blue sedan. I saw two

heads above the back seat. I recognized Jessie. Then the other head turned. It was Stallworth.

"Open the trunk," the smaller man said to his partner, who kept his hand firmly on the machine gun while he worked the key.

It was a small trunk for a big car.

"Climb in," the big man said and moved the muzzle of his little gun into the small of my back. Jessie turned and looked at me through the back glass. Her face was drawn and exceedingly pale but there were no marks or cuts. I winked at her.

"Come on, asshole," the man said and pushed the muzzle so I felt it against my spine.

I climbed into the trunk and lay down, curled around the spare in a kind of grotesque fetal position.

"Comfortable?" the big man with the gun said.

When I didn't answer, he slammed the trunk.

The little space went dark and seemed to shrink by half. For a long, long thirty seconds or so I fought against a rising wave of panic that seemed about to break over me and leave me without air, screaming and kicking in desperation. All the old horror of close, dark places—steel and concrete cells, earth and timber bunkers, and, worst of all, a long moldy tunnel I'd gone down into carrying a pistol and a flashlight, trailing a rope behind . . . all of that washed over me in a wave of dread.

Easy. Easy. Easy. I told myself to hold on and breathe. Hold on and breathe.

My chest was heaving. I could start by getting that under control.

Easy. Breathe in . . . now out. In . . . and out. Just hold on.

The car started.

Just hold on.

I could feel the wheel near my head begin to turn.

In and out.

We moved slowly for a while.

Hold on. Breathe.

Then stopped to pay the toll.

In and out.

Moving again.

The tires began to move faster and the car swayed ponderously on the shocks.

Easy.

My chest was no longer heaving and my breathing felt almost

normal. Now I needed to work on not getting seasick as the big car rocked like a tubby boat on a following sea.

I imagined a horizon, a long level vista where land merged with sky, and as the body of the car moved, my mental horizon remained fixed, giving me a reference. I concentrated on that horizon like a pilot making sure he was in level flight.

After a few minutes the car accelerated and settled into what felt like a kind of steady cruising speed, so we must have cleared town and reached a highway that would take us wherever we were going.

I worked on my breathing and my horizon. On fighting vertigo. And I thought about Jessie. Whatever else I did, the first thing I had to do was get her away from these apes. Then I could go back and deal with them in detail. I needed a plan and I worked on one while the big car rolled along the road toward wherever we were going and whatever Stallworth had in mind.

When the car stopped, I was stiff and my ears were ringing, but otherwise I was in good shape. I heard the key sliding into the lock and then the lid of the trunk rose and a flashlight beam was in my face.

"All right, Slick. End of the road. Out. And if you get cute . . . you get hurt. The babe, too."

My legs were stiff and I had a deep, precise cramp in my back but I made it out of the trunk, moving in stages, and it felt good to put my feet on solid ground and breathe fresh air.

I blinked and looked around. We were parked in front of the river house.

"You don't have some kind of big old mean dog in there, do you, Slick? A pit bull or a Doberman I'm going to have to shoot?"

"No dog."

"Well, good. Then lead the way."

I walked, still a little unsteady but gaining, across the yard and up the steps. I could feel the others coming behind me in the night. No one said anything. I opened the front door and turned on some lights.

"Move real slow, Slick, until we're all inside."

The big man with the machine gun followed close behind me. Then Jessie and the other biker. Stallworth was last in and he closed the door behind him.

His face was pale, with the skin drawn tight as stretched canvas over the bones. His eyes were narrow and hot. He carried nothing in his hands but looked like he might be ready to kill me with his fists. The rage came off him like steam.

"You sit down over there," he said to Jessie and pointed to a sofa. "Pancho, I want you to watch her and if she does anything but sit there like a nice, well-behaved little sorority girl, you knock the shit out of her. Got it?"

"Yeah, coach," the big man said, smiling like he couldn't wait to slap Jessie around and then get on to something else.

"Rusty, you come with me while I talk to this meddling bastard."

"Okay, coach," the little one said happily.

I looked across the room at Jessie, sitting on the couch. Her body seemed drawn in on itself for protection, and her face was a perfect, pale blank, giving nothing away.

"Move," Stallworth said.

"Where do you want me to go?"

"Looks to me like you've got lots of rooms in this house. You pick one where we can talk."

I went down the hall to an empty room that I had been putting off rebuilding. The floors were eaten up with dry rot and the plaster was crumbling and mildewed. A little blood wouldn't hurt it a bit.

I opened the door and turned on the light. Stallworth pushed me into the room. Hard, but not hard enough to make me fall. I suspect that he would have liked to kick me and that it was all he could do to restrain himself and stick to business. He wasn't used to people messing around in his business.

He pulled the door shut and nodded to the man with the machine gun. "You stay right there," he said, "by the door. And if he does anything I don't tell him to do, shoot him in the knees."

"Whatever you say, coach."

Stallworth glared at the man. He wasn't used to backtalk either.

The man at the door gave him a grin. He was missing three or four teeth and those he still had were moldy green.

Stallworth turned away from him and looked at me.

"We could kill you and the woman right now. And we could make sure nobody ever finds the bodies."

I didn't say anything.

"I ought to just go ahead and do it," he said. "Just because it would make me feel so goddamned good."

"You'd still have a problem," I said.

His head snapped back and he sucked in some air, like he'd been slapped.

"*Me?*"

I nodded.

"My problem is nothing next to what you're looking at. You *and* the woman."

"I'm your problem," I said. "That's why you're here."

"You're just something on my shoe."

I didn't say anything.

"If I killed you right now, my problem with you would be all over."

I shook my head. "Then you'd have done it already," I said.

"You are a real smart-ass," he said. "And I don't put up with that."

He walked over close to the man at the door and held out his hand. The man reached in the pocket of his leather jacket and took out a short length of polished chrome chain. He handed the chain to Stallworth, who swung it two or three times. It sounded like the wind as it cut the air.

"Get on your knees," Stallworth said.

I did what he told me to do.

He came across the room slowly and stopped when he was about three feet from where I was kneeling. He moved quickly, without telegraphing it—the man was an athlete—and the chain came at me in a blur. I tried to react but I still took it on my shoulder. The force of it knocked me over so my face was on the floor, and my arm went numb. I rolled away as the chain cut through the air again and caught me across the ribs. I heard Stallworth grunt with the effort he put behind the swing and then heard the air leave my own lungs in a rush when the chain hit. I felt a sharp, hot, stabbing sensation low in my chest where the chain broke a rib.

"On your knees," he said. Beads of sweat popped off his forehead like blisters. The man at the door grinned, showing more of his green teeth.

I got up on my knees.

"Now tell me again about my problems, smart-ass."

I didn't say anything.

"All right," he sighed, and a measure of control came back into his voice. He was smart enough to know that he couldn't save himself just by stomping me. He needed to know how things lay.

And to find out, he had to talk to me. That's what I'd been counting on. Now that he'd knocked me around, he'd expect me to be grateful for the chance to talk and eager to tell him what he wanted to hear. I'd also been counting on that. He thought he'd hurt me but there were things he didn't know. He might have played hurt but there were whole worlds of pain that were foreign territory to him.

"Now suppose you tell me why you think I'm here and what I want from you."

"You're here because Griggs called you. And you don't want to go down in flames because of Stitch Folsome and William Coleman. You want whatever I've got that can burn you."

"Very good. Stitch told me about the tape and the letter."

"I've got them," I said.

"And I want them."

"People in hell want ice water," I said.

He swung the chain again, hard and fast. So fast that even though I tried to duck, the chain caught me high on the face. That eye exploded in red flame and hot white sparks.

I rolled over on the floor and the chain came down on my back. I felt a numbing seizure of pain all along my body.

"Up," he shouted. "Get up on your knees."

I did it.

"You'd better be careful with me." His face was damp and his lips were pulled away from his teeth so he looked like a snarling, cornered animal.

"The tape and the letter wouldn't be enough, even if I gave them to you right now," I said. My tongue felt thick.

"It's a start," he said.

"You'll need more."

"Why?"

"Because too many people know what I've been up to. Even if you had the tape and the letter and killed me, they'd still be running hot on your trail."

My mouth was full of something and I had to spit. Half a cup of blood.

"There's more," he said. "Lots more."

"I'm sure of it. It might make you feel better but it won't help your problem."

My voice sounded thick and distant. But my head felt clear.

"*My* problem?"

"You're the one working up a sweat with that chain."

"Tell me about *my* problem."

"There's Griggs, for starters. The lawyer I work for knows about him and he's not going to quit if I disappear along with the letter and the tape. He'll just bear down harder on Griggs. I don't think it would take a chain to break him."

Stallworth turned his back on me and walked the room for a minute or two, like an agitated coach pacing the sideline.

"So what's your solution?"

"I'm not interested in solving your problems," I said, spitting more blood. "I'm interested in making a deal."

"Deal?"

I nodded.

"You don't much look like a man who is in a position to deal."

"And you don't look like you've got a handle on Griggs. Or the tape and the letter."

"I could get them," he said. "Real quick."

He came across the room, swinging the chain but without as much conviction or force as before. I rolled up on the floor and took it across my shoulders and my back. He didn't even try for my face. He was thinking and he wanted to talk more. Through the pain, I knew that I had him.

"Up."

I raised myself to my knees again. Spit more blood. And looked up at him. He didn't know it, but I was winning. And I didn't want him to know. Not as long as he had Jessie.

"Listen to what I have to say," I said. "Just listen."

"All right," he said. "I'm listening."

"I can get you out of it. Clean. But I want something."

"Like you said, people in hell want ice water."

"If I don't get it, you'll go down. Even if you can get me to give you the paper and the tape, and then kill me and the woman, the lawyer and the other people who know will come down out of the trees on you. I can keep that from happening."

"Go on."

"First, the woman goes home. With you. Not the motorcycle apes."

The man at the door gave me an evil look and showed me some of his green teeth when I said this. Stallworth looked at me with a mix of curiosity and contempt and said, "Then what?"

"When she's at her house and you're there with her, you call over here on the phone and I'll get the key to a safe deposit box and give it to these boys. They'll tell you they've got it and you come back over here. Leave the woman at her own house."

"So she can call the law. What kind of bullshit—"

"She won't call the law as long as you've got me and can kill me anytime you want to. She won't say *boo* until she sees I'm safe."

"So we get a key," he said. "Assuming the stuff I want is in the safe deposit box . . . so what? You already said I've got that lawyer on my ass."

"What do you know about me?"

"Grant told me about you. Vietnam and an ex-con. Errand boy for that lawyer and all-around pain in the ass."

"What if I met with Griggs and his lawyer—I'm sure he's got one. Met with him tonight and made a sworn and witnessed statement that I was part of the whole thing all along. Stitch had the idea and I muscled in, figuring I could sell it to you and Griggs. I was conning the lawyer I work for."

"Why should anyone believe that?"

"Why shouldn't they? I'm an ex-con. Makes me a credible blackmailer. Credible enough to cover you and Griggs."

He thought for a moment.

"What do you get?"

"Two things. First I get some money from Griggs. This afternoon he was looking at losing everything. He'll deal and I suspect he'll be generous."

"And you'll keep quiet? Even if you have to do time?"

"If I change my story, nobody will believe me. If I do time, I'll figure I'm earning Griggs's money."

"You said two things. What's the other?"

"Like I said, the woman leaves here, with you, and I know she's all right when you come back. Nothing happens until that's done."

The biker at the door shook his head. "Shit, he's that worried about the babe, just bring her in here and work on her for a while. That'll make him play."

It was the exposed nerve in my plan, and when the biker touched it I felt the sensation—dread mixed with alarm—through my whole body.

Stallworth looked at me. He grinned.

"Kill me and the woman," I said, "and you are still in a bind.

Hurt the woman and let me live . . . you'll never know when you wake up in the morning if this is the day."

I said it like I meant it. Because I did.

Stallworth studied my face. A nerve in his cheek twitched and his eyes narrowed as he thought it over. If it had been up to the bikers, there wouldn't have been any question. But Stallworth wasn't here primarily for sadistic kicks. He was scrambling to salvage what he'd spent a lifetime putting together and he thought he saw a crease he could slip through. He was a gambler.

"All right," he said. "When I get back here and I have that key in my hand, we're going to work on your story until it is airtight."

33

Jessie looked at me with something like horror before she left. Her face was pale and still.

So it was me and the two motorcycle boys now. Pancho and his partner, Rusty.

While we waited for Stallworth and Jessie to get to her house, Rusty went into my kitchen and looked through the refrigerator. He came back with a jar of peppers and a can of beer, sat down and opened them both. He ate two peppers for every swallow of beer and he looked bored. Which was fine with me.

The phone rang. Rusty put down his beer and picked up the receiver.

"Yeah," he said. "Okay. Give me a number and I'll call you just as soon as we've got it."

He hung up.

"Okay, Slick, on your feet. You and me are going after the key. Where is it?"

"Upstairs."

"Lead the way. You stay here, Pancho. Have a beer."

I stood up, making it look harder than it was. One leg was sore but not gimped. But it might help if they thought I was hobbled.

I started up the stairs with Rusty and his little machine gun behind me.

At the top of the stairs, I turned on a light and moved past two closed doors to open another. It was dark in that room, too. I stepped in past the door, then kicked back with my foot so the door slammed hard in Rusty's face. Then I took three or four quick steps across the room and launched myself through the window.

There was no glass. I'd been waiting for a special-order window for over a month and had covered the frame with a sheet of clear plastic. It gave easily and I was in the air, falling fifteen feet to soft ground covered with thick centipede grass.

I took it on the balls of my feet, my thigh, and the big muscle under my shoulder. The impact pushed some air out of my lungs and stung the leg that had been chain-whipped, but otherwise I felt nothing. I rolled to my feet and started running.

I could hear Rusty shouting from the window and then the abrupt hammering sound of the machine gun as he got off a couple of sloppy bursts. I didn't hear the impact or the crack of a round passing over my head, so the shots must have been wild. If he'd hit me at that range at night, with me moving, it would have been absolute blind luck.

But I staggered, trying to make it look like I'd been hit. Went to the ground. Rolled. Got up again. Then moved around the shed, out of sight. There was a stump behind the shed that I used for splitting firewood and I kept an ax stuck into the stump. The ax felt good in my hands.

I stepped into the woods on a little path that led down to a slough. Not very far. Twenty or thirty feet. Waited and watched the house.

Rusty and Pancho came through the back door erect and close together. If I'd had a rifle in the shed, I could have dropped them both and would have had a hard time resisting the temptation. I wanted them and I wanted Stallworth. The ax would have to do.

"I nailed him," Rusty said, much too loudly, his heavy composure gone. "Got him at least once. And he wasn't moving too good before that. He can't get far. Look for blood."

They had a light. But they would be looking down for a blood trail. I knelt and picked up a handful of soft, wet earth. Smeared it on my face to cut the glare and wondered what sort of microbes I was rubbing into the wound from Stallworth's chain. Well, I could worry about infections later. I tested the ax blade with my thumbnail. It was sharp enough to peel the nail like an orange.

Rusty and Pancho reached the shed and stopped.

"Okay," Rusty said. "We'll go down this trail here. If you see him, put the gun on him and yell."

"I'll blow him away."

"Later. We need that key first."

They started into the trees, moving clumsily. I heard Rusty in the lead, moving like an old fat sow, crushing whatever got in his way.

I was behind the top branches of a blowdown. The big tree would channel them right past me and the leaves and broken branches would break up my shape and give me some concealment so they wouldn't see me, even with their lights. That was the plan, anyway. The best I could do under the circumstances.

I wrapped my hands around the ax handle. Hard, like I was trying to wring sawdust from the butt. My mouth tasted like copper from the blood but there was something else in the taste. Something bitter and hot. I could hear my pulse in my ears.

The beam of their light played over the ground, searching.

"Come on, goddamnit. Where's the *blood*."

Coming right up, I thought.

"You think he came this far?"

"The fuck should I know?"

"Maybe we ought to go back. Call Stallworth."

"And listen to his shit? No way. That guy was limping when he went up the stairs and I know I clipped him. Once, at least. He ain't going far. He might be curled up gutshot or dead under a bush already."

"And maybe not."

"So what. We got two men who haven't been shot and two guns. I think we can take him. Now shut the fuck up and help me look for blood."

It was almost unfair.

I let Rusty go by. One heavy, sloppy step, then I came up off my knee and swung the ax so the blunt end caught him in the back of the head and crushed it like the shell of a melon. I felt something splatter on my face as I went back to the ground and rolled away. Rusty had had the light and it was on the ground, useless. Pancho tried to run but I caught his leg with mine and he went down. Before he could move the hand that held his little machine gun, I swung the ax, using the blunt end again, and broke his arm just below the elbow.

He screamed.

I took the gun from his useless hand.

"Up," I said.

He moaned.

"Get on your feet before I break your other arm."

He stood, rocking clumsily and holding his arm.

"My turn," I said. "And I've got an ax."

"No, man."

I hit him on the arm just above the break, this time with the sharp end. It bit and his leather sleeve parted like paper.

"Arrrgh."

He sagged to his knees.

"Get up."

He tried. Fell back to his knees and vomited.

"Feel better?" His good arm was across his body so the hand could cover the cut on his upper arm. Blood seeped through his fingers.

"Is Rusty dead?"

"Let's see," I said and swung the ax so the blade caught the big, inert man in the back of the thigh. The flesh parted easily and the bone broke. I left the ax in his leg, like it was a billet of firewood.

"Jesus," Pancho said, bringing up peppers and beer. "Jesus."

"I believe he's dead," I said. "And I'll do the same thing to your leg, while you're alive, if you don't do exactly what I want you to do."

"All right, man. Jesus."

I pulled the ax out of Rusty's leg and held it in front of Pancho's face. "You forget about all of this. Me and the woman and the whole thing. Pretend you never left Tampa. Stick to what you and your brothers do best, drinking beer and fighting each other in the parking lot. You understand?"

"I understand, man. You won't never see me again."

"I guess I'll have to take your word for that. You swear on your sacred colors?" I ran the ax blade along his face, stopping at the throat.

"Yes. Jesus."

"You sound like a preacher, Pancho. Now the second thing, you walk back to the house with me and call Stallworth. Tell him you've got the key and he can come on over. If he asks where Rusty is, tell him he's in the can. You'd better do as good a job for me as the woman did for you. All right?"

"All right."

"Remember, I'll be right next to you. Me and my ax."

34

Stallworth was easy. I put the muzzle of my own pistol in his ear almost as soon as he stepped out of the car.

"There's a sheriff's lieutenant on the way," I said. "He'll be here in thirty minutes or less."

I led him inside and made him sit on the floor. I kept my eyes and the pistol on him while I called Jessie.

"You all right?"

"Yes. What about you?"

"I'm fine. Stallworth is here, sitting on the floor until Tom Pine gets here to take him in. Rusty is dead. And Pancho is walking back to Tampa with a broken arm."

"Morgan, how—"

"I'll tell you later. As soon as I'm through with Tom."

"Be careful, Morgan."

"You told me that earlier, I believe," I said.

"You should have listened."

I put the phone down and sat in a chair ten feet from Stallworth. He looked older and beaten down, but still defiant.

"What is your interest, anyway?" he said. "You worried about William Coleman? Shit. That kid has it made no matter who gets him. Me or somebody else, makes no difference. Three or four years from now, he'll have an agent who'll sign him for a bonus that is more that you'll make in your entire life. For playing basketball, something he'd do for free. Comes as easy as dancing to someone like him. You believe he's getting a tough deal from life?"

"He's a good kid," I said.

"He's a *baby*," Stallworth said, nearly spitting the word. "He ought to be on his knees to people like me. We do the hard work and heavy lifting and he puts on a pair of short pants and goes out and does what comes as naturally to him as breathing. And he thinks he's got a bitch. You know who sweats and bleeds so he and his agent can go talk to some GM about a five-year no-cut, ten-million-dollar contract and *then* start shopping around for endorsements? You know who that is?"

"I feel sure it must be you."

"You got it," he said, glaring back at me. "That kid was born at the right time, but he don't have a clue. Time was, he would have spent his life looking at the back end of a mule and taking his shots at a peach basket. But he got lucky and now he thinks he's got a bitch. Poor little thing. People trying to put *pressure* on him. He doesn't know what pressure is, friend. Pressure is what bears down every day on the grown men who have to crawl to him and others like him, every day, and kiss their black asses. Most of them, they know what the deal is. They stick their hands out, take what we put in them, and shut up. But some . . . they want people to feel sorry for them because folks want to give them money and cars and clothes to go somewhere and play ball and take a few dink courses a half-bright high-school freshman could walk through. And some, like this Coleman, think they've got a grievance with the *system*. Makes me puke."

He looked around the room with furious eyes. I'd seen people look that way at the inside of a jail.

"You know what I played for?"

"Tell me."

"I got a grant-in-aid and I waited tables for some spending money. In the summer I went home and worked on the farm trying to keep the bank from taking it away from my folks. I had two pairs of pants and four shirts to my name. I never missed a practice or a game. I never backtalked a coach or complained to the newspapers about how I wasn't getting the ball enough. I kept my mouth shut and I played my ass off. I even went to class and got my degree. Not in physical education, either. Business, because I knew I didn't have the natural stuff to play pro ball and I was going to have to

work when I couldn't play anymore. I was not going to steer mules
on that little farm or sell cars or insurance somewhere for the rest
of my life.

"But now I've got to beg—literally *beg*—kids who look at you
like it is all they can do to keep from going to sleep while you're
talking and then they say, 'Yeah, man, well tell me about the
package, you know.' They want to know what kind of car they'll be
driving and who's going to be putting them in some threads so they
can strut properly when they walk across campus. I've had mothers
and fathers wanting to talk annuities, for Christ's sake, when they're
used to buying groceries with food stamps. But *I'm* the bad guy.
The corrupt one. And some ex-con from out of the swamps steals
a contract and makes a tape and talks to a newspaper man so he
can prove it to the whole world and fry my ass."

His face had relaxed slightly now that he made his speech and
vindicated himself once again in his own mind. I wondered idly
how he justified the bets on the games he'd gotten Randolph to
tank.

"You and all the rest of them . . . the NCAA, the newspaper
boys, the crybaby university presidents . . . you're all working on
the wrong side of the street.

"You think I want to pay kids money, give them cars? You
think people who come up with the money don't have anything
better to do with it? You think I have to *force* that money on these
recruits? I played for nothing but pride and a chance to beat you,
and I'd run a program in a heartbeat where everyone played the
way I did. And you know how long I'd last? One season. Maybe
two. Because I wouldn't be able to get any talent. And you know
who would fire me? The same chickenshit university president who
likes to talk about 'integrity in athletics.' He's not going to fire the
physics department when MIT gets a grant instead of the U. But
he'll fire me when we don't win the conference.

"It isn't me *buying* you ought to be looking at, it's the players
selling. I'm not the one who turned it into a game about money,
and buying and selling players. But if that's the game, I'm going to
play to win and no apologies."

"You're wasting that on me," I said. "I don't care if basketball
is clean or dirty. Might as well be Chinese politics. I'm interested
in one man."

"William Coleman," he said, sounding a little calmer now.
"I might have been wrong about him. He might be the one kid

who comes along every now and then who doesn't have his hand
out."

I shook my head. "Wrong man."

He looked at me, not quite comprehending.

"I'm working for his brother, Jackson."

Stallworth shook his head. "A worm. What's he got to do with
you?"

"He's in jail," I said. "Looking at felony murder because he
was set up."

"That's all there is to this?"

I nodded.

"You're going to burn me to get him out of jail?"

I nodded.

"How long before he's back in? A week? Two?"

I said nothing.

"How much are you getting paid?"

"It would break your heart."

"Dumb. All-world dumb," he said. "But I think we can make
a deal. One that's good for both of us."

"Griggs's money."

"Sure. But no time. Just say you had it wrong. It was just
Stitch all by himself all along."

"I'll pass."

"You still might have a hard time proving anything," he said.
Like the coaches say, there was no quit in him.

"We'll just add kidnapping," I said. "I think Jessie would be
glad to testify on that one."

"Maybe. But I've got friends in this state I've never met. It
would just take one of them to make a hung jury."

He was already talking like a convict, holding on to something,
the possibility of a mistrial. Some error that comes up on appeal.
Early parole. You never run out of those things. Not even on death
row, where there is always a chance of a last-minute stay.

"I wonder how your friends will feel about your deal with
Ricky Randolph?" I said.

His face went limp. "You do a thorough job, don't you?"

"Were you figuring on the same kind of deal with Coleman?
Talent like that, if he scored twenty-five on a night when he should
have hit forty, nobody would think anything about it, except that
maybe he'd had a bad night. Didn't get enough sleep or something.

You could make a bundle if you spread the action around so no one bookie got suspicious."

He shook his head wearily. "It's the easiest money there is."

"But not enough. Is it?"

"No," he sighed. "It never is. I get ahead every now and then. But you know what happens."

"You bet heavier."

"Every time."

"How much?"

"Christ, I don't know. I'd go crazy trying to come up with a number. The money isn't the point. Isn't that what they say?"

"It's the action," I agreed.

"The action," he said bitterly.

"Who came up with the plan?"

"Stitch. He wanted a job. He didn't know anything about tanking games. He wanted to coach. What a loser."

"Could you have gotten to a prosecutor?"

"Ask Griggs. He knows them all. Maybe one of them would have cut a deal and let Jackson plead to something small. Griggs could have promised to help the guy when he ran for Congress or something."

"You tell Griggs you wanted him to do that?"

"Yeah. He was game. He always is."

"Stitch was betting too."

"I know. He was in deep. That's how I kept him on the reservation. He was long on mouth, short on guts. After you made that tape and took the paper from him, he wanted to run. I was afraid he'd make a deal."

"So you sent him to the Iron Horseman?"

Stallworth nodded.

"Where did the motorcycle boys come from?"

"A bookie in Tampa uses them to collect. I'm a good customer."

"Not anymore."

He laughed. Out of relief, I suppose, that it was all over. "No. There will be a few of them stuck, won't there? That's one thing I won't have to worry about ever again. No more calls from the boys wanting to know when can I pay. I'm so sick of that. And all that stuff I told you earlier. About kissing up to nineteen-year-olds?"

I nodded.

"All true. I just didn't know how true until tonight. Now I don't have to do that anymore. I've hated it longer than I can remember. Right now, I feel better than I've felt in a long time."

That would change soon enough.

Pine locked him in the back of the cruiser and walked out back with me to look at the dead biker.

"Done a job on him, Morgan."

"Look at what he was holding." I'd left his machine gun on the ground next to him after I'd taken Pancho's.

"Yeah. All that firepower sure let him down. Got himself killed with something they used back in the Stone Age. That's the trouble with those little boutique guns. They make a dumb man think he's invulnerable.

"You know, we had a battalion commander in the Hundred and First once who had a standing order that any man who killed a VC with an ax got himself an extra ration of beer and the time to drink it. I got thirsty, but never *that* thirsty."

"It was all I had," I said. "I'd have called in an air strike if I'd had a radio."

Pine smiled mournfully. "Yeah. Well, I'll call a wagon, get them out here to clean up this mess. You look like you could use some cleaning up yourself."

"Feels like the side of my head is made out of sand," I said.

"It'll tighten back up. Hurt like a bitch tomorrow, though."

"I know."

"All right. Let's get back inside. Get warm and get some coffee. You can give me a statement."

It took an hour. Then I called Jessie. She came by and cleaned my face with warm towels and alcohol.

"Stop squirming," she said.

"It hurts."

"Don't be such a baby. I didn't hear you moaning and carrying on when he was hitting you with his chain."

"It didn't hurt like this."

"Oh, poo. Now be still."

When she finished, she looked at her work and said, "You're going to look ugly for a few days. But I think I can stand it."

* * *

In the morning, the eye had swollen until it was almost shut. Jessie drove me to the airport, where I picked up my truck. Cost me a fortune for short-term parking.

I went by to see Semmes. He wasn't happy that I hadn't told him right away about Ricky Randolph.

"I didn't want to bother you at home."

"Call next time, you hear?"

"I will," I said, relieved to hear there would be a next time.

"Meanwhile, take some time and go somewhere. You could fly to Paris on what you'll make on this one."

"Leave it in the account," I said. "I believe I'll stay here and finish the drinking room. I didn't leave anything in Paris."

I went by the radio station and told the story to Mike Grantham. Most of it, anyway. He reacted like an old Klondike gold digger who'd found the mother lode after twenty years of looking.

"I'll put it out tonight," he said. "It'll be the biggest thing in sports in ten years. This baby will be everywhere. I'm going to have to buy me a new suit because I'll be on ESPN tonight."

He wanted to meet me later, after his broadcast, at Pepper's. To celebrate. I thanked him and said I didn't feel up to it. Maybe later.

My last stop was at Dinah Coleman's. She had already talked to Nat, who'd told her that Jackson would be out in a few days. She hugged me and thanked me and said there was no way she could repay me. I told her it wasn't necessary; Semmes had already taken care of it. She invited me to dinner that night, too. I asked if I could bring Jessie.

William Coleman was there along with Denise. She wanted to apologize. I told her there was no need.

Dinah Coleman served red beans and rice seasoned with country ham. Also greens, cornbread, and fried chicken. It all tasted wonderful, even though it was hard to chew. It occurred to me that Tom Pine would have liked to be sitting at my place but that if he had, Dinah Coleman would have had to cook another chicken.

Jessie asked for the recipe. "I've eaten chicken at all the New Orleans places," she said. "Mister Eddie has the best, but this is better."

"You got to soak it in buttermilk," Dinah Coleman said. "Most of them use sweet milk, but the buttermilk is what does it right."

I asked William if he'd made up his mind about a school yet or if he was tired of thinking about it.

"No, sir. I want to go to Duke."

"That's a good one," I said. "You couldn't do better."

"Only thing is, it's a long way off. Too far for Mama to come see the games."

"Not necessarily," she said. "They've got airplanes and I've never flown on one before. If I had to go somewhere, I always took the bus. But I'd like to take a plane to North Carolina. It's a place I've never been."

"We'll all go," Denise said, "to your first game. And every time you play Carolina. I'm already learning to hate the Tarheels. Got to start getting up earlier every morning so I can hate them a little bit longer."

Everyone laughed.

"I was wondering," William Coleman said to me, "if you'd like to come up to the first game."

"He'd love it," Jessie said, before I could answer. "And I'll go with him. I've got lots of friends in Carolina."

William Coleman looked at me.

Even eight months away, it seemed like a long way to go just to watch a basketball game. I've never cared that much about basketball. But I've always believed you should witness greatness whenever you get the chance. I still remember watching Sayers run the ball and listening to Coltrane play the sax.

"Sure," I said. "I'll be there. I'd be honored."